Paula,
Hope

THE WICKED GAME OF THE HUNTER SERIES, BOOK #2

WICKED SHADOW

—— OF THE ——

HUNTER

TRACEY L. RYAN

LUMINARE PRESS

WWW.LUMINAREPRESS.COM

Please consider donating to Boston Children's Hospital. Log on to childrenshospital.org for more information on how you can donate and make a difference in a child's life.

This is a work of fiction. Names, characters, places, and incidents either are the product of the author's imagination or are used fictitiously and any resemblance to actual persons, living or dead, businesses, companies, or locales is entirely coincidental.

Printed in the United States of America

Cover Design: Melissa Lund

Luminare Press
438 Charnelton St., Suite 101
Eugene, OR 97401
www.luminarepress.com

LCCN: 2018947933
ISBN: 978-1-944733-80-3

To my loving and devoted husband who has provided me tremendous encouragement on this fantastic journey.

TABLE OF CONTENTS

Prologue

AFTER A RELAXING CHAMPAGNE BRUNCH, EMMA, Morgan, and Hannah opted to head to the North End for some Italian pastries. While at the bakery, they decided to load up on decadent treats to take to their respective workplaces. The day was bright and warm with the birds singing the sounds of spring. Normally, Emma would walk home from the bakery, but today she decided to take a cab. It pained her to know that her life had already changed because of an unknown stalker hiding in the shadows.

When she got out of the cab in front of her condominium building, she noticed the people enjoying a beautiful Sunday afternoon in the city. To them, this was a typical weekend spent with family and friends. Only Emma recognized the darkness that hung over the city like a volcanic cloud. Once inside the lobby, Emma noticed the two security guards stationed at the front desk. Both nodded in her direction and went back to looking at the security monitors in front of them.

Emma wondered if these were the men who had helped Ryan on Friday night but wasn't about to ask due to sheer embarrassment. The quicker she could forget that night, the better. Immediately, Emma's mind lurched back to that dreadful night. The would-be stalker's gift of lingerie, the creepy text message, and Ryan rushing to her rescue when her psyche couldn't take any more of these games. Emma desperately wanted all of this to be over and to be able to get back to her normal life.

The elevator doors slid open to a faint hint of Versace Pour Homme cologne. There was only one person that Emma knew who wore that brand. The champagne's effects had started to wear off, which didn't help. Emma's pulse elevated slightly at the thought of her potential guest.

She entered her apartment. Everything was quiet until the floor creaked ever so slightly. Emma spun around to see Hunter come out of the darkness. His hands were in the pockets of his Lucky Brand jeans. For the next few seconds they both stared at one another like they were sizing each other up for a gun fight at the O.K. Corral.

"I realize that you own the building, but you're invading my privacy by showing up unannounced." Emma glared at Hunter as if challenging him to a fight.

"Ryan told me what happened on Friday night." Hunter's response answered one of Emma's recent questions—Ryan was still keeping Hunter apprised of incidents involving her. "I won't tell you how disappointed I was to learn of this latest episode from Ryan and *not* you."

"Well, Hunter, we all know how extremely busy you are with business these days. Your influencing and negotiating skills are getting a real workout from what I can see."

Hunter couldn't hide his bewilderment. "I'm not exactly sure where you're going with this, Emma. If you have something to say, just say it." Hunter was chillingly calm like a great white shark before the kill.

"It's not even worth getting into. As you can see, I'm perfectly fine. I survived another day and plan on continuing to do so. Now, if you'll excuse me, I have some work to catch up on. I believe you know your way out." Emma strutted to her home office, leaving Hunter in the foyer. She had to admit that it felt good to have the upper-hand in the conversation.

When she heard the faint sound of her front door closing, Emma emerged from her office, once again, to a silent apartment. A slight pang of disappointment washed over her at the thought of Hunter not even trying to find out why she was acting so cold towards him. Emma considered that a sign that he was indeed preoccupied with someone else. When she looked around the empty apartment, Emma noticed a note on the island in the kitchen.

The handwritten note was on Hunter's personal stationary and read, "Don't believe everything you see or hear." Emma stared at the note. It was indeed Hunter's handwriting, but she had no idea what he was trying to tell her.

CHAPTER 1

———

E mma replayed the last few hours in her head, going over every possible scenario like a chess player does with their matches. Nothing made sense, and she wished she could turn off the alarm bells in her head. Seeing Hunter with another woman at his office building, him showing up unannounced at her condo, and the damn note in his handwriting. She really wanted off this roller coaster ride.

"Just another mind game from the almighty Hunter," she said aloud. Emma tossed the note in the trash and didn't give it a second thought for the rest of her Sunday. After she finished a few emails and looked over the final details for the gala, she poured herself a glass of 2014 Francois Lurton Les Fumes Blanches Rose Reserve while she contemplated her dinner options.

Emma decided on a turkey wrap with avocado and Swiss cheese plus low-salt potato chips. Just as she was taking the perfect wrap from the cutting board to her plate, her cell phone rang. When Emma looked at the phone, she saw her brother's handsome picture on the screen. Emma put the call on speaker, so she could eat and talk at the same time.

"Hello, sis! How're they hanging?" Robert always laughed at his own jokes.

"Sorry I didn't call you back the other night. Was caught up at work." Emma fibbed a little bit. If her brother ever knew what was really going on, he'd be on the first plane to Boston. She didn't want him anywhere near the tangled web she was somehow trapped in. "How's London treating you?" she managed to ask in-between bites.

"Oh, you know. Work hard...play harder. I have a surprise for you!"

Emma dreaded whatever this surprise was and prayed it wasn't some engagement announcement to one of his floozies.

"I'm taking the redeye back to Boston Tuesday night, arriving Wednesday morning, on business and decided to stay to show-off my little sister at the Boston Children's Hospital Gala!"

Emma was silent for a few seconds. This was definitely something she had not expected. "Did Mom put you up to this?" she asked cautiously. Her mother always meant well but wasn't happy about Emma being single at her age. Victoria Sharpeton wanted grandchildren and knew her best chance was with her daughter and not her son.

Robert feigned disappointment like only he could to Emma. "*No!* I'm hurt that you think I couldn't possibly think of something *so* generous all by myself." Emma felt Robert's smile radiate through the phone.

"Okay, okay. Just checking. I would *love* to have you be my escort on one condition…you are *not* to take off with the first hot chick you see at the party. I mean it, Robert!" Emma knew this was a very real possibility.

"For the record, I only did that *one* other time, and I have to say it was worth it. Wow, that chick was *amazing*! But, no, I'm *not* going to leave you by your lonesome…especially given the predator that will be in the vicinity."

Emma chuckled while she took a bite of her wrap, "Ahhh…so there it is! You don't like the thought of Hunter and I being in the same vicinity. I *knew* there was more to this than brotherly love."

"Okay, I can't stomach the guy, *and* I want to make sure he knows that I'll pummel him if he does anything to upset you or ruin your big night."

"I think it's very sweet. And, for the record, I can't wait to see you. What time does your flight get in? I can pick you up at Logan Airport."

"I'm here for some meetings and staying at one of the hotels in the Seaport District, so I'll just take a cab to the hotel. I booked a two-bedroom suite so you can stay with me for a few days and we can catch-up. All the room service you want on the company."

"Sounds cool. Text me the details, and I'll see you when you get here...I really *do* miss you," Emma said sincerely.

"Miss you, too! See you in a few days." With that, Robert disconnected.

Absently, Emma put another potato chip in her mouth, smiling at the thought of seeing her overprotective brother. Emma was relieved that her brother would be here for the gala. She had dreaded being there alone, especially given the last few days. Who knew who Hunter would bring. Robert's presence ensured that Hunter would not come near Emma that night unless absolutely necessary. That was one of life's certainties—Hunter and Robert loathed each other and could barely be civil. Emma knew it was an added bonus that her brother was just as handsome as Hunter.

Although Emma would be mostly consumed with work during the gala, she knew it would bother her to see Hunter enjoying the evening with another woman. Her mind drifted to what she had witnessed in the lobby of Hunter's headquarters. Who was that woman and how is she connected to Hunter? Would he actually bring her to the gala? Emma stopped herself from silently asking any more questions that she knew she didn't really want the answers to and scolded herself for letting her mind run away from her yet again. Instead, she focused on cleaning up the dishes from her early dinner without another thought of the mystery woman or Hunter.

The day had faded into evening with the usual TV selections. Emma wrapped up as much as she could from a work standpoint and decided it was time to try to relax. She made a mental note to look into spa retreats after the gala was over. Just as her mind drifted to the sensation of an aromatherapy full-body massage, a new text chimed on her phone from Ryan.

"Just checking 2 make sure u were OK & u set the alarm."

Emma thought for a split second that maybe Hunter told Ryan to check on her but quickly dismissed the thought. "All's fine. Alarm set. Thanks for checking! :-)."

"NP. I'll pick u up 4 work around 7. no arguments! NON-NEGOTIABLE!"

Emma thought Ryan was being a drama king but also knew not to push it with him, so she simply replied, "OK."

Emma cleared up her dinner dishes, turned off the TV in the living room and headed to her bedroom. Suddenly, she got the eerie sensation she was being watched, which gave her goosebumps. She went back to check to make sure the alarm system was armed—which it was—and then checked each room and closet just to be sure. Satisfied, Emma made her way to the bathroom to take the hottest shower she could tolerate in hopes of washing away any hint of Hunter.

With the steam overtaking the shower stall, Emma mentally reviewed and compartmentalized the various experiences since Hunter came back into her life—some good and some not so great:

Winning the contract for the gala—definitely the top of the good list

Her office being vandalized—definitely on the bad list

Making love with Hunter—probably on both lists

Some psycho taunting and stalking her—top of bad list

Finding out her father worked for Hunter's father in some secret lab—too many questions to decide which list

Given she was a bit spooked before the shower, Emma decided on pale yellow cotton pajamas instead of her usual *au naturel* bedroom attire. Although she knew that no one was in her condo except for her, Emma still felt the need to check under the bed. She felt ridiculous but knew she wouldn't get a wink of sleep if she didn't. Tonight, she was safe from any monsters...or so she assumed.

What Emma didn't know was that a camera had been installed in her bedroom and turned on remotely. The camera was so small it was barely visible, even if someone was specifically looking for it. The little red light showing it was on and recording was no bigger than a pinhead. The camera was in the perfect position to watch Emma as she slept.

Emma's perfect form was displayed on a 38-inch monitor in a darkened room across the city. With Emma drifting to sleep, a man's hand gently stroked her onscreen image. A sinister smile formed on the man's face, as he settled in to watch the live streaming show. He was disappointed, though, to see Emma had chosen to cover herself this evening.

This was no different than a lion silently stalking its prey—extremely dangerous yet filled with adrenaline and excitement. The man always appreciated the skill and patience of the lion—using the camouflage of the terrain to hide and then attack their target without prior warning. He thought of himself as the lion—hiding in plain sight and waiting for the perfect time to pounce. His employer would be pleased with his progress, he thought.

"Sleep well, dear Emma. You will need your rest—the games have just begun," the man said softly to the computer screen.

CHAPTER 2

———

The alarm jolted Emma out of a deep sleep on Monday morning. She surprisingly felt refreshed and ready to tackle whatever the week threw at her. Given all the frenzy in the office, she chose a more casual appearance. With her hair pulled back into a ponytail, a dab of perfume, and light pink lip-gloss, she dashed to the elevator to meet Ryan downstairs. When the elevator doors opened, Ryan was already there chatting with one of the security guards about a Premier League match that happened over the weekend.

Ryan smiled at Emma and said his goodbyes to the security guard. Ryan bowed and greeted Emma in a horrible fake British accent, "Your chariot awaits, my lady."

Emma giggled as Ryan ushered her out the door to the familiar Ares Logan Industries Mercedes parked in front of her building. Her heart stopped for a brief second as she wondered if Hunter might be sitting in the back behind the dark privacy glass windows. Her hopes were dashed when Ryan opened the front passenger side for Emma. They sped off toward her office.

It was another crisp morning with the sun glistening off the Boston skyline as they made their way through the Seaport District. The cirrocumulus clouds looked like rippled sand on a beach after the tide went out. Traffic was amazingly light for a Monday morning, and both Emma and Ryan were deep in thought. Ryan was getting that tingling sensation that always warned him trouble was brewing. He observed his passenger, staring out the window.

"You must be crazy busy finishing up things for the gala," Ryan stated matter-of-factly.

Emma didn't take her eyes off the skyline and the shimmering Ares Logan Industries building in the distance. "Yes. A lot to do."

Ryan wasn't offended by the lack of conversation. In most instances, he preferred it. Not today— he was worried about the whole situation, especially the woman next to him. So many pieces just didn't fit, like trying to put together a jigsaw puzzle with pieces from all different puzzles. In his past life, Ryan always had at least some intelligence around either who was involved or what the motive was. This whole thing seemed random, yet very strategic at the same time, which perplexed him.

The deep thoughts for both of them came to an end when Ryan pulled up in front of Emma's office building. Without a word, Ryan ran around the car to open Emma's door for her. He bowed slightly and held out a hand to help her get out of the car. "My lady."

Emma smiled as she allowed Ryan to walk her to the front door.

"I'll be back to pick you up at around five. I'll text you when I'm on my way." Ryan could see the protest forming on Emma's face. "Non-negotiable, remember?" Emma nodded.

Emma opened the doors to the building and watched Ryan speed off towards Ares Logan Industries' rose-hued glass building that mesmerized so many in the city. It was by far the tallest building in the city with a modern sophistication that couldn't be rivaled. It could be seen from virtually any point in Boston, which made it the unofficial beacon welcoming visitors to this vibrant city. Thousands of tourists came to Boston each year to walk on the streets where the American Revolution had been instigated. Even back in the 18th century, Boston had been vivacious and electrifying.

Once inside, Emma was greeted by the friendly security guard, Stan. "Morning, Ms. Sharpeton. Hope you had a nice weekend. Almost time for your big party, isn't it?"

"Morning, Stan. Weekend was nice. And, yes—coming up soon. Thanks for asking. How was your weekend? Anything fun with the grandkids?" Emma always enjoyed her morning chats with Stan. He was 6'5," in his early 60s with thick grey hair, and some extra girth that proved how much he enjoyed his wife's cooking. Stan was also a retired Boston police officer and one of the most caring people she knew. He had given the city of Boston thirty-eight years on the police force and had been lucky enough to retire without ever firing his weapon or being shot.

"Those grandkids are going to be the death of me!" Stan chuckled. "We brought them to Salem to see that witch museum stuff. Then went for ice cream and back here to the aquarium. I needed a nap by the time we were done!" Stan gave one of his big belly laughs that made Emma grin.

"Well, it sounds like you had a great time. I'm sure the kids really had fun." Emma waved to Stan before she stepped into the elevator to begin her hectic day.

She was relieved to have work to focus on since her personal life was currently in shambles. The soft classical music playing in the elevator was the last bit of peace she would have as the workday began.

The office was already as busy as a bee hive. Ashley, Emma's administrative assistant, waved to Emma while simultaneously typing and talking on the phone. This gave Emma a chance for a few more minutes of quiet time before the "Ashley tornado" blew into her office.

While Emma was turning on her laptop and taking off her navy blue North Face three-quarter trench coat, her faithful assistant appeared in her office. "How was the weekend, boss?"

The last thing Emma wanted to do was relive the weekend but knew she needed to indulge this ritual of Ashley's. Ashley was an amazing assistant, so humoring her on these little things was an acceptable price to pay. "Weekend was good. Very relaxing. And, yours?"

"Oh, no! You aren't getting away with that! Did you see tall, dark, and British or what?" Ashley gave Emma a wink and a smile.

"Actually, I only saw him briefly. He had to work this weekend, so I got to spend some much needed 'me time' relaxing."

"Oh. Okay. Well, Greg and I spent the whole weekend together. You know what is so great about him, besides the obvious, *if* you know what I mean." Ashley chuckled and turned a little red. Emma had all she could do not to roll her eyes. She gave Ashley a smile to encourage her to continue with this torture. "He's always so interested in my work here. I've told him all about the cool stuff we're doing for the gala and how great it is to work here. I wish you were here the day he surprised me."

Emma almost tripped over her chair when she heard Ashley's last revelation and tried to quickly compose herself. "I didn't realize he had ever been up to our office."

"Ya, it was a while ago. He was in the neighborhood so decided to pop in. I gave him a little tour." Ashley confessed. "Hope you don't mind."

"No, why would I mind? I'd love to meet him sometime." Emma needed to play this very cool and calm. Ashley brought new meaning to the phrase, "Loose lips sink ships."

"Great! He said he might bring me lunch sometime this week since he knows how busy we are with all the gala stuff going on. I'll definitely let you know. You're going to love him!" With that, Ashley flew out the door to answer the phone at her desk.

Emma's heart was pounding out of her chest as she thought about the not-so-coincidental timeline. This Greg guy had been in her office when she wasn't around, about the same time of the break-in. Ryan and Hunter both thought Greg may have had something to do with it. There seemed to be a lot of coincidences, but not enough proof. Emma needed to tell Ryan, but it would have to wait until after her office's daily status meeting.

As the troops poured into the conference room, Emma decided to forego her morning English breakfast tea ritual until after the meeting. She gazed around the room and beamed with pride. The company was a small start-up, but already they had achieved great things in the world of marketing.

Every person in the room deserved to be there, and she hoped their hard work would bring rewards for each of them.

"Morning, everyone. Hope you all had great weekends. We are in the home stretch!" The room erupted with cheers. "This week and next week are going to be busy ones, and I know we'll get everything done that we need to. The gala is going to be a great success, in large part due to every person in this room."

Emma paused to look at the team. "Now, what I'm about to tell you is in *no way* mandatory. It's a bit of a reward for those that want to partake. We are all invited to the gala!" The room once again erupted in cheers. "Again, it is up to you if want to come. It might be fun to see all your hard work in action. Plus, there will be great food and drinks. Do remember it's a black-tie event."

Once the team settled down, they reviewed outstanding tasks and then dispersed to their respective desks. Emma walked to the windows of the conference room and gazed out across the city. She couldn't help but think that somewhere, hidden in this incredible city, was a stalker who could strike at any minute. Her mind drifted to the mysterious and elusive Greg, and a shiver went up her spine.

Back in her office, Emma closed the door and decided to text Ryan what she had learned about Ashley's boyfriend. A few minutes after the text was sent, Emma's cell phone rang with Ryan on the other end.

Ryan skipped the usual pleasantries, "It's looking more and more like this Greg guy could be the one who vandalized your office."

"I admit that it all seems too coincidental, but we still don't have any real proof, Ryan." Emma didn't want to accuse someone unless they were absolutely sure.

"I know. That's why you have me—to find the proof. Listen, don't do any amateur sleuthing on your own. I mean it, Emma! This isn't a game." Ryan tried to sound calm but knew that each passing minute they didn't find any answers could mean disaster. And Ryan didn't even know how deep the plot really went or who the real target was.

Emma knew that Ryan was right, but she also couldn't simply standby and let this stalker play mind games either. "I know you'll do everything you can to find out what's going on, Ryan." Emma hoped that Ryan would assume that this meant she wouldn't interfere.

"Okay. There is one thing you could help me with." Ryan understood that she wasn't going to stay out of it, and he couldn't blame her. If roles were reversed, he wouldn't have been able to sit on the sidelines either. The difference was, Ryan was trained in these type of spy games and Emma wasn't.

Emma was exhilarated that Ryan asked for her help. "Sure! Just name it."

"Ask your assistant for Greg's last name. Obviously don't be too conspicuous about it, just act casual."

"Gee, Ryan, I *never* would have thought to be casual." Emma rolled her eyes.

"No need for sarcasm, my lady."

Emma couldn't help but smirk into the phone. "Let me see what I can do. I'll text you if I find anything out. Ryan?"

"Ya?"

"Take care of yourself."

"Always do, my lady." Ryan disconnected and stared at the phone for a minute. Emma was definitely more scared than she let on, he thought. There was something in her voice that put him on guard. He was also worried that Emma seemed to be handling the whole Hunter situation so maturely. In Ryan's experience with women, when they were too calm about something, watch out for the explosion.

Emma jerked back to reality when she realized she still hadn't heard from Joe Bonamassa's agent. It would be a nightmare if she needed a "Plan B" for music this late in the game. Just as Emma let out a sigh at the prospect of not having entertainment, Ashley knocked on her door. "Emma, there's a Joe Bonamassa here to see you. He doesn't have an appointment, but he said it was very important.

What do you want me to tell him?"

Emma blinked a few times while it registered who was in the lobby of her office. "Um, send him in."

"Mr. Bonamassa, Ms. Sharpeton will see you now." Ashley escorted one of the world's greatest guitar and blues musicians into Emma's office.

Emma rose to meet him as they shook hands.

"Ms. Sharpeton, I do need to apologize to you for not returning your message earlier. I've been touring in Europe and just got back to the States last night."

Emma motioned for the musician to sit in one of the brown leather wingback chairs in front of Emma's desk. "Please call me Emma. And I completely understand—no apology necessary. I have to say, this is incredible for me to be sitting across someone with your musical talent. I'm a big fan!" Emma tried hard to control her giddiness without much success.

"That's so kind of you to say, Emma. And, please call me Joe. What's your favorite song? If you don't mind me asking," Joe asked as he got comfortable in his chair.

Without hesitation Emma said, "I can give you my top three: *Livin Easy*, *Wild About You Baby*, and *When the Sun Goes Down*."

"Nice choices," Joe said as he smiled at Emma. "So, let's talk about this gala. As luck would have it,

I'm in Boston that weekend for a family function after doing some concerts in the area. My manager gave me all the specifics, so it would definitely fit into my schedule if you still want me to play."

"We would *love* to have you play at the gala!" Emma's heart was beating a mile a minute.

"Fantastic! It would help me with my play list if you gave me some more specifics around the event. I know it's to support Boston Children's Hospital—which, of course, is a great cause. Are these the typical stuck-up society types?"

Emma laughed, loving his casualness. "Trust me, there will be lots of money in the room. Yes, some are the typical stuck-up society types. What I want to do is create a new atmosphere for these type of charity events. I want this to be fun, with everyone letting loose."

"Now, you're talking. I can definitely help with that." Joe was starting to really like the woman sitting across from him.

Emma couldn't help but smile. "Great! I'll have Ashley get in touch with your manager with all the specifics."

Both rose and shook hands once more. Emma walked Joe to the elevator. "Thanks again, Joe, for doing this. This is a great event and will be even better with you there." She couldn't help but gush. Joe waved goodbye before he was whisked away in the elevator.

Ashley just stared at Emma. "Who was that, and why are you blushing?"

Emma was not completely surprised that Ashley had not recognized her unexpected guest. Ashley's taste in music was whatever was pounding through the local dance clubs.

"That, my dear Ashley, was one of the greatest musicians in our lifetime. He's agreed to play at the gala, so I'll need you to send over all the details to his manager as soon as possible today." Emma didn't stick around to get into a musical debate with her assistant—she had too many other things that were taking over the little brain capacity she had left.

CHAPTER 3

———

The day flew by, and before Emma realized, Ryan was texting her that he was on his way to pick her up. She quickly shut down the laptop and threw everything in her bag. Emma was putting her coat on when Ashley popped in the doorway.

"Oh. I didn't realize you were leaving," Ashley said.

"Taking some stuff home with me and will be in bright and early tomorrow. What's up?"

"Just wanted to let you know Greg will be picking me up tonight. I was hoping that you'd get to meet him, but I guess not." Ashley appeared sullen and disappointed.

"I could wait. What time is he going to be here?"

"I don't want to hold you up. Greg won't be here until around six. He had some work to finish up, and we're going to grab dinner at the Mexican place down the street."

Emma's mind was racing. "I'm sorry, Ashley.

Definitely next time. By the way, I don't think you ever told me what Greg does for work?"

Ashley started smiling again. "Greg is some sort of consultant. He doesn't talk much about it—says it's rather boring. I know he makes a lot of money, so it must be important whatever it is he consults on."

"Interesting." Emma was doing her best to be casual. "Well, have fun tonight! I'll see you in the morning."

Ashley waved goodbye as Emma stepped into the elevator. Emma was relieved when the doors finally closed. All she could think of was getting this information to Ryan. At the ground floor, the doors slowly slid open, and a very anxious Emma burst through them.

Ryan was startled to see Emma sprinting towards him. Emma grabbed Ryan's arm and literally hauled him outside. "Get in the car!"

Thoroughly confused, Ryan slid into the driver's seat. "Okay. What the *hell* is going on?" Ryan instantly went into protection mode in case of an imminent threat lurking.

"Sorry, but I need to get this all out before I forget anything." Emma rehashed the conversation she just had with Ashley word-for-word while Ryan sat there speechless.

"So, are you going to say anything?" Emma demanded when she had finished.

Ryan tried to put his thoughts together quickly. He turned to look at Emma, "Well, I have to say that this was excellent detective work." Emma flashed him a smile and Ryan continued, "I'm going to drop you off at home, make sure all is good at your place, and then I feel in the mood for some Mexican tonight."

"Ryan, Ashley's met you. What if she sees you?"

"Oh, my dear Emma, have you no faith in my abilities? I'm eternally hurt." Ryan flashed a devious smile.

Emma shook her head, "Okay, okay. I didn't mean to wound your pride. I'll let you do whatever it is that you do."

"Why, thank you. Look, by the end of tonight, we'll hopefully know exactly who this guy is. *Trust me*." Ryan tried his best to reassure Emma.

Emma nodded, and the car zipped off towards her condo. Ryan talked to the security guards and then checked Emma's place. He hesitated before leaving. Emma could tell he wanted to say something and needed a little prodding. "Ryan, what's on your mind?"

Ryan sighed heavily before responding. "Emma, I know that you don't understand everything that's going on right now."

"That's an understatement," Emma responded softly.

"Please trust me that I will figure this out and

keep you safe. And, also trust that Hunter is doing everything in his power to do the same."

"Ryan, I trust you completely. Hunter…not so much. Let's just leave it at that." Emma groaned.

"I get it. I'm not here to defend him. He doesn't always go about things in the best way, but his intentions are genuine." Ryan wanted Emma to recognize that she had both of them in her corner.

"What's that saying about the road to hell being paved with good intentions? Or, no good deed goes unpunished?" Ryan was about to respond when Emma held up her hand and continued, "I recognize that I'm a pawn in some game that is *way* larger than me. I also know there is a lot at stake. So, *for now*, I won't do anything foolish. That's all I can promise—is that good enough for the moment?" Emma would only be able to take so much of this whole situation before she hit her breaking point, and she needed Ryan to understand she had her limits.

It was Ryan's turn to nod in consent which was something he wasn't used to doing. He kissed Emma's forehead before he left to start his clandestine operation. Emma closed the door behind Ryan and made sure everything was locked up tight. Her stress level was off the charts, and she just wanted all of this to be over.

When the gala was over, it didn't necessarily mean the rest of this mess would be over. Emma thought about the gala and pondered the one thought she'd been trying desperately to avoid: "What if everything up to now was leading up to something happening at the gala?"

This notion sent a chill down her spine.

CHAPTER 4

———

E mma settled into what she thought was her "safe place" while Ryan prepared for his last-minute surveillance operation. Given the resources Ryan had access to, it wasn't hard to get all the necessary equipment and people for the job in a short amount of time. Emma's office building was already under surveillance, and the camera footage streamed to both Hunter's laptop and a backup server in the security office. Therefore, Ryan only needed to worry about having eyes and ears at the restaurant.

Ryan had three men available for live surveillance. He had worked with them in his prior life and trusted them. He wasn't sure if it was luck or something else when Ashley and Greg had chosen that specific restaurant, because Ryan happened to know the owner very well. In fact, the owner and Ryan worked together at a certain cagy government agency before they moved into their current careers. Within an hour, Ryan had two bus-boys and a bartender planted in the restaurant. He also brought in specialized high-tech equipment including state-of-the-art listening devices. The plan was for Ryan to sit in a nondescript beige mid-size sedan outside the restaurant and take pictures with a high-powered zoom digital camera, while the inside team focused on listening to the conversation and gathering any additional information.

At 6:46 p.m. the plan launched into action. The office video footage, which Ryan also had streaming on his tablet in the car, showed someone fitting Greg's general description walk into Emma's office building and get on the elevator. Inside the elevator, Greg was calm, but did not glance at the camera. All Ryan could tell was that Greg fit the overall description they had so far. Once inside the lobby area, the video showed Ashley running over to greet Greg with a very passionate kiss. Greg once again positioned himself so that there wasn't a clear view of his face, as if he knew where the cameras were.

Ryan half expected them to hop on the desk and get down to business. Instead, Ashley grabbed her coat and purse while Greg pushed the down arrow for the elevator with his right index finger. Ryan made a mental note to have the elevator dusted for prints, since Greg wasn't wearing gloves. It seemed odd that Greg would be so careful not to show his face clearly, but then be so careless about leaving a fingerprint. Ryan knew from experience that the more a criminal got cocky or comfortable, the more mistakes they usually ended up making. Al Capone was found guilty of tax evasion and sentenced to eleven years in federal prison due to his arrogance. Whitey Bulger was finally captured after being a fugitive for fourteen years because his girlfriend liked a stray cat outside their apartment in Santa Monica.

The couple rode down the elevator in silence with Ashley occasionally peeking at her man with a twinkle in her eye. They walked out of the building holding hands and continued that way the two blocks to the restaurant. Fortunately, it was a Monday night, and the restaurant wasn't too crowded, which made it easier to listen to their conversation. The hostess sat them by the window facing the street as previously instructed by Ryan. The high-tech listening device was part of the lit candle and would record everything that was said, then transmit it to Hunter's office.

To anyone walking by, they looked like any other normal couple on a date. There was subtle hand-holding, and Greg seemed to listen to Ashley attentively, smiling and nodding at appropriate times. This guy was good, Ryan thought. He didn't think the couple knew they were being watched, although Greg was definitely being careful. He never glanced in the same direction for more than a few seconds. Ryan was able to get some pictures of him, but only his profile. Halfway through their meal, Greg excused himself, presumably to go to the restroom. Ryan waited patiently for Greg to rejoin Ashley, who seemed anxious for her date to return. Ten minutes later, Greg returned to the table with what looked like sweat on his forehead. Maybe the food didn't agree with him, Ryan supposed.

Greg signaled for the waiter to bring the check and quickly paid cash for their bill. He escorted Ashley out of the restaurant, not waiting for her to put on her jacket. On the curb, he hailed a cab and appeared like he apologized to Ashley. Ashley seemed disappointed but appeared to understand. Before she got into the cab, he gently kissed her cheek. Greg waved goodbye to the cab then sauntered back toward Emma's office building. Ryan quickly alerted his team to the change in the couple's plans, so everyone was on guard for whatever happened next. To Ryan's surprise, Greg hailed his own cab in front of Emma's office building. Ryan was able to snap a photo of the cab and its license plate before it quickly sped off. This was unusual behavior for a man whose dinner didn't seem to agree with him a few minutes prior, Ryan thought.

Ryan quickly did a U-turn to tail the cab at a safe distance but briefly lost sight of the cab in the typical Boston evening traffic. Finally, after weaving through the traffic, Ryan spotted the cab heading

Tracey L. Ryan

toward the Massachusetts Turnpike entrance and followed it heading west. After about 15 minutes, Ryan realized they were headed toward Route 95 north to Waltham. Ryan realized that he was on a wild goose chase—there was no passenger in the car, only the driver. Ryan got off at the next exit and headed back to the city in a fury.

On the drive back, Ryan called Hunter. "Dude, this guy is good. Almost had me going to Maine with a little diversion onto the Mass Pike and 95! I'll be at the office in about ten minutes." Ryan disconnected when he heard Hunter's grunt of acknowledgement.

He knew Hunter hadn't left the office, and Ryan knew that Hunter wouldn't be happy with what he just heard. Both men were really hoping Greg was some amateur, but that dream had faded into a nightmare tonight.

When Ryan pulled into the parking garage at Hunter's office, he called his team to get any fingerprints from Emma's building. Something bothered Ryan about the casualness of Greg pushing the elevator button. It was springtime, so it would have looked bizarre for him to have gloves on, but why not wait for Ashley to push the button or use his knuckles? It didn't sit well with Ryan. He hopped out of the rental car and headed up to Hunter's office to face the inevitable wrath.

Ryan knew that Hunter was going to be like a

startled rattlesnake. He opened the office door and was not disappointed.

"What the *hell* took you so long?" Hunter growled.

"Oh, I don't know. I thought I'd take in the scenery around the city before I leisurely drove back here. What the hell do you think took me so long? There was a little thing called *traffic*. Ever hear of it, your highness?" Ryan wasn't afraid to jab the rattlesnake when the situation called for it.

Hunter recognized that he was being an ass and always secretly commended Ryan for his ability to hit him head-on when he was. "I'm just sitting here twiddling my thumbs and feeling absolutely useless. *Please* tell me that you have something—*anything*."

Ryan could clearly see how much this was tormenting his friend. "Nothing concrete yet. Obviously, you saw the video from Emma's office. It'll take us a little while to analyze it and hopefully get facial recognition on this guy. You heard their conversation; very benign to say the least. He didn't overtly ask about Emma, or you for that matter—played it cool the whole time."

Hunter sat at his desk with his back to Ryan and stared out the window at the city skyline that was slowly transitioning to darkness. Hunter was only half-listening, focused on Emma, until Ryan snapped him back to reality. "Are you listening to me?"

"Yes. Go on." Hunter continued to focus on the blanket of darkness falling over the city.

"Okay, then. As I was saying before you went into La La Land, I have a feeling that this guy has at least some training. He's very organized and methodical. Not your average psychopath."

"What do you mean by training?" Hunter was a bit puzzled and turned to face Ryan.

"I mean that this guy has avoided showing his full face to every camera out there. He's been very careful up to the point where he purposely pushed the elevator button when leaving Emma's office. There is this little voice in my head screaming that it was deliberate. Something is completely off here. I learned to trust my instincts years ago."

Ryan studied Hunter to make sure all of this was sinking in before he continued, "And then he leaves the table at the restaurant for ten minutes, comes back visibly flushed, and puts Ashley in a cab a few minutes later. Now, I know what you are thinking, maybe it was the food, but after Ashley's gone, suddenly all is right with the world, and he casually walks back to Emma's building to get his own cab. What's *wrong* with this picture?"

He didn't give Hunter a chance to answer. "I'll tell you what's wrong with the picture—you *don't* recover that quickly from eating bad food! And, then there's the little bait-and-switch he pulled with the cab ride. There are so many things that just don't add up right now. I think he was playing a cat and mouse game, testing us to see if we were watching him."

Hunter pondered all of this and let it slowly seep into the crevasses of his brain. He knew Ryan was right—this guy just didn't add up. "This just keeps getting better, doesn't it?" he said sarcastically.

Ryan laughed as he plopped down on the dark brown leather sofa. Hunter watched him and was reminded of when Emma first came to his office. He had wanted to dazzle Emma with all that he had achieved without the help of his father. What he didn't expect at that luncheon, which seemed like a lifetime ago, was how much his heart still ached for her.

Spring was an absolutely enchanting time to be in Boston—everyone seemed to wake up from their long winter slumber with a renewed energy. Hunter got up from his desk and once again gazed out the floor-to-ceiling windows at the city below. The city skyline was now fully encapsulated in darkness. The blackness reminded Hunter that the city had a wicked undertone that Emma and he had been dragged into.

"Fine, Ryan, what do you suggest we do next?" Hunter never stopped staring out the windows.

"I've got my team at Emma's office now trying to see if they can get some usable fingerprints. We're going through the surveillance footage frame-by-frame plus the voice recordings. One silver lining—you can change your appearance, but you really can't change your voice in live conversations. Well, not for very long. And you can't change your fin-gerprints." Ryan paused and looked in Hunter's direction, "You're the big-time chess player. If this was a game, what would his next move be?"

"I'd say this guy is an expert chess player. He's controlled the board from his very first move. In chess, you know the objective is to get checkmate. This game he's playing seems different. It feels like checkmate is not his end-game. This all feels like a diversion for something much bigger and, I hate to say it, more sinister."

Ryan pondered all this at the same time his phone vibrated. "What do you have for me?"

Hunter could only hear Ryan's side of the con-versation, and it didn't sound promising. A lot of "uh-huhs" before Ryan disconnected. Hunter stared at his friend and waited for Ryan to deliver the bad news.

"I don't know what the hell is going on! I *knew* something was off when the guy pushed the ele-vator button without a care in the world." Ryan started pacing around Hunter's office. "Here's the deal—there were NO fingerprints on the elevator or anywhere else in the lobby of Emma's office. None, nada, nothing, zero!"

Hunter was befuddled and didn't comprehend what Ryan was implying. "That's impossible, right?"

"You got it! The guy didn't care about leaving his fingerprints because he doesn't have *any*!" Ryan continued to pace around the office like a wild cat.

"Will you stop pacing? You are making me dizzy!" Hunter's head was spinning.

Ryan plopped back on the sofa and sighed. "I don't know about you, but I could use a stiff drink."

Hunter nodded in agreement and grabbed the bottle of Jameson 18-Year-Old Limited Reserve plus two Waterford crystal tumblers from his private fully-stocked bar. Neither put ice in their whiskey— it watered down the smooth taste too much.

While Hunter poured two-fingers in each glass, he summed-up the situation, "So, we aren't any closer today than we were last week *or* the week before. Emma is *still* in danger. The guy is enjoying watching us fumble all over each other. *And*, to top it off, I'm going to have hundreds of society's finest downstairs for the party of the year in less than two weeks."

Hunter handed the glass to Ryan who swallowed the contents in one swig. Ryan poured himself another. "You're correct, my friend. No better—no worse."

Both men sat in silence and drank their liquor hoping it would diminish the sting of the night's failures. Just as Ryan was about to pour his third glass, his phone vibrated again. "What?" Ryan once again had a few "uh-huhs" before he ended the call.

"Well, there might be a sliver of sunshine. My tech guys were able to get a frame with half of this guy's face in it."

"And, what does half a face get us exactly?" Hunter tried not to sound irritated.

"Well, the funny thing is, there was a reflection of the other half in a different frame. So, the boys put them both together and *voil*à, we have a full face! *And*, we have this guy's voice recording. All we need to do is match them to a name." Ryan's spirits finally lifted a little, although he knew it was still a far cry from finding out Greg's true identity. "I'm going to head downstairs to see exactly what the tech gurus put together. Wanna join me?"

Hunter was back at the windows looking out at the twinkling city lights against the dark nighttime sky. "I'll swing down in a few minutes. Need to finish a few things here first."

"This may be another wild goose chase, but it's something. Hang in there. I care about her, too, you know." With that, Ryan made the high-speed journey down to the basement, which contained some of the world's best security systems and people.

Hunter stood like a statue, blankly staring out of the windows contemplating the last few days. He'd been reminded how tricky fate could be. A long-lost love popped back up only to be clouded over by sinister forces beyond his control. Hunter was used to being in control. He was always the one who controlled the chessboard, except now, he thought to himself. At the moment, he felt like an amateur at a game he didn't know how to play.

He desperately wanted to call Emma but knew that she more than likely wouldn't answer the call, plus it was too dangerous. Instead, Hunter brought up her picture on his phone. She hadn't even realized he had taken the picture the day she was in the lobby examining the space for the gala. The sun's soft rays had filtered through the atrium and picked up the blonde highlights in her flowing hair just as she smiled to herself, not realizing she was being watched. He had been able to capture her pure essence and beauty with one picture. He swallowed the rest of his whiskey and headed downstairs to meet Ryan.

When Hunter entered the elaborate security office he spotted Greg's picture on the large screen against the back wall. The entire room was filled with the latest in technology and security experts going about their work. Ryan was in deep thought, staring at the image of their potential perpetrator. The guy seemed like he was military or law enforcement— he had the "high and tight" haircut, square jawline and muscular build. More than likely, Greg was some sort of freelancer—meaning he would do about anything for the right price, which unsettled Ryan.

"So, what're you thinking?" Hunter startled Ryan.

"Hey—didn't hear you come in. Well, this guy is probably some sort of gun for hire. To him, it's just another job. Obviously, that's just my gut feeling with *absolutely* nothing to back it up." Ryan sighed. He needed to have more than a facial image and voice print—Ryan needed to know what made this guy tick and why if there was any hope of solving this mystery before it went down the path of no return.

Hunter stared at the screen for a few more minutes before he silently left. He knew that Ryan and his team were doing everything possible to find more leads, but Hunter needed to think about his own next move in this dangerous chess game.

Against his better judgement, Hunter decided to swing by Emma's condo on his way home, even if he could only sit outside for a few minutes and peer up at her place from the car. He really hoped that Emma could read between the lines of the note he had left her yesterday—he was doing all this for her safety and not by choice. Hunter would do whatever he needed to in order to protect Emma, even if it meant completely walking away from her.

CHAPTER 5

Emma was nestled on the couch in the living room of her condo finishing a bit of work on the gala to keep her mind off tonight's clandestine mission. She had no idea that she was being watched—not only by the most eligible bachelor in the city, but also by a mysterious stalker. Hunter, feeling unsettled, pulled away after a few minutes and headed to his own empty penthouse. He was feeling more anxious than usual while he sat outside of Emma's. The situation was escalating, which would be cause enough for increased anxiety, but Hunter knew it was more than that. He just didn't know exactly what. While outside of Emma's condo, he thought he saw movement in the shadows outside the building. He decided it was his mind playing tricks on him.

The stalker had a perfect view into Emma's living room from his hiding spot, cloaked in the shadows across the street, where he watched through high-powered binoculars. He could see every curve on her body as she lay stretched out on the couch amongst files and her laptop. The binoculars were so powerful, the stalker could see her chest moving with each breathe she took and how her emerald green eyes reflected in the light of the laptop.

He panicked slightly when he thought Hunter had seen him, but when the Mercedes drove away the stalker realized Hunter was too focused on the prize inside the condo to notice his shadowy outline. The plan was all coming together perfectly, he thought. This was going to be one of the easiest jobs in his career—easy money and low risk. It was nothing like the work he was used to, and this could set him up for an early retirement, he mused.

While Emma tried to focus on work, she wasn't able to block out thoughts of tonight's covert activities with Ashley and her boyfriend. She was not known for her patience. It was taking every bit of strength she had not to text Ryan and ask for an update on Ashley and Greg's date. She was reviewing the final draft of the contract for Joe Bonamassa, and making sure every detail was correct, when her phone alerted her that a text was waiting.

"Hi, my lady! Still working on things but got some info. Will tell u tomorrow when I pick u up for work. Sleep well."

Emma breathed a sigh of relief at the sight of Ryan's text. She hadn't realized just how worried she had been, not only about the surveillance, but also about Ryan. Emma surmised from the text that things were moving forward in figuring out this whole mess. The gala was fast approaching, and Emma didn't want anything to ruin that night. In typical Emma fashion, she was more concerned about the potential damage to the gala than the danger to herself that lurked undetected right outside her window, hidden in the depths of the night.

With the news that Ryan was safe, Emma decided to call it a night and try to get some sleep. The stalker observed her turn out the lights in the living room and then move down the hall to her bedroom. He turned on the bedroom video camera to keep close tabs on his prey. With the feed for the camera being routed to the stalker's cloud account, he could replay these nightly adventures at his leisure.

Although his employer was adamant that no harm was to come to Emma before the designated time, he fantasized about being able to touch her in the flesh, instead of through these other means. With each day, his imagination grew more vivid and convoluted. In his mind, he was in a twisted relationship with this beautiful creature; however, he understood that his job came before any personal pleasure.

As the condo went dark and blended into the night like a chameleon, he stepped out of the shadows and walked a safe distance before grabbing a cab. To the cab driver, he looked like any other businessman who worked late, with his messenger-style laptop bag and business casual attire. The stalker smiled to himself when the cab departed, and they melded into the cityscape.

CHAPTER 6

———

Ryan was at Emma's building promptly at
7:30 a.m. He waited for her in the lobby.
Once again, Ryan was chatting with the
security guards about sports, specifically the Bruins
and their run for the Cup. Ryan flashed Emma his
typical smile when she came off the elevator, and
they both walked to the Mercedes parked out front.
It was another picturesque morning in the city with
a slight chill in the air and wispy clouds far above.
A pair of robins were chirping in the oak tree in
front of Emma's building—the sign that spring had
officially arrived.

Emma buckled her seat belt before she started
to interrogate Ryan. "So, what's the deal? Did you
figure out who this schmuck is? Why does he seem
to be part of this whole crazy situation? Is he some
sort of crazy psycho?"

Ryan cautiously pulled out into the morning
traffic and let Emma finish with her barrage of
questions before he responded. "Emma, take a

46   *Tracey L. Ryan*

breather. You're exhausting me." Ryan laughed and winked at her. "We finally have a picture of him—which is good news." He quickly glanced at Emma to catch her reaction, which was reserved.

Emma stared intensely at Ryan with her big green eyes as the car continued to follow the flow of the heavy morning traffic. "That implies there's bad news."

"I wouldn't say that there's *bad* news—just not really any other news," Ryan said matter-of-factly.

"You need to spell this out for me, Ryan. I don't speak 'secret agent' like you do." Emma wasn't trying to be snarky, but she needed to know exactly what Ryan meant.

"You do crack me up. Okay, here's the deal. We have the picture and a voice recording, *but* we still don't really know who the guy is. There are no fingerprints and no record of him anywhere. I'm ninety-nine percent sure his name is fake. Until we get his supposed last name, I can't prove that." They pulled up in front of her office building, and Ryan turned to face Emma. "Look, I know that it's not what you wanted to hear, *but* it's a start. Now, go have a great day and try not to worry about any of this."

Emma exited the car and gave Ryan a wave before she entered the building. Dependable Stan was at his desk, watching the security monitors. Like clockwork, he beamed a big smile when he saw Emma. "Good morning, Ms. Sharpeton. Great weather out there, huh?"

"Morning, Stan. Yes—it's a beautiful morning. Have a great day!"

"Same to you!" Stan called after her as Emma made her mad dash to catch the elevator.

Once in the office, she noticed that Ashley wasn't at her desk. Emma figured she was in the kitchen getting coffee. After Emma dropped off her maroon spring anorak jacket and turned on her laptop, she headed down to the kitchen to make herself a cup of tea. When she entered the kitchen, Emma saw a few of her graphic designers and exchanged pleasantries. There was no sign of Ashley, which sent a tinge of panic through Emma given last night's escapades.

Emma asked one of the graphic designers, "Have you seen Ashley by chance?"

"Nope. Haven't seen her at all this morning come to think of it." The graphic designer grabbed his coffee and went back to his desk to start his day.

Emma meandered back to her office, becoming increasingly concerned. What if Greg knew what they were doing last night and hurt Ashley as a result? Just as Emma considered the worst, Ashley blew into the office like a hurricane.

"I'm *so sorry* that I'm late this morning. I completely overslept." Ashley was out of breath.

Emma tried not to show her relief. "No worries, Ashley. How was your dinner date last night?"

"It was okay, I guess. We went to that Mexican place down the street from here. It was Greg's idea—I could take or leave Mexican, but he insisted that's where he wanted to go. He ended up getting food poisoning or something, so it was an early night. He was really sweet about it, but I haven't heard from him since I took a cab home. He hasn't returned any of my texts. I just hope he's all right." Ashley looked genuinely worried.

"I'm sorry your date got cut short. Maybe you should bring some chicken noodle soup over to him." Emma tried to sound empathetic.

"I would, but I don't know where he lives," Ashley responded sheepishly.

Emma was puzzled. "What do you mean, you don't know where he lives?"

"He always comes to my place or picks me up here. Says it's easier since he's always traveling around the city all day for work. I'm sure I'll go over there eventually." Ashley couldn't hide her disappointment.

"Well, I'm sure that he probably just doesn't want you to see his messy place. You know how guys are." Emma tried to sound like Greg was just another guy, even though she suspected he wasn't.

Ashley smiled and headed to her desk to return calls from yesterday. As soon as Emma was sure that

Ashley was preoccupied, she texted Ryan this new tidbit of information, especially the part about Greg insisting on eating at that specific restaurant. Ryan replied "thanks" a few minutes later.

Emma had just settled into her chair and leaned back when her phone rang.

"Emma Sharpeton speaking."

"Hello, Ms. Sharpeton This is Wendy Aucoin from the Boston Times."

Emma had completely forgotten about the follow-up to the newspaper interview. "Hello, Wendy."

"I hope I didn't catch you at a bad time."

"No, not at all. What can I do for you?"

"I was hoping that I'd be able to come by today or tomorrow to finish part two of the article for the paper. I know you're very busy with the gala fast approaching but thought it might be the perfect time with all the excitement in your office. I can see the team in action," Wendy said enthusiastically.

Emma hesitated then said, "Today would be better. Later this afternoon, if possible."

"Oh, splendid! I can make that work. How about two o'clock?"

"That's fine. I'll see you later today." Emma hung up and called Ashley into her office.

"What's up, boss?"

"Wendy Aucoin from the Boston Times will be coming here around two to do the second part of the newspaper interview. Can you rearrange my calendar to accommodate?" Emma asked drudgingly.

"Sure thing! That's fantastic about the next article. Can't wait!" Ashley skipped out of the office.

The article would be good exposure for the company, but Emma really didn't have the time or the mental capacity for it. The full article was going to be a two-part piece on Sharpeton Consulting and its owner. The first part of the piece had been completed and published over a week ago. Most of it was benign and almost boring, Emma thought when she read it. This next part of the article was going to focus on Emma·as the owner and CEO of the company. Emma was hesitant, but Wendy had assured her that it would give the article the human touch readers wanted. Emma hoped she wasn't throwing gasoline on the fire with the newspaper article. The last thing she wanted to do was put more of a spotlight on herself with her shadowy stalker.

CHAPTER 7

——————

When Emma was originally approached by the Boston Times reporter several months ago, she had decided to do her own research on Wendy Aucoin. Emma wanted to know more about the reporter's background, including how she got her start and the types of interviews she'd done in the past. The internet search pulled up numerous articles that Wendy had written plus photos of events she had attended in the Boston area.

The results from the search produced the standard resume-type information Emma had expected. Wendy graduated from a small private college in western Massachusetts with both journalism and business degrees. She started her career at a few small, local Massachusetts' newspapers before being hired by the Boston Times.

Emma skimmed through the human-interest type stories that the reporter focused on early in her career and fixated on the business topics Wendy was fast becoming known for.

Emma had been taken aback when she did the initial research. It turned out that Wendy Aucoin had interviewed Hunter's father, Philip Logan. That wasn't necessarily unusual—Hunter's father was interviewed frequently, which always helped feed his enormous ego. Emma thought it was strange, though, that there was a connection between this reporter, herself, and Hunter. Normally, Emma wouldn't have given it another thought, except for all the other bizarre incidents lately. A spider's web was being spun, and Emma felt like the fly captured in the middle of it.

To help prepare for today's unplanned meeting, Emma decided to review the series of articles once more. This time she'd pay particular interest to those previously written about the Logan conglomerate. Emma noticed something strange in this reading. One of the articles was on a cancer charity event at a posh Boston hotel in the Seaport District. The article included a photo of Philip Logan with his arm comfortably around the waste of an exceptionally lovely blonde. The caption underneath the photo read, "Philip Logan, owner of Ares Logan Industries, and his companion, Wendy Aucoin, enjoying the charity event being held in Logan's sister's honor."

Emma was dumbfounded that Wendy and Philip went to an event together. She couldn't believe she had missed this article the first time around. In the picture, Emma noticed Philip and Wendy were smiling at each other and seemed very relaxed. Other pictures she'd seen of Hunter's father at those types of events weren't as flattering—Philip never seemed to smile and looked like he wanted to be anywhere else. Then, it hit her like a ton of bricks—she was almost positive that Wendy was the woman she had seen Hunter with in the lobby of his building a few days ago. The one that he seemed very comfortable with, and she with him. For a brief moment, Emma felt her chest tighten, and she couldn't breathe. Emma couldn't believe that she hadn't put the pieces of the puzzle together before now. She tried to calm herself down and apply logic to this new revelation—it could be as simple as Wendy wanting to interview Hunter, like she had his father. Darker thoughts that Hunter and Wendy were somehow involved on a more personal level clouded Emma's mind.

Abruptly, Emma came back to reality. She appreciated that she needed to be coy with Wendy during the interview. This wasn't something she wanted to screw up for her employees. Emma was glad she was armed with the additional information—it would help her avoid going down any rabbit holes during the interview.

The clock on Emma's laptop read 1:55 p.m. Emma sighed. Ashley knocked on the door and poked her head in. "Ms. Aucoin is here. Would you like a few more minutes, or do you want me to show her in?"

"Go ahead and show her in. I didn't realize it was already two o'clock." It was best not to procrastinate.

Ashley fetched the reporter and escorted her into Emma's office. Emma stood to greet her, and they exchanged the typical pleasantries. "Please, Ms. Aucoin, have a seat. It's nice to see you again."

"Thank you very much for taking the time to meet with me today. I know you're extremely busy, Ms. Sharpeton. I really do love the space you have in this old building. They did a great job restoring it, didn't they?" Wendy made a show of glancing around.

"Yes, they did. I was very lucky to find the space." Emma wanted to move this along, "I'm not quite sure how you'd like to proceed. I'm happy to answer any questions you have and give you the twenty-five-cent tour, if that would help with the article. I know we ran out of time for a tour when you were here previously."

"Fabulous! Yes, I'd love a tour. Why don't we talk a little bit first? I'm sure I'll have more questions while you're showing me around." Wendy reached into her large, traditional-style Louis Vuitton tote and pulled out her notebook and pen. "I know what you're going to say—I'm very old-school with a notebook and pen." Wendy smiled as she sat back in the chair across from Emma's desk and crossed her very long, sculpted legs.

It took all Emma had in her not to roll her eyes. "No, not at all. Sometimes going low-tech is much easier."

"How about some background information on you? More than what I can find on the web," Wendy prompted.

Let the games begin, Emma thought. "Sure. I received my MBA from Harvard, and basically right after graduation I started Sharpeton Consulting. To most people, it seemed like an incredibly risky endeavor, but it felt right for me. I really wanted to see what I could do on my own." Emma smiled and continued while Wendy furiously wrote notes, "The company now has fifteen fabulous employees, and I'm hoping—*fingers crossed*—to double that in the next year."

"Amazing! What's it like being your own boss?"

"I wouldn't say that I'm my own boss. I really report to every employee and client," Emma said honestly.

"That's an interesting way to look at it. The CEO who reports to her employees. Can you talk a little bit more about what you mean?" Wendy seemed genuinely interested.

"Sure, Wendy. Think of it this way, a CEO in a publicly traded company must report to their Board of Directors and shareholders. That's basically how

I consider my employees. They're looking to me to make sure we have the most successful company possible, and I know that I can't do that without them. It truly is a team here. No one is a one-man-band. I don't mean to sound like a cliché." Emma chortled.

"I've interviewed CEOs from large conglomerates, and I have to say, none of them ever talked about their employees like you do. They could probably learn a few things from you." Wendy gave Emma a sly smile.

Emma suspected the game had started with this—likely a vague reference to Hunter's father and his fake charm. "Well, I'm sure that I could learn more from them than they could from me. That's just how I am. It doesn't work for every CEO but seems to work here."

Wendy was disappointed that Emma didn't go for the bait and moved on. "Let's move on to the Boston Children's Hospital Gala. That was a big win for your company. I could feel the creative vibe when I entered the lobby. It must be very satisfying for you."

"It's such a worthy cause, and I'm honored to be part of it. I'd be remiss if I didn't say it will also be a boost for the company." Emma wasn't sure how long she could continue with this performance.

"The event is being held at Logan Industries' headquarters, is that correct?"

Emma sensed Wendy was trying to act like the cat tormenting its prey and refused to indulge her. "Yes, it is."

"It's a beautiful building. If you don't mind me asking, Emma, why choose that location over some other, more traditional venue in the city?" Wendy hoped that this would throw Emma off-balance a little.

"Mr. Logan is one of the sponsors of the event and offered his lobby free of charge, so it was great from a budget standpoint, not to mention that the lobby is an incredible space." Emma did her best to stay on point and not offer any additional information.

"I know the Logans can be very generous when they want to be." Wendy glowered at Emma almost daring her to bite, and when Emma didn't, she continued, "I'm sure all of Boston's finest society people will be in attendance."

"We're hoping for a sell-out crowd and lots of donations. Every penny counts when it comes to helping kids get well." Emma could tell she had started to get under Wendy's skin and secretly found some satisfaction from it.

"I do agree." Wendy decided to change tactics. "Okay—let's get into more fun topics. So, Emma, what do you do for fun? You can't possibly eat, sleep, and drink work."

"Oh, I don't know. The usual—spend time with

friends and family. I live a rather boring life, if you must know." Emma tried her best to chuckle.

Wendy baited Emma, "A beautiful, successful, young woman like yourself? I'm sure that your personal life is more exciting than you let on."

For a brief instant, Emma thought she saw an evil glimmer in Wendy's eyes with her last statement. "That's very kind of you to say, Wendy. Sorry to disappoint you and your readers. I just don't have much time for a personal life right now. Maybe after the gala is over, and I've had time to catch my breath." Emma smirked at Wendy. "How about a quick tour?"

"That sounds lovely." Wendy knew she couldn't push the topic and gathered up her belongings.

Emma was polite and accommodating during the 20-minute tour. She made sure that Wendy saw how energized and hard working her employees were. Most of the employees didn't even realize who Emma was showing around their office. The only person who happened to notice was the king of office gossip, Evan Stewards. Although extremely creative, Evan was a complete introvert and would rather fantasize about life than living it. As the two women walked past Evan's cubicle, Wendy winked and gave Evan a cunning smile without Emma noticing.

After the tour, Emma walked Wendy to the front waiting area and extended her hand. "It was very nice to see you again, Wendy. Please don't hesitate to call if you have any follow-up questions. The team is really excited to read your next article."

Wendy reciprocated the handshake and said her goodbyes when the elevator arrived. Once Wendy was behind the closed elevator doors, and Emma could see the floor numbers descending, she felt a wave of relief. When she looked up, she noticed Ashley staring at her quizzically.

Emma didn't feel like delving into every aspect of the interview with Ashley. "It was a long interview but hopefully it went well. Did I miss anything?"

"All's good. Contracts were sent by messenger to Bonamassa's people, and they promised them back to us today or tomorrow."

"Did you hear from Greg yet?" Emma tried her best to sound interested.

"I got a text that he's still feeling lousy, so he won't be able to see me tonight. I offered to take over chicken soup like you suggested, but he said that he really just wanted to rest." Ashley sounded deflated.

"Well, I'm sure that rest is the best thing for him right now. Hey, I have an idea. Why don't you bring him to the gala?" Emma couldn't believe what spontaneously just came out of her mouth.

Ashley beamed at the thought. "Really? You wouldn't mind?"

Emma wasn't sure if this was a good thing to do or not, "Not at all. You've done a lot of hard work and deserve this. Consider it a thank you from me."

Ashley unexpectedly hugged Emma and grabbed her phone to text her elusive boyfriend. "Thank you *so* much!"

Emma had a sinking feeling that she just invited the devil to the dance, and Ryan was going to be furious with her impulsiveness. She sighed and meandered back to her office to finish up for the day. Instead of texting Ryan, Emma decided to tell him in person when he picked her up. It was better to face the wrath head on, she thought.

CHAPTER 8

W hen the elevator doors opened, and Emma stepped out, she was surprised not to find Ryan waiting in the lobby area. At that point, she realized she didn't get the usual text from Ryan letting her know he was on his way. Emma hadn't put much thought into it since Ryan always seemed predictable. Hunter's personal driver suddenly appeared in front of her, which perplexed Emma even more.

"Ms. Sharpeton, are you ready to go?" Jared said with his usual formalness.

"Sure. Thanks." Emma really didn't know how to respond and didn't want to ask Jared too many questions.

Jared opened the back door for Emma and waited until she was securely buckled in before heading to the driver's side. Emma felt strange riding in the back of the car, since she was accustomed to being in the front with Ryan. As they merged into traffic, Emma wondered when Hunter had last sat in the very spot she now occupied and if he was alone. Her mind drifted to Wendy and her apparent connection to Hunter.

The more she thought about it, the more she was convinced that Wendy was the woman she had seen Hunter embracing in the lobby of his building. Emma's blood pressure started to rise when she remembered she had told Hunter about the interviews. Hunter had acted like he didn't know who Wendy was during the conversation. Cleary that was a lie, Emma fumed. She had a strange feeling she would be seeing the striking vixen reporter again very soon.

When Emma returned from examining her deep thoughts and insecurities, she realized that they were not heading toward her condo. In fact, they were going in the complete opposite direction toward Hunter's office building. Emma groaned and watched the concrete and glass buildings pass by in a haze. She wasn't up for whatever was going to happen, and a knot quickly formed in her stomach. For the next few minutes, she fantasized about being on a Caribbean island with an umbrella drink in her hand listening to the relaxing sound of the ocean waves.

Emma knew that Jared was just following orders, so she shouldn't be mad at him, but there was a piece of her that felt deceived. Jared pulled the car into the parking garage, which was new for Emma.

After parking the car in its designated spot, he opened Emma's door and silently escorted her to the private elevator.

In the elevator, Jared pushed the button for the basement. Emma was more confused than during the car ride. The doors slid open to a very high-tech open space with monitors in every direction, people engrossed in their tasks, and Ryan at the helm. Emma breathed a sigh of relief. It was obviously Ryan who had summoned her here. She guessed this was where all the corporate surveillance was handled for the Logan conglomerate.

"Emma, my dear. So glad you could join us." Ryan bowed in front of Emma.

Emma loosened up and gave Ryan a faint smile. "Ryan, why did you have me commandeered and brought here? It's been a long day," she said as she tried not to sound irritated.

"And I thank you for indulging me. Come, I want to show you what we have so far. It was easier to do this here, so I apologize if I overstepped," Ryan said sincerely.

Emma could tell Ryan was being honest. She knew her safety was a priority for him.

Ryan led her over to one of the workstations, and Emma wondered if Hunter was in his office or if he even knew she was here. Before Emma could contemplate Hunter any further, Ryan began providing information to her. "Take a look at this picture. Have you seen this guy before?"

Emma studied the image of the handsome but mysterious-looking man on the monitor before answering Ryan. "I think I actually have. This looks kind of like the guy that I bumped into in front of my condo a few weeks ago. I can't say for sure, but he's definitely similar. Why?"

"This is your assistant's boyfriend, Greg." Ryan watched Emma as the information sunk in. When Emma didn't say anything, Ryan continued, "We still don't know if that's his real name. Although, I doubt it is. We have a recording of his voice from the night at the restaurant. I want to play that for you to see if you recognize it, okay?"

Emma nodded. Ryan handed her a pair of Bose over-ear wireless headphones. She listened intently to about ten minutes of the dinner conversation before taking the headphones off. She straightened out her hair and replied, "Yes, that's the voice of the man I bumped into. I remember it because it was very deep and almost sultry."

Ryan gave the headphones back to one of the technicians. "I'd say this pretty much confirms that the mystery man on the street is the same as this Greg guy. I know it's not a huge step but it does help put some pieces together."

Emma peered at him curiously, "How so?"

"We know that you bumping into him wasn't an accident. He more than likely planned the whole thing. Was probably waiting for you outside your building until you came around the corner. And, it may not have been the first day he did this. I don't mean to freak you out, *but* he probably has been watching for a while to learn your routine."

Emma felt sick to her stomach. "So, this guy's probably been keeping track of my routine? That means he knows more about me than just where I live and work. He probably knows who my family and friends are. Oh my God! Could they be in any danger?" Emma started to shake.

Ryan put his arm around Emma to try to calm her down. "Trust me, I don't like this any more than you do. At least now we know who to watch out for. I wish I could tell you definitively that your family and friends aren't in any danger, but I just don't know right now."

"Wait, then he's definitely using Ashley. What happens when he doesn't have a need for *her* anymore?"

"We won't let anything happen to her. I promise."

Emma remembered her conversation about the gala invitation. "Um, Ryan, I think I really screwed up today." Emma took a deep breath and looked Ryan straight in the eyes, "I kind of told Ashley that she could bring Greg to the gala as her date if she wanted to." Ryan began to protest, and Emma cut him off, "In hindsight, it probably was a stupid thing to do. At the time, it seemed like it would help the situation. We wanted this guy out in the open, so what better place? The security will be impenetrable, and there are cameras everywhere."

Ryan tried to stop himself from strangling this woman. "What's done is done. Do you know if he accepted the invite?"

"I don't know yet. I know Ashley texted him, but she hadn't heard back before I left work. Did I really screw things up, Ryan?"

"No, sweetheart. It may work to our advantage. We'll get to see how he operates in the open, if he decides to attend."

Emma felt a little better. "I'll let you know as soon as I hear from Ashley."

"Sounds like a plan. Don't worry. You have your knight in shining armor: me!" Ryan laughed and hugged Emma. Even though he could throttle her for going off on her own with this, he really did believe it might give them an edge that they desperately needed.

As Ryan walked Emma to the elevator he said cautiously, "You know, I think Hunter is still in his office if you want to go see him."

Emma didn't know how to respond. "Did you tell him I'd be here tonight?"

Ryan blushed, "Well, no, but since you *are* here…"

Before Emma could respond, her attention was drawn to one of the security monitors. It was clearly the camera that was in Hunter's office. When Ryan saw what Emma was watching, he tried his best to block her view without much success.

On the monitor, Hunter was having dinner with a leggy blonde, who happened to be a Boston Times reporter. Candles were lit the table, showing a bottle of chilled white wine and the main course: stuffed lobster tails. Both Hunter and Wendy were laughing and smiling during their conversation. Wendy, casually but affectionately, rested her hand on top of Hunter's as she locked eyes with him. Hunter didn't pull his hand away and appeared to be thoroughly enjoying himself.

Emma didn't say a word to Ryan as she whirled around and headed straight toward the elevator. Her impulsive plan was to confront Hunter in his office, but Jared was waiting in the elevator to take her to the car. Ryan didn't know what to do. He was furious at Hunter for putting him in this awkward position. In a spur of the moment decision, Ryan resolved to go break up Hunter's little dinner party himself. During the express ride up to the top floor, Ryan contemplated what he would say to his best friend and boss. One thing he decided was that he was tired of being caught in the middle. This whole situation was crazy enough without Hunter adding fuel to a growing inferno that was already engulfing the trio.

CHAPTER 9

T
he doors opened into the waiting area outside Hunter's office. Ryan heard more laughter coming from behind the closed door. He turned and went back down to the basement. He could only imagine what was going through Emma's head, but he knew that there was usually a method to Hunter's madness. Ryan would interrogate his boss later. Sometimes, Ryan saw flashes of Hunter's father in his best friend and this was one of those times. Philip Logan was a bastard on a good day and wouldn't hesitate to use anyone to get what he wanted, whatever the cost. He just hoped that Hunter wasn't headed down his father's wicked path.

Back down in the basement, Ryan texted Hunter. "Emma confirmed Greg & guy outside her building the same." He figured the text would bring Hunter downstairs eventually. And when Hunter did venture to the depths of the building, they could have a man-to-man chat about his covert activities. While

Ryan waited for Hunter to finish his dinner with the reporter, he decided to do his own research on this woman. Ryan needed to uncover Wendy's motives before Hunter dug himself into a hole that he couldn't easily get out of. Under normal circumstances, Ryan wouldn't interfere in Hunter's liaisons. Given all the recent chance encounters and coincidences, something made the hairs on the back of Ryan's neck stand-up.

Ryan went into his private office and logged onto his laptop. He had access to countless databases across the world but settled on a standard internet search. When he typed "Wendy Aucoin" into the search engine, all the same references popped-up that Emma found during her quest for information. Ryan also noticed the same photo that Emma had seen of Wendy and Hunter's father at the charity event. One detail Ryan picked up on that Emma hadn't was the lack of information about Wendy's early years beyond the basics. With his hands clasped behind his head, Ryan sat back in his chair and looked up at the ceiling while he tried to wrap his head around what all of this meant, if anything at all.

A rough knock at the door broke Ryan's deep thought. He looked up to see Hunter filling the space that was the doorway to his office. Both men glowered at each other for a few seconds waiting for the other one to initiate the robust discussion that was about to happen. Ryan continued to lean back in his chair completely at ease. He wanted to make his best friend start the conversation. He knew this tactic worked well with Hunter. Hunter always needed to feel in control, and Ryan knew how to effectively maneuver around Hunter's ego to get what he needed.

The tall, dark, handsome Brit stayed virtually monotone as he verbally replied to Ryan's text. "You're confident that the visual we have and the voice recording are the same person?"

"As confident as we can be at this point." Ryan wasn't going to give Hunter an inch. He could do this dance all night if he needed to.

"So, where does that leave us?" Hunter knew that Ryan knew more than he was letting on.

Ryan began to recap the information they had. "What we know is that this guy was most definitely stalking Emma. There was no way that he just happened to be in front of her building that day. More than likely he'd been watching her for a little while." Ryan stopped, not for dramatic effect, but to ensure all of this was resonating with Hunter regarding the danger that seemed to be lurking.

"So, we aren't any closer to figuring this out." Hunter was getting more impatient by the second.

Ryan went head-to-head with his friend. "No, you ass, we aren't any closer! We're always two-steps behind this guy!"

Hunter still hadn't moved from leaning against the doorway. "What the fuck am I paying you for then? I could get a rent-a-cop to do this non-investigation!"

Slowly, Ryan rose from his chair and walked to the front of his desk. Hunter straightened up and stepped inside the office a few feet. Ryan casually leaned against the front of his desk trying to diffuse the situation that was about to erupt. "Just so we're clear, you pay *me* to be *your* head of security and eliminate any threats that come *your* way. I've done that to the best of my ability with the information that we have. This becomes increasingly harder when *you* go off on your own to do God knows what and add complications to an already insane situation." Ryan folded his arms across his chest and waited.

Hunter took two more steps closer. Ryan didn't flinch and continued to stare directly at Hunter. He was used to assessing dangerous situations in a split-second. This was not one of those times, but he also knew the stress Hunter had been under. Stress always made people unpredictable, Ryan believed.

"If you have something to say, Ryan, just spit it out! Let's get this over with."

"Fine, here's the other part of the situation. The only way for me to get confirmation on this guy was to have Emma come here and look at the photo, plus listen to the recording. I had Jared pick her up from work tonight and bring her down here through the garage elevator." Ryan watched Hunter closely to try to detect any change in expression. "Emma wasn't happy about coming here but was willing to help in any way she could. As I was walking her out, she saw you and the leggy blonde reporter whooping it up in your office on one of the security monitors."

Hunter cringed slightly. Someone who didn't know him wouldn't have noticed—Ryan did. "So, while you were enjoying a lovely lobster tail dinner in your office, Emma's dinner consisted of trying to deal with knowing who her stalker is for the main course and seeing you in action for dessert. *And*, it wouldn't hurt to remember that whatever happens in your office goes on a live video feed down here."

Ryan knew he had Hunter's attention just before Hunter lunged at him and both landed on the floor. Ryan tried to block the wild punches coming his way. This probably wasn't the best approach he could've taken.

Hunter knew that at any minute Ryan could end this so-called fight with a few very quick moves but didn't care. He needed to punch something or someone. This was his release for the moment— even if it was his best friend.

One of Hunter's fists was headed toward Ryan's face, but Ryan managed to move to the right before impact. He rolled Hunter on his stomach to stop the punching frenzy. With Hunter's hands subdued, and Ryan sitting on him to keep him still, Ryan asked, "Are you all done using me as your punching bag? I can sit like this all night if we need to."

Hunter's response was muffled because it was getting harder for him to breathe with Ryan on top of him. "Yes."

"Okay, I'm going to let you up now. But one more punch comes my way, and you're going down for the count." Ryan slowly got off Hunter and released his arms.

Hunter rolled on to his back and sucked in several deep breaths before opening his eyes to see Ryan looming over him with a satisfied grin. Ryan extended a hand to help Hunter up off the floor, which he grudgingly accepted. Hunter sat in one of the chairs that hadn't been knocked over in the scuffle while Ryan leaned against his desk.

"Now, would you like to tell me *what the hell* you were thinking having dinner with that reporter?"

"Hey, if I'd known Emma was coming here, I would've been more careful." Hunter glared at Ryan.

"*More careful?* The correct answer would be that you wouldn't have been having dinner with her to begin with! You *are* an ass of monstrous proportions!" Ryan glared back at Hunter.

"Fine. It wasn't the smartest thing I've done lately." Hunter became sullen as the implications of what Emma thought she saw registered.

"That's an understatement!"

Ryan started to continue, and Hunter cut him off. "The reporter had dealings with my father. I was trying to figure out how much she knew about him."

"And, what *exactly* did you find out over a bottle of wine and lobster tails?"

Hunter sighed. This wasn't going according to his plan, although at the moment he wasn't exactly sure what his plan was. "When Emma told me that she was being interviewed and by whom, I did some internet research on the reporter. It came up with the usual stuff, until I saw something that seemed out of place."

Ryan knew where Hunter was going with this— the picture of the charity event. "I saw it, too, if you're talking about the picture with your father at that charity event." Hunter was stunned but allowed Ryan to continue, "After tonight's events, I did my own quick research and pulled up the same things you probably did. Look, you're my best friend and like a brother to me, but you're going down a path you may never recover from. This is twice now that Emma has seen you with this woman in, let's say, compromising positions."

Hunter was perplexed, "What do you mean *twice?*"

"I didn't tell you this before because, frankly, I thought it was a one-time deal. Emma came to the office one day to get measurements or something. It happened to be the same day that Wendy showed up unannounced. I saw Emma coming through the front doors and tried to head her off and put her in a cab back to her office. Told her it wasn't a good time. Unfortunately, you picked that moment to escort Legs out of the building."

"So, still not seeing the big deal. Emma saw her in the lobby of my building. So, what?"

"She also saw Legs give you a very suggestive hug. Hunter, this was the *same day* that she received that package of lingerie from her stalker. This girl has had *nothing* but trouble since you came back into her life." Ryan regretted the words as soon as they came out.

"You're right. This *is* all *my* fault. Don't you think I don't know this?" Hunter's ice blue eyes seemed to turn crimson with anger. "I don't know what the fuck is going on, and I can't do anything to stop it. I haven't slept in what feels like months. I can't see Emma because it's too dangerous. Do you know I sat outside her condo building last night just to catch a glimpse of her walking past a window? Now, I'm a bloody stalker!"

Ryan could see how much this was tearing Hunter apart. "Oh, man. I know this is tough for you, but you need to let *me* do my job without any help. I'm begging you for both of our sanity."

"I know you're doing everything you can to put an end to this." Hunter took a deep breath. "I love her. Guess I always have."

"I know you do. We'll get this guy." Ryan had never seen Hunter like this. He'd seen Hunter with plenty of women over the years but nothing like this. This was definitely different, and he knew it caused Hunter's judgement to be clouded. "Why don't you go home and try to get some rest. We can start back up in the morning. Not to mention, you need to focus on your other project."

Hunter got up and started toward the door, then stopped. "What if this Greg and Wendy are somehow connected?"

Ryan had also contemplated this idea and wasn't surprised that Hunter jumped to the same conclusion. "How do you mean?" Ryan sat in his desk chair to be more comfortable while Hunter provided his theories.

"Think about it. Greg shows up, there's the break-in at Emma's office, and the mysterious stalker. Greg also takes you for a wild goose chase which probably means he knows we're watching. At almost the same time Greg is testing the security fence, per say, Wendy shows up suddenly to try to interview me and Emma. *Plus*, Wendy knew my father—from the looks of it quite comfortably, too."

Ryan rubbed his temples. This was getting more confusing by the minute. "Hmmm. I must admit that I've had similar thoughts. You know how I hate coincidences." Ryan stared at the ceiling. "Let me see what else I can dig up on Miss Legs. I'm calling it a night. Need some sleep. You should do the same. We can reconvene in the morning." Ryan paused. "Tomorrow, I want you to tell me everything that was discussed at your dinner party tonight. And, I do mean *everything*. Understood?"

Hunter nodded. Both men strode to the elevator in silence. Once at the parking garage level, each said "goodnight" and sauntered to their separate company cars. Ryan knew that Hunter was going to go sit in front of Emma's condo building before heading home and figured he'd probably do the same exact thing if their roles were reversed. "Oh God, I hope I don't get hit with Cupid's arrow someday and get all mushy with ass for brains," Ryan thought as he drove away from the Logan headquarters and into the night.

Just as Ryan predicted, Hunter sat in front of Emma's condo for about thirty minutes, hoping to catch at least a peek of her in the window. Hunter had never known that Emma had seen him with Wendy at his building that day. He also hadn't realized that the note he left Emma in her kitchen would have even more meaning than he intended. At the time, he meant it as a preemptive strike for what he was about to do relating to the gala. Hunter sat in his idling car, completely unaware the watcher was being watched.

Emma was mentally exhausted from the day's myriad of peculiar events. She daydreamed about lying on a beach with the sun and waves washing over her and promised herself a Caribbean vacation after the gala. After leaving Hunter's office building, she had Jared make a slight detour to the deli down the block from her condo for a large meatball sub with extra peppers. Jared made sure she made it safely into her building before he made an illegal U-turn and headed back to the behemoth skyscraper in the distance.

Once inside her condo, Emma conducted her now normal routine of disarming and then re-arming the sophisticated security system. When all the proper lights were lit on the panel, she moved to the kitchen to unwrap her sub. Emma opted for easy cleanup with a paper plate and replayed the events of another long day. Emma knew her strong suit wasn't in jumping to conclusions, especially in matters of the heart. She decided to focus on the things that she could control—like the gala preparations.

Emma had skipped lunch, so she devoured the sub like it was the last food on Earth. After she cleaned the small mess she made on the kitchen counter, she walked over to the floor-to-ceiling windows in the living room. The darkness fell fast on the city skyline, and the stars glimmered above. As she briefly peered down to the street, she noticed there were cars parked on both sides as usual. She hadn't noticed the Mercedes parked across the street and diagonal from her building, nor did she detect its occupant watching her intently. Emma also didn't spot the stalker cloaked in darkness on the next block, lurking between one of the buildings, with a tablet in his hand that streamed her live image on the screen. Emma felt a sudden shiver go up her spine and quickly closed all the drapes.

With that, the Mercedes slowly pulled out of its spot and drove back to where it came from, still unaware of the stalker lurking nearby. When the Mercedes was a safe distance down the street, the stalker stepped out of the shadows, as he had done numerous times before, and walked to the corner to hail a cab. While one of the city's many cabs whisked him back to his lair, he thought about the next phase of the plan.

CHAPTER 10

———

Emma woke at her usual time to the sound of a reminder chiming on her phone calendar. She rolled over in bed to grab the phone to see what she had forgotten. Suddenly, she realized that Robert was flying into Boston today.

"Shit, I totally forgot!" She flung herself out of bed. Emma was ready in record time and packed a bag to take with her to Robert's hotel.

She sent a quick text off to Robert to let him know she'd meet him at his hotel after work tonight and they could catch-up over dinner. He had taken the redeye from London and the plane was landing in about an hour at Logan International Airport. Emma hadn't seen her brother in over a year and was elated to spend some quality time with him. Plus, she thought the change of scenery might give her new perspective. Robert's busy schedule in London and Emma's in Boston had made it virtually impossible to find time to see each other.

The siblings had the typical brother/sister relationship growing up. There were more than enough fights between them, but they always stuck together when it counted. Robert knew he could be a typical guy when it came to relationships but was unforgiving if someone did the same to his sister. Emma never knew to what lengths Robert would go to protect her—he gave new meaning to the definition of being overprotective.

Emma smiled as she thought of her brother while on the elevator to meet Ryan. Ryan and Robert would definitely hit it off. She was worried about how Robert might react when he saw Hunter at the gala and made a mental note to have a stern conversation with her brother as the doors slid open.

Ryan whistled as Emma stepped off the elevator. She was dressed in a similar casual look she had on earlier in the week with khakis, a Tommy Hilfiger pale green cotton V-neck sweater and Sperry's. "Good thing you have me here to protect you. There's no knowing who might try to chat you up looking like that."

Emma couldn't help but laugh. "Chat me up? If I'd known the casual outfits would get all this attention, I'd have tried it sooner." Ryan always had a way of putting me at ease, Emma realized.

Ryan deposited Emma in the front seat of the car and whisked her to the office in record time. Before Emma left the vehicle, she looked at Ryan intently. "I know that I don't know what the hell is going on, *especially* with Hunter. I'm trying my best not to jump to conclusions and let you do your job, although that's not one of my strong traits." Before Ryan could respond, Emma hopped out of the car and sprinted into the building. On a good day, Ryan was confused by women, today was no different. He pulled the car into traffic and headed to his own office while he shook his head in amusement.

Emma came barreling through the front doors and stopped in her tracks upon seeing a new security guard at the desk instead of Stan. "Morning. Where's Stan?"

"Don't know. All I know is I got a call telling me to come cover this building today. Do you have ID?" the security guard said gruffly.

Emma searched for her ID to show him, and he grunted in acknowledgement. On the elevator, she thought about Stan and hoped nothing was wrong. He wasn't a young man and had some health issues but always had a smile on his face that lit up the entire lobby. Before Emma could contemplate the reason for Stan's absence any longer, her phone vibrated with a text message.

"Just landed. Will see u @ hotel around 6. Can't wait 2 see u! xoxo."

Emma desperately wanted to be able to tell her brother everything that had been going on. He was always her rock and a good sounding board when she needed it. She rarely kept secrets from him but this would have to be one of those times—it was imperative that she did. Ryan had been crystal clear when he forbade her to tell Robert or anyone else. It was for his safety, Ryan had said. Still, Emma was torn about lying to her brother. What if something happened at the gala? Wouldn't it be better if Robert was aware and not kept in the dark?

When Emma entered the small but finely appointed lobby area of her company, Ashley popped out of nowhere and almost scared Emma half to death. "Sorry, boss. Didn't mean to startle you. I put your tea in your office and also put the last of the contracts for you to sign on your desk."

Emma and Ashley walked into Emma's office to begin the day. "Thanks, Ashley. You've been a life-saver during all this." Ashley flushed at the compliment. "Has Greg decided if he'll accompany you to the gala yet?" Emma knew she told Ryan she'd let him do all the sleuthing but didn't want to let an opportunity pass.

"He said he'd *love* to come! He was totally surprised." Ashley beamed with delight.

"That's fantastic. I hope you both enjoy it." Emma did her best to hide her distaste given she now knew that Greg was probably her stalker.

"Thanks again for letting me invite him. It means a lot. I think we might get a hotel room that night so that we can both have a few drinks after the event."

"Probably a wise decision. There are lots of great hotels in that area." Emma tried to not push the information flow too much. "Let me know which one, and we can probably get a discount."

"Thanks, but Greg said he'd take care of all the arrangements through his company. I think they get discounts, too."

"Okay, let me know if you change your mind. Do you have a dress to wear?"

"I borrowed one from a friend. We're both the same size, so it worked out great! It's a long, black gown with a low-cut back. And she loaned me strappy 3-inch sandals with rhinestones on them. Hope I don't break my ankle."

Emma chuckled. "I'm sure you'll be fine. You'll look radiant. I'm excited to finally meet Greg."

"And, he's very excited to meet you. He was asking me all about you last night. Wondering what you're like and stuff like that." Emma raised an eyebrow. "Nothing creepy. He just wants to make a good first impression." With that, Ashley flew back to her desk to start the day.

Emma sat in her chair and replayed the conversation in her head. She wondered what game Greg was playing and hoped that Ashley wouldn't end up as collateral damage. Ryan had assured Emma that he wouldn't let anything happen to her assistant. Emma couldn't help wondering if Ryan was busy keeping everyone safe, who was keeping him safe. Although Ryan was ruggedly handsome, Emma wasn't attracted to him in the traditional sense, instead she felt a fondness towards him that she couldn't define.

Around noon, Emma's office phone rang with Ashley on the other end. "Sorry to disturb you. Your brother is on the other line. Do you want me to transfer him?"

"Yes, please transfer the call." A smile instantly spread across Emma's face.

"Hi, sis! Was that the hot little number you have for an assistant? She still sounds enticing."

Emma rolled her eyes at her brother's typical commentary. "Yes, Ashley is still here. You never give up, do you? Anyhow, she has a boyfriend." Emma figured this was a benign piece of information she could tell him.

"Why should I? I'm an eligible stud in the prime of my life." Robert laughed. He knew this side of him drove his sister crazy. "I'm heading to the hotel to check-in and then am going to finish up some phone calls there. I'll have dinner sent up to the suite, so we can dine in peace and quiet. Six still work for you?"

"Sounds divine!"

"When you get to the hotel, there'll be a key waiting for you at the front desk. It's the penthouse suite so you'll need the keycard to get up here in the elevator."

"Perfect. And, Robert?"

"Yes, my darling sister?"

"Thank you for doing this. You don't know good it will be to see you." If only Robert understood the double meaning, Emma pondered.

"Right back at ya. See you later." Robert hung up the phone, leaving Emma smiling.

CHAPTER 11

———

Like clockwork, Hunter showed up at Ryan's office as Ryan came through the door. Ryan was surprised that he genuinely got through to Hunter the previous night given how stubborn Hunter could be.

"Morning, mate!" Ryan said enthusiastically.

"You're definitely chipper this morning," Hunter commented somberly.

"It's a fine spring day—the sun is shining, and the birds are chirping. *And*, I get to hear all about my best bud's dinner date last night. What more could a guy ask for at nine in the morning?" Ryan's sarcasm wasn't lost on Hunter.

Hunter sat in the same chair he occupied the night before with a glum expression. Ryan went about getting organized for the day while he waited for Hunter to begin his intriguing tale.

"First, I want to acknowledge that you were right about last night."

Ryan lifted an eyebrow at this admission but

held his commentary.

"Probably wasn't the smartest thing I've done lately."

Ryan continued to stay quiet.

"After Wendy showed up unannounced the other day, I decided to delve a bit deeper into her background. Something was nagging at me, and I couldn't figure it out, until I saw the picture of her and my father at that charity event."

They had covered this the night before, but Ryan had learned ages ago to let Hunter move at his own pace.

"It wasn't just the picture—it was the way they both *looked* in the picture. My father only posed for those type of things if he benefited from it. And that's what I've been trying to figure out. So, in a total lapse in judgement, I decided to invite her here for dinner. It was obvious that she was trying to flirt the last time I saw her, so I figured I could use that angle to try to get information from her."

"Unfortunately, that backfired a bit, wouldn't you say?" Ryan couldn't help but point out the obvious.

"Never said I thought the whole thing through. Give me a break, Ryan." Hunter realized that he had done something that his father would've done and with the same disregard for anyone else.

"All right, I'm not going to pile on the guilt anymore. Continue."

"Wendy very enthusiastically accepted my invitation. I tried to keep the conversation light during dinner—I know my way around reporters so wasn't about to give away any trade secrets." Hunter sighed. "Wendy absolutely made her intentions known. She was actually running her foot up my leg to my crotch!"

Ryan tried hard to stifle a laugh. "Sorry. Go on."

"Glad to see you're enjoying this. I did my best not to encourage her, but since it may be the one way I was going to find out more information I couldn't be too unfriendly. I tried to play dumb and asked her if she ever interviewed my father."

"Did she bite? I mean figuratively and not literally." Ryan chuckled.

Hunter didn't acknowledge Ryan's double meaning. "She did a bit. She said that she knew my father briefly when they did some charity work together."

"Is that all she said? Doesn't sound like much."

"It was the *way* she said it that was strange. Wendy's eyes got a little glassy before she regained her composure. It was only for a few seconds, but not something that you'd expect if they barely knew each other, wouldn't you agree?"

Ryan contemplated this. "Seems a bit odd. What else did she say?"

"One thing she let slip was her contempt for Emma." Ryan's ears perked up. "She couldn't hide it when I asked how the article was going. Don't get me wrong—she said all the right things. But, she went from whimsical when talking about my father to loathing when talking about Emma in a matter of seconds."

"Interesting. Did she know Emma before this?"

"Not from what I could gather. They didn't move in the same circles, colleges were different, not the same hometowns. I think she's jealous of Emma, but I'm not exactly sure why."

Ryan let out a belly laugh. "Dude, are you really that naïve? Wendy's freaking jealous of Emma because Emma has what she wants: you!"

Hunter sat back in his chair and felt even worse than he did when he first entered Ryan's office. "So, what you're saying is I'm a total schmuck."

"That about sums it up. I think that Emma had the final interview with Wendy yesterday afternoon. You need to tread lightly with this reporter. I think she's accustomed to getting what she wants, and she's set her sights on you. Just not sure how far she'll go to get you."

"What about the connection to my father. Another coincidence?"

Ryan was perplexed about this. "I don't know. Could be a total coincidence or she's somehow involved in all this. Let me see what I can dig up on her. Anything else come up about her and your father?"

"No, not really. She talked about Logan Industries and the empire my father built. Almost to say that this is still his company and not mine."

"What's your gut tell you?"

"I think she was, to your point, staking a claim and letting me know her intentions. *And* I think she was having an affair with my father. I keep going back to that picture of the two of them. It was one of the few times I ever saw my father enjoying himself. You can tell by their posture that both were relaxed and happy to be together."

Ryan breathed a sigh of relief. "Okay. Good. I wasn't sure how to bring that up to you. It was the way he had is arm draped around Wendy in that picture that did it for me. There's no way that was a casual thing. Plus, how she gazed at him gave it away."

"My guess is they thought they were hiding it well. Look, it's the only 'proof' we have that they even knew each other. So, they did a fairly good job of covering their tracks—unusual for my father. He usually didn't give a rat's ass about who knew he was playing around."

Hunter got up and started for the door. "Ryan, I'm sorry about last night. Truly. I hope I didn't jeopardize our friendship."

Ryan also got up and extended his hand to shake Hunter's. "No, you didn't. Just think before you do something like this again. We've got a lot of balls in the air, and I'm getting tired of juggling."

"I'm guessing Emma is none too pleased."

"She, amazingly, was very calm. Which kind of terrifies me, to be honest."

Hunter let a small smile slip. "I promise no more clandestine activities." Hunter retreated to his office at the top of the tower.

CHAPTER 12

Emma dove into the rest of the day with a vengeance. She absolutely couldn't wait to see her brother, although she groaned at the thought of hearing about all his recent conquests. Settling down was not something her brother had in mind, at least in the near future. At 5:30 p.m., Emma packed up her bags and headed out the door. When she passed by Ashley's desk, she noticed that Ashley wasn't there, but her cell phone was. Emma scanned for her assistant's other belongings, didn't find them, and figured Ashley forgot her phone, or it fell out of her bag when she left.

An impulsive idea struck Emma, and she did a quick check of the area. She felt foolish since this was her company, but what she was about to do was probably technically a crime. As casually as she could, Emma pretended to be writing an innocent note to Ashley, but instead picked up the cell phone. To her relief and surprise, she found that Ashley's phone wasn't password protected when she turned it on. While she scrolled through Ashley's very long contact list, Emma kept one eye to the elevator in the event Ashley returned to retrieve her phone. Emma's finger landed on the contact entry for Greg. There wasn't a last name, but there was a phone number, which Emma quickly jotted down on a piece of paper.

As Emma slid the piece of paper in her pocket, she noticed the elevator's indicator lights climbing up to the office's floor. Emma gathered her things, put the phone back where she found it, and hurried to the elevator, where she waited patiently for the doors to open. Ashley bounced out of the elevator and almost knocked Emma over.

"Oh, my God! I'm so sorry! I forgot my phone, and Greg's waiting downstairs in the car for me." Ashley grabbed her phone as Emma held the elevator for both of them.

While Ashley was distracted, Emma texted Ryan letting him know that Greg was out front in one of the parked cars.

Ashley bolted off the elevator when it reached the ground floor and yelled a goodbye to Emma. Emma purposely waited a few minutes to see if Ryan could identify which car Ashley got into. When she thought enough time had passed, Emma walked out and climbed into the waiting Mercedes. Without a word, both Ryan and Emma headed to her brother's hotel. Instead of Ryan just dropping her off at the front entrance, he parked in the garage, and they went into the hotel lobby together.

The hotel was relatively new and luxurious, and Emma could now understand why it was rated five-star. The lobby floor was done in a polished Italian white Carrara marble with interlocking earth tone circles around the center of the floor. The furniture featured velour sofas and whimsical chairs in eye-popping color schemes. Brilliant crystal chandeliers dangled high above and radiated off the floors. The front desk was also made of earth tone colored marble, and the entire lobby was filled with enormous vases of fresh vibrant flowers.

While they waited at the front desk for her room key, Emma was noticeably fidgety. After she received her key, they decided to sit on one of the maroon velour semi-circular couches in the lobby. "Did you see what car Ashley got into?" Emma anxiously inquired.

"Yes. And before you get too excited, it's a rental."

Emma was disappointed as she hoped this would be a break for them. "Makes sense." Emma hesitated slightly. "Please don't yell at me, but I was able to get some more information on Greg."

Ryan wasn't sure where this was going, so he let Emma continue. "First of all, Greg will be at the gala. He accepted Ashley's invitation, and they're going to stay over at one of the hotels close by. I don't know which one. Ashley said that Greg's company was taking care of the reservations. Well, that's what he told her at least."

"I can have my team try to dig into that to see if we can find out which one. Go on."

"Apparently, he was asking Ashley a lot of questions about me last night. Things like how I was to work for, do I have a boyfriend, where do I like to hang out—stuff like that. She said he wasn't being creepy, he just wants to make a good first impression." Emma couldn't help but roll her eyes.

Ryan was getting that uneasy feeling again. "So, the boy is trying to do some research through your assistant. Do you think she told him anything of consequence?"

"I doubt it. She may have told him about Hunter, but that's probably it. Now, this is the part where you're probably *not* going to be happy." Emma could see Ryan's jaw clench. "Ashley forgot her phone on her desk when she left tonight. I just happened to look at it and copied down Greg's cell phone number." Emma stopped there and waited for Ryan's wrath.

Ryan counted to ten before he responded, "First of all, that was extremely dangerous. What if both of them came back to grab the phone and caught you? You not only put yourself in danger but your assistant as well." Ryan paused and gave Emma the sternest stare he could. "Did she catch you?"

"Nope. Here's the number." Emma handed Ryan the piece of paper. "You're welcome." Emma sat back on the couch with a smug look on her face.

Ryan didn't know if he should strangle her or kiss her. "You did good, but *please* don't do this again. We've talked about this—no more playing amateur detective. Look, I gotta run back to the office. Enjoy your time with your brother. And remember, not a word to him about *any* of this. I know this will be hard for you, but it's extremely important." Ryan kissed Emma on her forehead and strode out of the very sophisticated hotel lobby.

CHAPTER 13

E mma sat in the lobby for a few minutes to decompress before heading up to her brother's suite. She knew that she needed to put on an Academy Award-winning performance with Robert in town. Unfortunately, he was the one person in the world who knew her better than she knew herself. Lying to him was not a choice, it was a necessity, she reminded herself. Emma knew that both of their lives depended on her discretion.

Even with her back to the front desk, Emma could sense Robert before he reached her. She turned to gaze at her devilishly handsome older brother sauntering across the highly-polished marble floors. The three-year age difference never mattered with the siblings growing up or as they got older. Even though they now lived on different continents, they were still a formidable pair.

Emma wasn't sure if it was the light from the crystal chandeliers above or maybe the jet lag but noticed that Robert looked like he had matured a little. His dark hair had a touch of grey on the sides and a few lines appeared under his emerald green eyes. Just the sight of him brought an ear-to-ear grin to Emma's face as she jumped off the couch and threw her arms around her brother's neck. He reciprocated by swinging her around like he used to do when they were young, which always made Emma giggle.

"Well, big brother, I was just about to head up to your suite. I literally just got here," Emma said.

Robert snorted. "Ya, right. You forget that you suck at lying to me, little sister." He continued to hug her like she was his lifeline. "I thought I'd wait for you in the lobby and saw you talking to some guy that, *thankfully*, wasn't Logan." Robert smirked.

"Just a friend who offered me a lift, Mr. Protective. You'll get to meet Ryan at that gala." Emma touched the specks of grey in his hair. "Looks like you're finally starting to lose the battle with age."

Robert playfully swatted her hand away. "I'm told it makes me appear distinguished." He sarcastically posed as a well-to-do gentleman. When he stepped back to take a look at his baby sister, Robert noticed something in her own emerald green eyes. He could tell she had a secret which she was desperately trying to hide from him and made a mental note to coax it out of her later. Robert just hoped it didn't involve the bottom-feeder, Hunter Logan.

Emma watched him with concern, "Everything all right? You have a strange expression on your face."

"Everything is perfect now that I've seen you. You make sunshine out of the darkest clouds. C'mon, let's head up to the suite." Before Emma could say anything else, Robert grabbed her bag in one hand and wrapped his other arm around her shoulders. "After we take the lift up to the suite, I'm going to take a super quick shower before we order dinner, if that's fine with you. It's been a long day."

"Lift? Wow, you've been Londonized!" Emma teased. "Sure. No problem. I'll just get settled while you do that." Emma paused before continuing, "I hope you know how good it is to see you."

Robert noticed her eyes glistened slightly and this confirmed that she was hiding something. He didn't want to get into any deep conversations on the elevator, so instead he chose the comical route, "I've been told that before. Women just love seeing me!"

Emma playfully punched his arm as they entered the elevator with several other hotel guests. As each floor passed, the elevator became increasingly empty until they were the only ones left heading to the penthouse suite.

"I can't wait to see this place. It was featured in one of the travel magazines last year for its lavish furnishings," Emma said with the enthusiasm of a child on their way to the toy store.

When the doors slid open, Emma's eyes widened. They were deposited into an Italian marble foyer with a similar design and color scheme as the lobby. The foyer opened further into an expansive living room and dining room combination. The staff had turned on the see-through glass fireplace that divided the living room from the dining area for added ambiance. Off the foyer were a study, powder room, wet bar, and pantry area.

Emma slowly walked into the living room area and absorbed every possible design aspect of the space. The floor-to-ceiling windows provided sweeping views of Boston Harbor on one side and the city on the other side. It also boasted a large half-circle plush sage-colored couch situated so every seat faced the breathtaking views. The space included additional seating with tufted accent chairs and a chaise lounge. Emma walked to the windows to absorb the sprawling view and noticed that the blinds were all remote controlled. The hotel had spared no expense in creating the suite.

Robert watched intently as his sister moved through each well-defined space with a look of wonderment. The formal dining area had cherry hardwood flooring with a mahogany table that allowed seating for up to six. Above the table was a stunning modern glass chandelier. The two doors down the short hallway off the living space led to the separate master bedrooms. Each had private marble bathrooms with a glass-enclosed shower, separate soaker tub, and small sitting room adjacent a walk-in closet. The bedrooms themselves each had a tray ceiling, king-size bed with luxurious bed linens in muted tones and views of the city.

Even Robert was a bit mesmerized by the suite. He had traveled around the world for work and always stayed in five-star hotels. This was definitely on his top ten, he concluded. "Okay, your highness, let me know which bedroom you want. I think they're both the same."

"I'll take this one. This is incredible! Thanks again for inviting me to stay with you. Not just to enjoy this very posh suite but so we can spend some time together. I've missed you." Emma hugged her brother for the second time that day.

"Don't get all mushy on me," Robert teased. "I'm hopping in the shower. You go unpack, and we'll meet back in the living room in a half-hour. Sound good?"

"You betcha!" Emma dashed off to her room with bag in hand. Her brother was the definition of punctual, so if he said a half-hour, he meant it.

Emma hung up her work clothes in the closet and put her toiletries away in the bathroom before changing into more comfortable loungewear that consisted of a pair of black Talbots full-length yoga pants and a sea green Talbots soft-drape jersey hoodie. She heard the shower in her brother's room still going full-throttle when she padded out in her bare feet to the living room. Emma plopped onto the plush circular couch and turned on the TV to watch the news. She took a quick peek at the room service menu. Just as she got comfortable, she heard the shower turn off.

The weather portion of the news came on predicting mild temperatures and no precipitation for the foreseeable future. Emma breathed a sigh of relief that, at least for now, there weren't any monsoons in the forecast, but New England weather was famous for changing in an instant. She didn't hear her brother come into the living area until he flopped on the opposite end of the couch wearing an Under Armour Patriots popover jersey with coordinating grey sweatpants. "Good—no rain! What are you in the mood for—pizza, steak? Your wish is my command."

"I snuck a peek at the menu while you were in the shower. I'm bushed. How about pizza, salad, and beer?"

"Now, I *know* we're definitely related! I was seriously hoping you'd say that. Let me call room service, and then we can catch-up a bit. Back in a flash." Robert hopped off the couch and strode over to the phone on the end table. Emma seized this opportunity to really inspect at her brother—his 6'3" broad muscular frame had been her pillar of strength, especially for the last few years. Her high school girlfriends always went crazy over him, and even back then, he loved the attention he got. Morgan and Hannah were the top of the list for turning to mush every time Robert was around. Emma chuckled to herself at the memory.

"Okay, spill. What are you giggling about over there?"

Emma gave her brother a big smile, "Nothing. Just taking a walk down memory lane."

"Oh, boy. That could mean anything." Robert positioned himself on the end of the couch he previously occupied. "Do I even *want* to know?"

"Just remembering how Morgan and Hannah would follow you around like puppy dogs, batting their eyes, hoping you'd pay attention to them. It was *so* annoying! I wanted to throw up in my mouth."

"Speaking of the dynamic duo, will they be at the gala? And more importantly, are they single?" Before Robert could finish, a pillow bounced off his head. "Now that was uncalled for!" Robert shot the pillow back in Emma's direction and hit her square in the face. For the next few minutes, the siblings laughed until they had tears in their eyes. They both remembered simpler times before their father's death and the overall stress of being adults.

"In answer to your question, neither will be there. *But*, they made me promise to setup time for the four of us while you're in town. Just remember that these are my best friends, and you hitting on them would be—how can I say this—GROSS!"

Robert pretended to be hurt, "So, now you think I'm gross? Wow! The sisterly love is just oozing out of you." Before the two could banter further, the doorbell to the suite rang with an announcement it was room service. Robert jumped off the couch to let their dinner in.

The waiter pushed the cart into the suite and set up the place settings and food they had ordered on the dining room table. He discreetly left the suite after accepting the twenty-dollar bill Robert slipped into his hand. Neither of the siblings realized how hungry they were until they sat down and devoured the Caesar salad and fully loaded pizza. To wash it all down, they each enjoyed a bottle of one of the local beers.

Robert was amazed at how good the local beer had become since he went to England. The beer in England was world-famous, but he thought this one was right up there with Boddingtons. "Who would've thought that a small brewery in Sturbridge would be able to compete with the big boys?" Robert marveled.

"My dear brother, you've been gone too long. You forget that we also know how to make beer here. This brewery uses local ingredients and has made it a point to stay small."

"Well, I may have to sneak a few of these on the plane home with me." Robert savored his beer before he swallowed the last of it. "Seriously, this was a perfect ending to a great meal."

Emma laughed. "Glad you enjoyed it. They offer tours, so maybe we can take a day trip out there while you're here."

"Count me in!" Robert exclaimed.

CHAPTER 14

A few minutes after finishing their beers, Emma called room service to collect the dirty dishes and the very little leftover food. Within ten minutes, the same waiter rang the doorbell, wheeled the cart back into the suite, and efficiently removed everything.

Once they were alone again, Robert decided to tackle the perceived elephant in the room head-on. "So, how about we talk about Hunter?" Robert gritted his teeth just hearing the name come out of his own mouth. It had been years since he thought about the tycoon, let alone said his name aloud.

"I was wondering how long it would take you to bring him up." Emma visibly tensed at having to discuss Hunter with her brother. She wondered how much she could divulge, so that he'd be satisfied and not know she was hiding a larger story or want to murder Hunter. Emma let out a sigh. "Fine. What do you want to know?"

"Something is obviously going on with you and

him. I don't want the gory details, but I do know when you're hiding something." Robert let this hang in the air before he continued, "You know I hate the guy for breaking your heart. I'll probably want to punch him in the head when I see him, but I won't ruin your big night. That's a promise. Unless, of course, he does something stupid and it's well-deserved." Robert crossed his arms against his chest and studied his sister.

Emma sighed again. She knew that Robert meant well and was only trying to protect her. "I do love you for being so protective of me." She leaned over and kissed his cheek before she delved into this tale she had spun in her head. "Hunter and I were thrown back together because of this charity event. I'd be lying if I told you that he meant nothing to me long ago. Sometimes, affairs of the heart run deep. I can tell you that we are *not* involved in anything beyond the gala." Emma spoke the truth because, at this moment in time, they weren't even speaking to each other.

Robert exhaled in relief.

Emma was determined to leave out the part that they had been involved for a short period of time until their world was turned upside down. "We actually straightened a few things out regarding the past."

Robert raised an eyebrow but didn't say anything.

"Turns out that Daddy Dearest didn't want Hunter to have anything to do with me and did everything in his power to make sure we were separated."

"And, you believe *him*? Sounds a bit convenient given the old man kicked the bucket, if you ask me."

"On this one thing, I *do* believe him. You'll just have to trust my judgement here." The last thing Emma wanted to do was fight with her brother. "Look, he's still a pompous ass and that won't ever change. The only reason we were brought together again—and I use these terms loosely—was because of this very worthy cause."

"I agree it's a worthy cause, *and* I agree that he's a pompous ass." Robert said with a self-satisfied expression on his face.

"Will you promise to be on your best behavior when you see him?" Emma pleaded.

"I will promise not to ruin the night for *you*." Robert agreed even though he had a feeling that she still wasn't telling him the whole truth.

Emma thought they had made some progress. She stifled a yawn and realized it was later than she thought. "I'm glad you're here. But right now, I need to go to bed. It's been a long day, and tomorrow is going to be just as crazy." She leaned over and wrapped her arms around her brother's neck and gave him a tight hug.

"Sleep tight, sweet Emma. I'm going to stay up a bit longer. Check some emails."

Emma retreated to her designated bedroom and,

after changing into her Kate Spade pink shadow dot pajamas, crawled under the 800-thread count Egyptian cotton covers. She was in dreamland before she knew it. The events of the last several weeks turned into a mish-mash of flashes in her dreams like a crazy movie trailer. The collage of images didn't prevent Emma from getting some much-needed sleep as she floated on a cloud in the soft bed.

CHAPTER 15

A gentle knock on her bedroom door roused her from deep slumber. "Morning, love. I let you sleep in."

For a moment, she thought the slight British accent was Hunter until she remembered where she was and who she was with. "Oh, my God! I forgot to set the alarm. What time is it?" Emma bolted out of bed and headed for the bathroom.

"It's 6:45. No need to rush. I gave you an extra fifteen minutes, that's all." Robert closed the door when he heard the shower come on and clanging in the bathroom. He remembered how growing up the two of them had to share the same bathroom. Robert laughed to himself as images of makeup, lotion, and hair products covering every square inch of the tiny space flashed into his mind.

When Emma emerged from the shower, she changed into her Lily Pulitzer Lillith tunic dress. Once she was presentable, she headed to the main living area of the suite. Robert sat at the dining room table reading the Boston Times in sweat pants and a plain white t-shirt that seemed to highlight every muscle. Emma was slightly confused. "Taking business causal to a whole new level?"

"Ha, ha. I don't have any meetings until ten this morning. And, lucky for me, it's just downstairs in the restaurant. Figured I'd relax a bit."

Robert turned to the sports section of the paper, while Emma poured herself a cup of English breakfast tea and grabbed a blueberry muffin from the basket of pastries.

With her mouthful, she commented, "Wow! These have got to be the best muffins."

Robert watched her inhale the muffin in three bites, drank her tea in a less than lady-like manner, and put on strappy heels that were sure to cause a broken ankle. "You did all that in record time."

"Funny. Now, where the hell did I leave my laptop bag?" Emma visually searched the room before she found it on the wet bar where she had left it the previous night. "I've gotta dash. Have a good day, and I'll see you around six tonight." She blew her brother a kiss and flew out of the suite. Robert could hear the chime announcing the elevator's arrival and yelled "goodbye" to his sister.

Good thing she doesn't know who my meeting is with this morning, Robert ruefully thought.

Since the hotel was close to her office, Emma opted to take a cab instead of Ryan picking her up.

Ryan hadn't been thrilled at the idea but had given in when Emma promised to text before she left the hotel and when she arrived at her office. Even though she got to sleep an extra fifteen minutes, she was still in the office at her normal time. The first part of the morning was filled with last minute details for the gala, including firming up the details with Joe Bonamassa's people. Emma was elated to find out that the blues musician was going to donate his time to the charity. The world needed more people like him in it. The office was at full throttle by 9 a.m., with even Ashley having little time for chit-chat, which Emma secretly appreciated.

While Emma had her next-to-final meeting with the caterer at 10 a.m., Robert was having his surreptitious meeting at the hotel. Robert was dressed in a pair of navy trousers, light blue checkered button-down shirt from Vineyard Vines and loafers as he sat patiently at the reserved table for two in the back of the restaurant, away from prying eyes. Just as the pot of coffee was delivered to the table, the tall, well-dressed, conceited-looking man walked across the room in Robert's direction.

Robert motioned for the man to take a seat and had the waiter pour two cups of steaming hot coffee. "Glad you could find the time to meet with me on such short notice."

"Oh, trust me, I didn't want to miss this. So, what is it that I can help you with?"

"You can't help me with anything except staying away from my sister," Robert said matter-of-factly.

The man relaxed a bit and sipped of his coffee. "That may be a little challenging given the upcoming gala. I'm going to guess you'll be escorting Emma to the event?"

"Yes. Which is why I thought you and I should have this conversation prior to the event." Robert also sipped of his coffee. Neither man took their eyes off the other one. "This is a big deal for Emma, and I don't want the likes of you screwing it up."

"It's a big deal for me as well. Contrary to popular belief, I do want to see your sister succeed."

"Oh, please. You only care about the billions in your bank account. Your family walks over whoever they must to get to the prize. This time, it WILL NOT be my sister!" Robert tried to control his anger, but his contempt was slipping through.

"I know I can't convince you that I'm different from my father, so I won't waste my breath trying. But we both have something in common—wanting the gala to be successful for Emma."

Robert began to speak. Hunter stopped him. "Please. Let me finish. I do care about your sister and don't want to see her ever get hurt. Whether the two of us rekindle anything is up to us, not *you*. And, since you know your sister so well, you'd have to agree that once she puts her mind to something there's no changing it."

"So, you're saying that you *are* involved with her?" Robert was losing the battle of keeping his anger in check.

"I didn't say that. And I don't know if there *is* a future for us. All I know is that this event is important to both her and me. I'm glad she has you here for her big debut. I'm sure it means a lot to her. Look, Robert, I don't want to spar with you, especially over Emma. You and I were friends once upon a time, not that I think we could get back to that state, but can we at least agree not to start a war right now?"

Robert had to admit that this conversation wasn't going in the direction he thought it would. "I'll agree not to start a war, as you put it. But I'm putting you on notice: if I find out you've hurt her in any way, I'll become your worst nightmare."

"Understood. Enjoy your time with your sister while you're back in Boston."

"Always nice catching up with you, Hunter." Robert watched his nemesis walk out of the hotel restaurant. He replayed the entire conversation in his mind and shook his head. There was something that Hunter and Emma weren't telling him, he was sure of it. Robert grabbed his briefcase and headed toward the lobby to grab a cab.

CHAPTER 16

E mma immersed herself in finishing up as much as she could before she left the office. Before she realized, it was five o'clock.

Ashley poked her head in Emma's door. "Do you mind if I take off, boss?"

"Not at all. I think we've done as much as we could for one day. I'm beat."

Before Ashley could answer, the phone on her desk rang. She trotted over to answer it and within a minute, Ashley was back in Emma's office. "Some police detective is on the phone for you. Do you want me to put him through?" Ashley had a perplexed look on her face.

Emma almost forgot about the break-in several weeks ago. It all seemed like a distant memory or a really bad dream. "Um, sure, put him through. Go on home. I'll be leaving as soon as I get off the phone." Emma tried to portray a stoic expression to her faithful assistant.

"Hello, Ms. Sharpeton. It's Detective O'Reilly.

Sorry to bother you at the end of the day."

Emma noted the detective's calming demeanor. "No worries, Detective. Have you found any leads?"

"Your friend, Ryan, has sent us everything he's been able to dig up on this guy, but we've come up with zilch so far."

Emma was surprised that Ryan shared information. "It's become a bit of a pet project for Ryan, so I'm glad he shared the information with you." Emma wasn't sure how much Ryan had shared, so she tried to stay neutral.

"I hate to admit it, but Ryan has other resources at his disposal that I don't have. Which, by the way, concerns me that he hasn't been able to come up with more on this guy. I don't mean to scare you." Detective O'Reilly tried not to sound alarmed.

"Not a problem. I don't scare easily, Detective O'Reilly."

She could hear him chuckle. "I do like your spirit, Ms. Sharpeton. I'll keep digging and leave no stone unturned. I know I don't need to remind you, but *please* be careful and don't take any unnecessary risks. If you think of anything, just give me a call. I'll keep in touch."

"Sounds like a deal. Thank you for all you're doing to find this guy."

"Just doing my job. You have your big event coming up, don't you?"

Emma had a sneaking suspicion she knew

where the detective was heading. "Yes, we do. And, trust me, security will be extra tight. Wouldn't want any issues with the Mayor there." Emma tried to sound jovial. "Say, maybe you and your wife would like to attend? I could send some tickets over to you."

"I really appreciate the offer. Unfortunately, it would be considered a conflict of interest."

"Oh, right. Sorry. I didn't think about that."

"No problem. I really do appreciate the offer. I won't take any more of your time today. Good luck with the event and remember, *please* be careful. This guy is still out there, and it makes me uneasy."

"I will be very vigilant, Detective. Thanks for checking in. Goodbye." Emma was perplexed that Ryan shared at least some of the information with the police. Not that she minded, it just seemed a bit out of character for Ryan and increased her concern about the whole ordeal.

Emma packed up her laptop and files with the intention of doing some work at the hotel. She figured Robert would also have work to do tonight. As she locked her office door, she heard the elevator's chime, announcing its arrival. Panic immediately ransacked Emma's body before she looked up to see Hunter step off into the lobby area.

Hunter noticed the color suddenly drain from Emma's face. "I'm sorry to show up unannounced and that I startled you."

"It's fine. I just got off the phone with Detective O'Reilly. I guess I'm still a bit tense. What can I do for you, Hunter?" Emma said as unruffled as possible.

"I know that things have been a bit...undefined lately."

"*Undefined?* That's one way to put it. Hunter, I'm tired and am about to meet my brother for dinner. I should probably warn you, he's in town and will be attending the gala as my escort. I know you two can barely tolerate each other. Keep it civil for the charity's sake, okay?"

"That's one of the reasons why I'm here. I had coffee with your brother this morning."

Emma was stunned but allowed Hunter to continue, "We ironed out an amicable agreement for the gala. There won't be any boxing matches at the event. We both agreed that we didn't want to spoil your time to shine."

Hunter's arctic blue eyes could still see straight through to Emma's soul.

"You met with Robert?" Emma managed to get out as she realized that Hunter had been Robert's morning meeting in the hotel.

"Yes. As I stated, it was amicable. Call it a truce. Now, you said that Detective O'Reilly contacted you. Does he have any leads?"

Emma was still shell-shocked. "A truce, huh? I won't even ask." Emma shook her head and resumed, "Detective O'Reilly doesn't have any new leads. Although, he did say Ryan shared some information with him but didn't elaborate as to what."

"Yes. I gave Ryan permission to share the basics with the detective. You never know, they may have information we don't." Hunter checked his watch.

"If you have a prior engagement, don't let me keep you," Emma snapped.

"No prior engagement. I didn't know if you wanted a ride to the hotel to meet Robert."

Emma contemplated her answer. It would be tough to get a cab during rush hour and, although the walk would do her some good, she was nervous given her stalker was still on the loose. "I'll take you up on your offer of a ride. *But*, only because Ryan would adamantly object to me walking alone to the hotel."

Before Emma could change her mind, Hunter pushed the down arrow for the elevator. Both of them rode down in silence. Emma didn't notice Hunter glance in her direction several times as she remained focused on the numbers for each passing floor.

Suddenly, between floors three and two, Hunter pushed the stop button and the elevator jolted to a halt.

Emma almost fell forward as Hunter reached out to keep her from falling. "What the hell, Hunter? Are you crazy?"

Hunter kept his arms around her, "Maybe I am. I've been called worse. All I know is that you're in danger and it's somehow my fault. And, I don't know how to fix it."

The smell of his Versace Pour Homme cologne in this close proximity intoxicated Emma. She knew she needed to come to her senses and quickly. "I recognize that somehow we're all entwined in this craziness. I'm some sort of target, but we don't definitively know it's because of you." Emma was surprised that she didn't try to wiggle out of Hunter's grip and scolded herself for still finding his touch electrifying.

Hunter hit the button for the lobby and the elevator resumed. Emma wondered why none of the security guards called the phone in the elevator when they noticed it had stopped. "Did you tell the guards you were going to stop the elevator and not to be alarmed?"

"No. That was pure impulse. Why?"

Emma was trying not to panic, "Unusual they didn't use the phone to call us to see if everything was all right."

"My guess is they saw us in the camera," Hunter pointed up to the corner of the elevator, "and they realized we were fine."

"Sorry. Just a little spooked tonight, I guess."

The elevator doors slid open to an empty lobby except for the guard who was covering for Stan.

The couple walked outside to the waiting Mercedes, and Jared opened the back door for the pair. Traffic was heavy, which was typical for this time of day in Boston. Emma texted Robert to let him know she was on her way and left out the part about who her traveling companion was.

The pair rode in silence for the next twenty minutes. Hunter occasionally glanced at Emma, who was intently watching the city buildings pass by in slow motion. The Mercedes pulled up in front of the hotel. Jared got out to open the door, as was customary.

Hunter slid out and extended his hand to Emma to help her out of the car. "Emma, please be careful, and *please* know that everything I'm doing, I'm doing for us." He released her hand but not before planting a light kiss on her lips.

"You speak in riddles, Hunter. I don't know if I'm coming or going with you. It's exhausting."

"Go enjoy time with your brother. He can protect you when I can't." Hunter ducked back into the car and disappeared into traffic, leaving Emma standing in front of the hotel wondering what just happened.

CHAPTER 17

This was all becoming too much for Emma to grasp. The beginnings of a migraine were taking hold. People came through the hotel's revolving door non-stop in various states of attire, while Emma stood in front of the hotel entrance to catch her breath. Emma eventually joined the flow of people to be deposited into the lavish lobby. Once inside, she casually glanced around on the off chance that her brother happened to be waiting for her.

When she didn't see Robert, Emma headed toward the elevators and grabbed her special key-card. When the elevator arrived and all its occupants exited, Emma maneuvered her way to the back-right corner. Emma realized she paid more attention to her surroundings than in the past. With the elevator filled to capacity, it started its journey to the top of the hotel.

Just like the previous night, with each passing floor, the crowd diminished until only Emma and one other passenger remained. Emma's mind drifted to earlier when it was only Hunter and herself in the elevator at her office building. The chime signaling the elevator was stopping at the next requested floor broke Emma's trance. The older gentleman nodded goodbye in Emma's direction before stepping out and proceeding down the hallway. Emma pushed her keycard into the special slot for the penthouse and was silently whisked to the highest point of the building.

Emma walked into an empty suite. She called Robert's name and was greeted by more silence. She dropped her bag on the wet bar and within seconds heard the elevator chime, signaling its arrival. Emma turned to see Robert saunter into the suite.

His eyes sparkled when he saw his sister. "Good evening, Miss Emma." Robert bowed in Emma's direction.

"I just got here myself. Long day?" Emma was ready to pounce on her brother regarding the secret meeting with Hunter earlier in the day. Robert started to respond, but Emma stopped him with a look. "I heard you had a very productive breakfast meeting downstairs. Care to elaborate?" Emma scowled at Robert with her arms crossed.

Robert muttered under his breath. "Em, I just wanted to set some ground rules. As long as Hunter follows them, we won't have an issue. Now, I don't want to ruin my evening talking about that slug."

Emma couldn't help but chuckle. "Fine, the slug is off limits for dinner conversation. I know you were just being your typical over-protective self, which I love. But you need to understand I'm not seventeen anymore. I can take care of myself." Before Robert could respond, Emma engulfed him in a big hug and swiftly changed the subject. "What do you feel like for dinner? I'm famished!"

"How about lobster tails? I haven't had great New England seafood since I was in Boston the last time." Robert could feel his mouth water just saying it out loud.

Emma flinched at Robert's dinner selection. "How about you get the lobster, and I'll get the ribeye?"

Robert let out a laugh. "I'll get the surf *and* you'll get the turf. That's perfect!"

Emma laughed at her brother's quirky sense of humor.

Once Robert finally stopped laughing, he placed the room service order. Emma sat on the couch. She contemplated firing up her laptop when she saw Robert staring at her. "I was going to finish a few more things before dinner, but I just don't feel like it."

Robert had been considering the same thing and agreed with his sister. "Let's boycott work for tonight and just relax. We both deserve it." He also knew this might be a good opportunity to try to get more information from his sister. Growing up, the only time she kept anything from him was when she thought he'd tell their parents about something that would get her grounded. Something told him that this was worse than her sneaking out and going to a party.

He wasn't sure what was troubling Emma and didn't want to pry into her personal life, but he had a bad feeling about whatever the secret was. Robert knew that Hunter was involved, which made things worse in his mind. Silently, he watched his sister snuggle up on the couch and start rapidly flicking through channels on the TV. One thought kept running through his head—was now the right time to be so far away from Emma or should he consider moving back to the States? Robert was always getting calls from recruiters for jobs in Boston and New York. He was just never ready to come back home until now.

The suite's doorbell broke his train of thought. When Robert opened the door, a different waiter from the previous night wheeled the cart in and setup everything on the dining room table. Robert noticed that the man was about his age with a high-and-tight haircut and chiseled facial features hidden behind a trimmed beard and glasses. The waiter smiled and nodded at Robert. The man briefly glanced in Emma's direction before placing the food on the table. After the food was ready, the waiter discreetly left the premises after Robert slipped him two twenties.

In the elevator, the waiter kept his head down and his back to the camera. He couldn't believe that he had been so close to his prey. He could've touched her. If his employer hadn't insisted on following the well-thought-out plan, it would have been utterly satisfying to eliminate Emma and her brother that evening. Back in the bowels of the hotel, the man disposed of his waiter attire in the designated locker room and left through the loading dock without anyone the wiser.

While Emma and Robert enjoyed their gourmet dinners, Robert eased into his questions around what Emma was keeping very close to the vest. "So, how's the gala coming? Must be in full swing with all the preparations." Robert gave Emma a warm smile across the table.

In between mouthfuls, Emma answered, "Everything is moving along except the actual stuff that can only be done the day-of the event." Emma swallowed a mouthful of her perfectly cooked ribeye. "It's sold out, so that's a great start. It's been great for the company, but part of me can't wait until it's over." Emma tried to sound nonchalant knowing her brother could pick up on the slightest change in her demeanor.

Robert dunked his forkful of lobster in melted butter, savoring how it delicately dripped from the lobster. The succulent meat melted in Robert's mouth, and he almost lost his train of thought. "And after this is all over, you won't have any reason to see Hunter, *right?*"

"I knew that was coming sooner or later," Emma said.

"I'm just watching out for you because I love you. I don't want to see you get hurt. With that being said, I know you're a big girl and can take care of yourself." Robert paused and gazed intently at Emma before he continued. "I know you've been under some stress lately with the gala, but it seems like there's something else going on. You haven't seemed quite yourself these last few days or on the phone the last couple of weeks. I just want you to know that you can tell me anything."

Emma was trying to think fast on her feet. Robert would ultimately pick up on her change in attitude; she just wished it would have taken him longer than a few days. "I appreciate your concern. I really do. I'm just stressed because of the gala and having to work closely with Hunter. Once the gala is over, I'll go back to my usual cheerful, witty self, I promise." Emma gave Robert a heartfelt gaze across the table.

"Okay. I'll trust you—which I always do. Just make sure that I'm your first call if you need to vent about the slug known as Hunter." Robert winked at Emma and knew he had to approach this delicately. He didn't quite believe his sister and was determined to find out what was going on. Unfortunately, Robert didn't realize the danger that he was potentially walking into by pursuing these questions.

After a different waiter cleared that evening's dirty dishes, Emma fired up her laptop to make sure there weren't any emergencies. A quick scan of her email showed that all was calm for tonight. "I'm calling it a night," she remarked and powered down her laptop.

"What? It's only nine o'clock! You're *definitely* getting old!" Just like the night before, Robert found himself dodging a pillow from the opposite side of the couch. "Okay, okay. No need for sibling abuse. Rest well, dear Emma."

Emma kissed Robert's forehead before heading to her bedroom. It still seemed strange to her to be in the hotel with her brother. She wasn't completely convinced that her mother hadn't played a role in all this. She smiled to herself as she walked into the marble bathroom—she loved her family more than life itself and would do anything to ensure their safety.

Tracey L. Ryan

CHAPTER 18

———

While in the shower, Emma's thoughts drifted to Robert's comments about her acting differently. It would completely send Robert over the edge if it turned out that Hunter was right, and he was the reason she was being stalked. But then there was also the bizarre coincidence about Craig Sharpeton working for Philip Logan. The hot water cascaded down Emma's slender frame while she wondered if Robert knew anything about their father's work. Emma made a mental note to carefully broach the subject with Robert over the next few days.

Emma felt only half-conscious by the time she dried off from the shower, climbed *au naturel* under the lavish sheets, and rested her head on the feather pillow. Once she slipped into REM sleep, her darkest thoughts infiltrated her dreams just like they had done so many times in these last few months.

It was a frigid, snowy night in the tranquil town of Hardwicke. The snowflakes were like millions of glittering stars falling from the heavens to earth. From inside the house, the snow resembled pieces of white cotton gently concealing the ground under the nighttime sky.

The only sound outside was the wind whistling through the pine trees—all else was silent. Emma felt an uncontrollable urge to go outside, like a moth drawn to a flame. She walked out the front door and down the path to the unplowed road in her sage green silk pajamas and slippers. She was surrounded by a sea of white as she gazed upwards, mesmerized by the falling flakes against a black sky. Her attention moved to a mound of snow about six feet long in the middle of the desolate road.

In the spot where the mound of snow was, the pristine white flakes started to take on a pinkish tone before changing to a deep crimson. Emma couldn't decipher what was in the road from where she stood, and curiosity inched her closer. When she reached the mound, she instinctively bent down to brush the red flakes away. Staring up at her was her brother's expressionless face, with his eyes wide open, gazing at the snow descending on him. She watched the white flakes continue to turn crimson as they enveloped his body. Next to his lifeless body was one word written in crimson: Whore. Emma stared at the word while the wind eerily whispered her name through the trees.

Emma jolted awake and frantically looked at

the clock. Her pulse raced, and she had broken out into a cold sweat. She had only been asleep for a few hours. The dream slowly became more vivid in her memory, which caused her to bolt out of bed and down the hall to where her brother was sleeping. Outside his door, she could hear him lightly snoring and tiptoed back to her room. Emma sat on the bed for a few minutes, afraid to go back to sleep.

She wholeheartedly believed that dreams were a combination of reality and fears. Although mostly embellished, there was always some truth to them. Emma had been having enough of these crazy dreams lately to not ignore them. In one of her college psychology classes, they had done a seminar on dreams. The professor had commented that dreams have always played an important role in civilization—some cultures thought they were a message from their gods and others believed it was a doorway into another dimension. Emma wasn't sure what her dreams were trying to communicate to her—only that she needed to pay attention.

Still breathing heavy and her pulse throbbing, she got back under the covers and lay down. There was probably little chance of going back to sleep, she thought. Instead she stared at the ceiling until the sun started to rise.

Hints of golden sunbeams gently broke through the one-inch crack in the drapes alerting her that the day had started. She sat up in bed and rubbed her hands over her face, while her nightmare crept into her conscious mind. Emma was sure that it was some subliminal warning for her to keep Robert out of her current situation. Based on the little pieces of information that Ryan had been able to gather, one thing was for sure, Emma's personal life was no longer private. What no one realized was, even with the hotel's best protection, sometimes danger lurked in plain sight rather than only in the shadows.

Emma strode over to the windows and threw open the drapes to allow the morning to fully infiltrate the room. "I'll be damned if you take my brother from me," she whispered out the window to the city below. She noticed dark clouds west of the city and wondered if this was a sign of things to come.

CHAPTER 19

R yan tossed and turned in bed at his small, but adequate, apartment not far from the Logan headquarters. He wasn't exactly sure why he was so restless this morning except that he knew this hunter and prey game was far from over. There were a lot of loose ends, which were slowly driving him insane. He didn't like the fact that this predator was taunting them. And he felt something wasn't right with the world this morning—he just couldn't put his finger on it.

Dawn began to overspread the city, and Ryan headed to the private gym at work. A good, hard workout could cure whatever ails you, he believed. After throwing his gym bag together and grabbing his work clothes to change into, he left his building and walked the two blocks to the rose-hued skyscraper looming in front of him. Storm clouds were brewing in the distance, which Ryan thought could be an omen.

After sweating more than he thought was

humanly possible, he showered and headed down-stairs to his basement kingdom. He barely turned on his laptop and put away his gym bag before Hunter moseyed into his office. "Do you ever sleep, dude?" Ryan asked. His friend probably slept less than he did these days.

Hunter forwent any pleasantries. "The answer to your question is a solid 'no.' I wanted to see if you came up with anything since last night." Hunter sat in one of the chairs facing Ryan's desk.

"Look, I got about three hours of sleep last night. I've been going over this whole thing up, down, and sideways. I appreciate that you think I'm a miracle worker, but I'm not. You need to be a little patient." Ryan cringed after he said the "P" word to Hunter.

"*Patient*? You want me to be patient? I'll just go up to my fucking office and have coffee and a blue-berry scone and think to myself what a beautiful day it is." Hunter was unusually testy this early in the morning.

"Yeah, 'patient' was probably the wrong word to use with you." Ryan tried to placate his friend. "I haven't even had my caffeine fix this morning, and you are banging down my door expecting answers that I don't have yet."

"I know I'm a raving lunatic! I've *never* not been in control—this whole thing is killing me from the inside out."

Ryan knew his friend was spiraling out of control, which made him incredibly dangerous. "I'm going to track down that cab driver that gave me the driving tour of Massachusetts to see what he can tell me about his mysterious passenger. I'm hoping that will provide at least a few morsels—although I'm not expecting too much to come out of it." Ryan sat down in his chair and watched Hunter's expression.

"That's good. Keep me apprised with your progress." With that, Hunter left Ryan's office.

This didn't surprise Ryan—it's how Hunter operated. As long as he thought that people were moving forward, he was reasonable. Ryan knew that he had to deliver news soon—good or bad.

Ryan didn't want to make assumptions, but he guessed the cab driver had a wad of cash thrown his way to take the scenic route. After several searches at the local cab companies, Ryan finally found the one with the correct license plate—Eight Spoke B Cab Company. Ryan made a quick call to the cab company to identify the driver and confirmed that the cab was in service that night. Ryan checked his Tag Heuer Formula 1 Chronograph Black Dial watch and figured he had about thirty minutes before his planned departure to the cab company. What he desperately needed was a very strong cup of coffee, otherwise he might fall asleep during the interview with the driver.

The caffeine kicked in just about the same time Ryan decided he needed to leave the office. Ryan slipped his GLOCK 9mm into his shoulder holster and put his navy-blue sport coat on to conceal it. Normally, Ryan would go to something like this unarmed but given how uneasy he'd been feeling lately, better safe than sorry. Luckily the cab company was on this side of the city, so Ryan only had a quick fifteen-minute drive to their office.

Ryan parked the Logan Industries' Mercedes in the designated visitor parking spot and strode in the front door. At the receptionist desk, there was a perky redhead who didn't appear much older than nineteen or twenty answering the phone. A very manicured finger went up in his direction signaling Ryan to wait a minute. While he waited, he visually scanned the place to make sure there weren't any unforeseen dangers lurking. Just as he deemed it was safe, a very high-pitched, girly voice asked, "Sir, how can I help you today?"

Ryan was now in full Hollywood mode. "Well, miss, I need to speak to one of your drivers if they're available. He was driving the cab with this license plate number on Monday night around 8 p.m." Ryan handed the young woman a slip of paper with the license plate number on it.

"Let me check." The redhead typed the information into the computer. "That would've been

Maxwell Smallwood. Let me see if he's available. Was there an issue with Mr. Smallwood?"

"Oh, no. Nothing like that. I realized that I didn't leave him a tip the other night as I was, let's say, feeling a bit under the weather." Ryan noticed the receptionist didn't question how he was able to get the license plate number.

The redhead brightened up since she wasn't going to have to deal with an irate customer. "That's very kind of you to come all the way here. This city needs more people like you." Her manicured nails busily clicked on the keyboard until she found what she was searching for. "Hmmm, this is unfortunate. It looks like Mr. Smallwood quit yesterday. I guess you're too late."

"Do you know if he left to go to another cab company? I *really* feel bad about not giving him a tip."

"Doesn't say in the computer. Just that his last day was last night's shift. Sorry."

Ryan was perplexed. "Okay, no worries. Thanks for your help, miss."

"My name is Lauren." Lauren winked at Ryan with the look of a vixen.

"Then, thank you, Lauren. You never know, maybe we'll meet again."

Before Lauren could sink her claws into Ryan, he hurried out of the building and hopped into the Mercedes. Ryan maneuvered into traffic and headed straight back to Logan Industries. On the short drive back, he mentally scratched his head. Every time they got a lead, it dried up faster than a drop of water in the Sahara Desert.

CHAPTER 20

Ryan decided to wait until he was back in the security office to call his boss with the disappointing update. He anticipated a lot of grunting and more than likely some vulgarity. Hunter answered on the first ring. "What do you have for me?"

"Hate to tell you this."

Hunter cut Ryan off. "Let me guess—another fucking dead end, Sherlock." Hunter didn't disappoint Ryan and grunted into the receiver.

"No need for sarcasm. I went to the cab company, but the guy quit. Lauren didn't know if he went to another company or just quit."

"Who the fuck is Lauren and what does she have to do with this?"

Ryan counted to ten before this became another shouting match. "Lauren is the receptionist at the cab company. She was kind enough to get me the fraction of information I have right now." Ryan could tell that Hunter was about to interject.

"Hunter, shut the hell up and listen to me for the next thirty seconds! I'm not done searching for this guy. It's just going to take me a little longer to get the story. My guess is the cab driver was seduced into this by a bundle of cash." Ryan disconnected before Hunter started ranting into the phone.

The security area was busy when Ryan ambled out of his office and headed to a very special computer. Ryan sat in the black mesh-backed office chair and entered his lengthy user ID plus password. His team was already searching through the usual government databases, like the Department of Motor Vehicles. With Ryan's top-level government clearance, he usually could find out anything about anyone—domestic or international. Since he had gotten that high-level clearance as part of his past life, Ryan tried to use these resources only when absolutely necessary. This was one of those rare times. This wasn't about corporate espionage—this was potentially a matter of life and death.

One of the challenges with the car service industry—besides Uber revolutionizing how people used it—was that virtually anyone could start their own livery service. Maxwell Smallwood luckily worked for a corporation, so he was just another employee and didn't own the equipment or registration. Score one point for the good guys, Ryan thought. Ryan typed in the cab driver's name and address on record at his employer to see what popped up. He narrowed down the search to three Maxwell Smallwood's living in Boston in the same general area as the address on his work file.

After about an hour of searching through various databases, Ryan and the team found the proverbial pot of gold at the end of the rainbow. He was ninety-nine percent sure that this was the Maxwell Smallwood they were searching for. Max was twenty-five years old, graduated from a Massachusetts state university, and was recently a casualty of corporate layoffs. He apparently took this job to help pay the rent while he was searching for a new corporate finance job. From a family perspective, he had relatives in the Boston area. His parents lived in Cambridge, while Max rented a small garden apartment in the South End of Boston.

Ryan sat back in his chair and contemplated what he'd learned thus far about Maxwell Smallwood. He seemed like he came from a decent home and had learned the value of working for a living. His mother was an administrative assistant in Waltham and his father was an operations manager at a manufacturing company in Needham. From what Ryan could tell from the DMV photo, Max was clean-cut, with that all-American "boy next door" appearance.

Max had no criminal arrests and only the occasional parking ticket in the police file. There had been no large deposits into his bank account over the last few days that would indicate irregular activity. All in all, the cab driver seemed respectable, not someone who would willingly be part of this situation. Ryan scratched his head. Something was wrong with the whole picture. Max was the definition of squeaky clean and he was nowhere to be found.

One of the technicians popped his head into Ryan's office. "I think we found something," was all he said before heading back to his computer. Ryan knew this wasn't good news and slowly walked to where the technician was sitting. The screen showed a picture of Maxwell Smallwood with a gunshot wound to his temple. Ryan stared at the screen for thirty-seconds before commenting, "Seems like we found Mr. Smallwood." Then without another word, Ryan walked back into his office and slammed the door shut.

Ryan left a message for Detective O'Reilly to see if he could get any specifics around this case. Within fifteen minutes, Detective O'Reilly returned Ryan's call. "Ryan, I have to ask. Why the hell do you want to know about some John Doe transient murder in Roxbury? Seems like you'd have better things to do sitting in that ivory tower." O'Reilly knew that Ryan had many resources at his disposal, which made the detective wonder why Ryan sought him out on such a trivial case.

"Call it morbid curiosity. Just placate me. What've you got on this one? I may have information that would be worth your while."

"We don't have much. Medical examiner said it probably happened around midnight—give or take an hour." Ryan could tell that Detective O'Reilly was drinking something hot while talking because he could hear him constantly blowing on his cup to cool it down. "No ID, and strange thing: no fingerprints."

Ryan was surprised. "What do you mean no fingerprints? Not in the database?"

"No—I mean his fingerprints were burnt off with some sort of corrosive material. He barely had fingertips let alone prints. Strangest thing I've *ever* seen. So, right now we don't have a way to make a positive ID. Looking at how disheveled and dirty his clothes were, my guess is he's homeless and maybe stumbled across a drug deal or something he shouldn't have seen." Detective O'Reilly took a big gulp of his cooled coffee while he waited for Ryan's reaction.

"Definitely strange, unless the killer didn't want you to be able to easily identify the body. In which case, it probably isn't your typical street thug or drug dealer. It was premeditated."

"I figured you'd say something like that. Once the lab determines what was used to burn off the tips, we'll have a better idea of what's going on. For this poor guy's sake, I just hope that was done post-mortem." O'Reilly took another swig of coffee. "You said you might be able to help. Let's start with telling me why the interest in this."

"He may be connected to the break-in at Ms. Sharpeton's office. I haven't put all the pieces together yet, but I may know who he is."

"Whoa—slow down! Connected to the break-in? How?"

"I think this guy was an innocent bystander in all this—wrong place, wrong time. You may want to explore Maxwell Smallwood from the Eight Spoke B Cab Company. He possibly drove the suspect in the break-in Monday night from a Mexican restaurant in the Seaport District."

"You've lost me. Do I even *want* to know how you know this? I probably don't, do I?"

"Let's just say, I ran my own sting operation. Unfortunately, the guy hopped in a cab, or so I thought, and sent me on a wild goose chase following a cab with no passenger. I tracked down the cab and the driver—Maxwell Smallwood—but this guy supposedly quit a few days after the joy ride." Ryan knew that he couldn't divulge all the details to the detective but needed to give him enough breadcrumbs to follow the trail. "Everything I could find on Smallwood says he was a hard-working guy with not even the hint of bad behavior."

Detective O'Reilly let this new information sink in before he answered. "I'll follow-up on this. The break-in suspect found out you were tailing him and then paid this cabbie to take you on a joy ride. Does that about cover it?"

Ryan flinched. "Yes. That about covers it."

"No wonder you aren't a spy anymore." Detective O'Reilly snickered into the phone. "Let me check out what you gave me. I know enough to not push you for details. I'll be honest—the scene looked a bit staged based on the photos I saw. That gunshot wound was point-blank and an expert shot in my opinion."

"That's what I was afraid of. My guess is the suspect offered the kid the type of payday you couldn't pass up but then when it came time to pay up—the kid got early retirement instead."

"All right. I'll let you know if this John Doe is who you think it is." Detective O'Reilly paused. "Ryan, what the hell is all this leading us to?"

"I wish I could tell you, but I honestly don't know. I just have a bad feeling about it."

"Make sure to keep a close eye on Ms. Sharpeton. She's got her big shindig coming up."

"Trust me, she's going to have more security on her than the President. Emma doesn't know anything about this Smallwood guy, so I'd appreciate it if you kept this between us."

"Gotcha—won't mention it to Ms. Sharpeton. Let me know if you get any more hunches." Detective O'Reilly disconnected and finished the last swallow of his now cold police department coffee. He leaned back in his creaky department-issued desk chair to try to make sense out of all this. A storm was brewing—he just didn't know if it was going to be a Nor'easter or an Alberta Clipper.

After the call ended, Ryan rubbed his temples. A soft knock on the door alerted him he had a visitor. Hunter once again stood in Ryan's office doorway wanting answers instead of more questions. "So, did you find this cab driver?"

Leaning back in his chair, Ryan gave Hunter all the details of his conversation with the detective. "So, we basically ran into another dead end. And, this time I mean it literally. I'll keep digging—see what I can find."

Hunter felt exasperated. "It's like I'm in one of those corn field mazes and there's no way out. This guy just upped the stakes by murdering someone."

"Agreed. This has all the makings of a professional job. It was calculated and planned. I really think this confirms he's a hired gun. I don't think we should tell Emma about this. It will only freak her out before her big event."

Hunter thought for a moment before he answered. "I agree. I don't want her to focus on the dead cab driver. She'll only think it's her fault, and that won't solve anything."

"Glad we're in agreement. Look, go back to being the corporate raider you are and let me dig into this more. I feel like there's something that we're missing and it's staring at us right in the face." Before Hunter left, Ryan told him, "Don't be calling me every ten minutes for an update. I need time to do my thing." Hunter shrugged and walked out of Ryan's office.

Ryan felt as frustrated as Hunter. And, Hunter was right—if this was a poker game, their opponent just upped the ante. This adversary was feeling them out to see if they were willing to call or fold. Ryan knew that he had to figure out this guy's motives soon or there could be a lot more bodies piling up like chips on the poker table.

After pacing around his office for ten minutes, Ryan decided to write down what they knew about Greg to start creating a profile. Ryan subconsciously tapped the end of the black Cross TracR ballpoint pen on his notepad as the outline of a profile formulated in his brain.

From watching the video footage, plus the information gained from the various other encounters, Ryan knew the following about their nemesis:

- Highly intelligent, methodical, and patient
- Probably had at least some police, and possible military, training given his knowledge of diversion tactics
- Manipulative with ability to charm those around him
- Callous unconcern for human life and lack of remorse

Ryan stared at the piece of paper in front of him and a chill went up his spine. His mind drifted to when he was working for a certain government agency— these were all the characteristics that were required for the job. This guy could be Ryan's twin from a psychological standpoint and that scared him down to his core. The one unknown was if Greg was the mastermind or just a pawn in a larger game. If Greg was a pawn, this added a whole new level of challenges.

CHAPTER 21

———

Emma wasn't quite herself at the office, and Ashley sensed something was amiss. "Hey, boss, you feel okay?" Ashley asked after she poked her head in Emma's doorway.

"I didn't sleep well last night. Getting a bit anxious for the gala, I guess." Emma knew she needed to be on guard with Ashley but just didn't have the strength today.

"I get it, but you know you have everything perfect. Unless it is more about Mr. Tall, Dark, and British?" Ashley probed.

This conversation was really giving Emma a migraine but made her curious at the same time wondering how far she could take it to find out additional information. "Oh, trust me, he's also causing some of this stress. Can't wait to see what kind of bimbo he brings to the gala."

"I thought things were going good with him. Apparently not. Sounds like you're maybe a little jealous."

"We've calmed things down—not that they were that hot to begin with. Maybe I'm a little jealous, but I'm not surprised by anything that he does. Been there, done that, as they say. Once the gala is over, I won't have to deal with him ever again. Truth be told, that is just fine by me." Emma tried to sound convincing while also wondering if this information would change the course of events if Greg knew.

Ashley seemed genuinely concerned. "As my mom always used to tell me—if it's meant to be, it's meant to be. That's how I think of Greg. I was in such a slump, going out with losers, and then one day Greg literally walks into my life. I know I'm just a pion here but here's my opinion: Mr. British gave you and this company a chance with the gala, so focus on the good that came out of it. Sure, romance is always nice, but you've worked hard to get this company going—enjoy the reward."

"Very good advice, I really do hope that Greg is your knight in shining armor—you deserve it. And, you are NOT just a pion here, Ashley. You are a lifesaver to me—I couldn't have made it this far without you. Please don't forget that." Emma was heartfelt in what she told Ashley.

Ashley blushed before turning to leave. "Thanks, boss!" With that Ashley fluttered back to her desk.

Emma was very concerned about Ashley being involved with Greg, if he was the culprit that Ryan and Hunter thought he was. She knew that love was blind, but Ashley was a smart woman. It was hard for Emma to believe that Ashley didn't have at least an inkling that something wasn't quite right about Greg, unless Greg was really that good at being a chameleon and hiding his true identity.

Emma's cell phone rang, breaking her out of her trance. When she looked down, she noticed Ryan's number was on the screen. For a second, her heart stopped as she thought he either found out more information or something had happened. "Hi, Ryan."

"Hello, my lady! Just wanted to check-in to see how you were doing today." Ryan sounded normal with no hint of worry.

"I'm just peachy." Emma couldn't hide her exhaustion.

Ryan immediately picked up on her mood. "Are you sure everything's good? You sound really tired."

Emma sighed. "I didn't sleep well last night. You know how it is, too much luxury in that hotel suite."

"Oh yes, happens to me all the time." Ryan chuckled a little. "Just wanted to let you know that I'll pick you up tonight around 5:15 if that's acceptable. Trying to finish up a few things here."

"That's fine. I've got a few things to finish, too. Did you find anything else out about this whole mess?"

"Sorry. I'm working every angle but keep coming

up with dead ends." Emma didn't catch the double meaning of Ryan's last statement. "While the team is focused on this mess, as you call it, I'm going over all the security plans for the gala. I might have some questions for you."

"Sure. We probably should talk about what you have in mind. God knows if all this crap is leading up to the big night or not." Emma was deflated.

"Cheerio! I'll see you later, and you can let me know when a good time is to meet on Monday." Ryan hung up before Emma could respond. He was concerned about how defeated she sounded. This situation was wearing everyone out.

Ryan just started conducting more research on his laptop when Hunter strode into his office for the second time that day. Hunter sat down and exhaled.

"You sound like Emma just did," Ryan observed.

Hunter was puzzled. "What are you talking about? You talked to her? Is there anything wrong?"

"Whoa! Slow down, cowboy. I just called her to let her know when I'd pick her up. She sounded defeated on the phone. *And*, really tired."

"We're all tired and want this mess to go away quickly!" Hunter snapped.

"I'd love nothing more than to make this all disappear with one wave of a magic wand, but I'm fresh out of wands. Look, this whole thing is a lot to handle. I need you and Emma to just focus on what you do best—your day jobs." Hunter grunted. "Speaking of day jobs, how are the negotiations for the acquisition going?"

Hunter rubbed his temples before he answered. "Basically, they're stalled. I was hoping to avoid playing hardball but seems like that is what I'm going to have to do, not that I haven't done that before. Just given the company and who works there, I have a feeling I'm in for a world of trouble."

Ryan couldn't disagree. "That should be an interesting conversation with brother and sister. I definitely don't envy you there. Does he know what's going on?"

"I don't think so. He would've said something at our little breakfast meeting the other day. It's not like his job is in jeopardy—I want him to stay on and even promote him. He's got a stellar reputation and can go far in the newly merged company. I'm not sure he'll see it that way, since he'll technically be working for me."

Ryan couldn't help but laugh. "You definitely take the saying 'go big or go home' to the extreme. When's the next meeting?"

"Tuesday morning. And Robert has been invited to the table."

"Okay, I'll make sure there's extra guys on stand-by." Ryan laughed again.

Hunter glared at Ryan. "You are NOT funny!"

As Hunter got up to leave, Ryan asked, "Do you

think that this acquisition could have anything to do with the other situation?"

Hunter contemplated his answer. "I've thought about it but can't see how. Except that Emma's brother would be affected. And, I don't think he'd resort to stalking and threatening his own sister."

"Good point. Just grasping, I guess."

"I think anything, *and* anyone is possible, just not this specific instance." When Hunter reached the doorway, he said, "The extra security on Tuesday may not be a bad idea." Then, as quickly as Hunter came into Ryan's office, he was gone.

CHAPTER 22

———

After another day of not getting any closer to the answers they desperately needed, Ryan realized it was already time to collect Emma. Before he left the office, he made sure that the overnight security team had their marching orders, and then proceeded to the parking garage. On the drive to Emma's office, Ryan thought again about the growing number of connection points that could no longer be defined as mere coincidences. There were just too many concurrences, he kept telling the voice in his head.

When Ryan pulled up to the curb in front of Emma's office building, Emma was sitting on the bench outside with her briefcase and phone in her hand. She waved when she saw him and walked to the passenger side of the Mercedes.

Before Ryan could open his mouth, Emma explained, "I thought I'd sit outside because it was sunny and warm. And, don't yell at me about safety, I'm too tired to argue."

"I won't yell but instead gently remind you that inside is safer than outside."

"That's not completely accurate since my office was vandalized," Emma said proudly.

Ryan smiled at Emma as she had a valid point. "You got me there. How was your day, dear?"

A small smile formed on Emma's face. "It was fine. Just finishing up the last-minute stuff. Oh, I checked my calendar. I can do either 10 a.m. or 1 p.m. Monday to go over the security details for the gala."

Ryan headed toward Emma's hotel. "How about ten? I can come here, so it'll be easier."

"And I won't risk my neck going out in public?" Emma questioned sarcastically.

"Yes, that too. You know me so well." Ryan winked in Emma's direction, which made her laugh. "Ah, there it is—the real Emma is coming out. I knew you couldn't make it the entire ride without giving into my enormous charm."

Emma shook her head. It was strange that she hardly knew Ryan but trusted him completely. "You always brighten my day."

Ryan pulled up in front of the hotel and put the car in park. Emma was about to open the door to exit when she felt Ryan's hand on her forearm. "Look, Emma, I know that you understand this situation is dangerous. So, I don't mean to be terse with you when you do stupid things." Emma cocked her eyebrow at Ryan. "How about I rephrase to unwise? Just be careful. *Please*."

"I know you're looking out for me. I just hate feeling like a prisoner. *And*, I don't even know what I did to be imprisoned."

"I know. I promise that I'll get to the bottom of this if it kills me."

Emma was taken back by Ryan's determination. "My turn to lecture. I know you are a super-spy and all that, but I couldn't live with myself if something happened to you because of me. So, it's my turn to tell *you* to be careful."

Ryan was touched by Emma's concern. "Let's pinky-swear that we'll both be careful." Ryan held up his left pinky in Emma's direction. Emma smiled and shook her head as she locked her right pinky in his before she jumped out of the car and headed toward the hotel entrance. She turned back and gave Ryan a wave before continuing into the lobby.

A thin smile formed on Ryan's usually hard face as he thought about the simple gesture that was exchanged between them. Ryan wanted to make sure that he stayed on Emma's good side. Once she found out about the pending acquisition, and how it related to her brother, things could get ugly.

One thing that Ryan never cared to get involved in was the business side of things—he didn't have the business acumen that Hunter did. Not that he didn't appreciate all the daily stresses Hunter went through, Ryan was just wired differently. Sitting through endless meetings, listening to people complain all day, and dying of boredom from reading financial statements wasn't his cup of tea. Ryan thrived on action, and he'd never admit this to Hunter, but he had even found his own job boring until recently. Solving these mysteries was what Ryan was born to do. At that moment, Ryan decided to call his team and put a few extra guys on for the meeting Tuesday morning, just in case.

CHAPTER 23

———

R obert was waiting in the suite when Emma arrived. When he heard the chime of the elevator's arrival, Robert announced, "Let's go out to dinner tonight instead of eating here."

"Fine by me. Just one request—let's go someplace cheap and cheerful. Pick a place, and I'll go freshen up." Emma dashed into her room. She decided on BLANKNYC embellished straight leg jeans with a navy-blue V-neck cotton sweater and lace-up wedge shoes.

When Emma returned, Robert was gazing out the windows toward the harbor. "Penny for your thoughts," Emma said wistfully.

"Just a penny? I figured it was at least a quarter with inflation." Robert smirked at his sister and headed toward the elevator. Emma pushed the down button and magically the elevator doors opened. They rode down the multiple stops in silence while others came and went.

In the lobby, Emma asked cheerfully,

"So, where to?"

"How about O'Ryan's Pub? I used to love that place when I lived here. Guessing it still has the same food and bar."

"Sounds perfect. I haven't been there in forever. Let's go, dear brother of mine."

O'Ryan's Pub was only two blocks from the hotel, so the pair decided to walk. Emma was hesitant at first. Ryan would be less than pleased at their decision. Outside was bright with the sun's rays filtering through the Boston skyline. Emma breathed in the refreshing sea air. The trees had started to fully fill-in with their leaves. It was a typical Friday night in Boston with the working crowd heading to the local bars for drinks with co-workers to celebrate the end of the workweek.

Emma and Robert spent the short walk people-watching and enjoying being outside. Neither of them noticed that amongst the throngs of people, a silent predator trailed a short distance behind them. The stalker looked like any other businessman, with his spring trench coat and backpack, on his way to meet friends for a few cocktails. Tonight, he was hiding in plain sight instead of the shadows, which made him even more dangerous to his prey.

At first, the stalker had been upset that Emma had moved into the hotel with her brother. Hotels were nearly impossible for surveillance, and cameras captured virtually every step inside, not to mention he wasn't getting the live video feeds, which was disappointing. Emma's schedule had remained basically the same, so he made some minor adjustments in catching her outside and bribing the hotel staff for inside.

It seemed like the unaware pair were headed to the Irish pub. The stalker smiled. He would fit in perfectly with that atmosphere. The key would be to make sure that he was seated close enough to them but not so close as to cause any suspicion. The stalker couldn't be sure that she hadn't seen his face from the clumsy surveillance the Logan rent-a-cop had tried to conduct. He wasn't one to take too many risks, unless the reward was worth it. All three reached their destination minutes apart.

The pub was hopping with both business people and tourists. Emma and Robert were shown to their table. The shadowing man was seated at the bar with an excellent view of the couple. Both enjoyed a Guinness with their fish and chips and decided to forego dessert. Dinner conversation was kept to discussing the gala and any other non-controversial topics, like the weather. What the pair didn't realize was that danger sat only a few feet away from them.

When the duo left the restaurant, Emma locked her arm in Robert's as they strolled to the hotel. She decided it was time to broach the conversation about their father's employment. "How much do you know about dad's job?"

"What do you mean? He was a chemist. He seemed to be good at his job. Why?"

"Oh, no reason. Mom asked me to start cleaning out the house, so I started in his office. I found some interesting—although *completely* over my head—files and stuff in there. Just didn't know if you knew more about what he did. I wasn't sure if I should toss them or not." Emma shrugged.

"Not really. I know he used to get a lot of job offers, but he never really talked about it. I remember asking him one time. All he said was that he was hoping to make the world a better place."

Emma thought about Robert's last comment. "That's interesting."

"I guess. He never told me how he was going to do that, though." Robert stopped in the middle of the sidewalk and glanced at his sister. "Everything okay?"

"Yes, it's fine. When I saw his files and his handwriting it just made me a little sad that I never showed more interest in his work. I was just feeling a little nostalgic. No need to worry." Although Emma was covering up the real reason for the question, what she told Robert wasn't a complete lie. She did feel guilty for never taking the time to show more interest in her father's work.

"I get how seeing that stuff would bring back memories. I can help with going through the house while I'm here if you want."

"Thanks. With the gala coming up, I probably won't get back to Hardwicke until after you leave. I appreciate the offer, though."

The pair continued their leisurely stroll as night started to blanket the Boston skyline. Commuters were on their way home after a long day at the office. Tourists were excited to go out and experience the Boston nightlife at the many restaurants and bars in the area. The Boston harbor cruises were starting to depart for their city tours on the water. To anyone else, it would be a perfect spring evening in one of the most historic cities in the country. This was the calm before the storm, the stalker thought, as he trailed the pair back toward their hotel. When the couple crossed the street and entered the lobby, the man continued walking, fading into the shadows of the crowd.

CHAPTER 24

The weekend was a blur for Emma. Her and Robert decided to act like tourists and do all the exciting activities like the duck boats, aquarium, and a harbor cruise plus dinner with her two best gal pals. For two solid days, Emma didn't think about stalkers or vandals or the gala. She was overjoyed to be spending time with Robert and just having some good old-fashioned fun.

Even dinner Saturday night with Morgan and Hannah proved to be some much-needed entertainment. Emma's best friends once again fawned over Robert just like in high school. Robert soaked up the attention and loved being out with three lovely ladies. They had a five-star dinner at a new fusion restaurant and then hit the bars on the block for a night of reminiscing, dancing, and relaxing. All Emma could do was laugh and hope that this weekend would go on forever.

Emma made sure she texted Ryan each time they moved to a new location. She knew he had installed some sort of tracking application on her phone, but figured he'd be happier if she gave the appearance of complying with his safety measures.

While the siblings were off on their tourist adventures, Hunter was busy at his office, finalizing the plans for the major acquisition. A big unknown was going to be Emma's brother and how Robert would react to the news. Hunter couldn't worry about Robert's state of mind—he needed to focus on the 30,000 employees that would be absorbed into the Logan conglomerate. This would be the largest acquisition Logan Industries had ever done, and although Hunter didn't want to jinx anything, he felt they were in the home stretch.

Hunter was beginning to relax and gaze out of the windows in his office when the door swung open. "Hey, dude, all work and no play makes Hunter a very dull boy." Ryan said.

"I'm trying to finish up all the paperwork for the acquisition, including that one very important packet of documents."

Ryan sat down on the couch and made himself comfortable. "Gotcha. What do you think the chances are that important packet is going to go your way?"

Hunter contemplated his answer. "Honestly, it's probably 50/50. Could go either way."

"Seems like Emma is having fun this weekend with her brother."

Hunter gave Ryan a suspicious look.

"I installed the tracking application on her phone, but she's been surprisingly cooperative and has been texting me her locations."

"My suggestion to you is to be wary when she seems to be cooperating," Hunter said flatly.

Ryan laughed. "I agree. They've just been doing all the tourist stuff. My guess is she's safe for now—this guy is going to want to make a big splash, and their spontaneity doesn't work well with his meticulous planning."

"That's what I'm afraid of. How secure will the gala be?"

Ryan got up and walked to the windows. "It will be as safe as possible. There will be metal detectors that everyone will need to go through. All workers have already been vetted with background checks. No one will be allowed in unless they have an invitation or valid identification badge. I'll be having the bomb dogs do their thing before, during and after the event. Best we can do."

Hunter grumbled at the potential for something to happen at the gala. "Sounds like you have it covered. I just hope that this guy's 'big splash', as you put it, isn't during the gala."

"Right there with ya. Hey, go finish what you need to. But don't stay here all weekend. I've got myself a hot date for tonight, so I'm off." With that, Ryan headed out.

Left in his office alone, Hunter realized it was a little creepy being the only one in the high-rise building. He wasn't ready to go back to his empty penthouse, so continued working through most of the night on the contracts he needed prepared for Tuesday.

While Hunter and Emma went about their lives with some normalcy, the stalker started to prepare for his next well-calculated move. His employer had very specific instructions on what should be done next. The stalker was getting antsy to try some of his creative methods on the chosen prey. He was only able to get creative one time during this job, and that was with the cab driver. His employer wasn't overjoyed about that deviation from the plan, but as the stalker had explained, it was unavoidable, given the circumstances.

For now, the stalker thought, it was in his best interest to let his employer call the shots. If anything went wrong, he had deniability since he was just following orders. Sitting in his one-room refuge, he began assembling the materials he needed to carry out the next phase. This was going to be a bit trickier than the other instances, and timing was going to be imperative. If the conditions weren't perfect, he would need to abort this part of the mission, something his employer would not appreciate.

"I'll give you this weekend to feel more safe, dearest Emma. But wait until next week—you're going to start to realize a storm is brewing," he whispered to himself as he stroked the piece of equipment that would cause terror in a matter of minutes.

CHAPTER 25

———

Ryan showed up at Emma's office promptly at 10 a.m. to talk about the final security measures for the gala. While waiting for Emma to end the conference call she was on, Ryan decided to try to obtain any tidbits from Ashley. "So, Ashley, everything coming together for the gala?" He flashed one of his brilliant smiles in hopes of softening up the assistant.

Ashley couldn't hide that she was captivated with Ryan. "Oh yes. It will be all-hands-on-deck this week."

"I'm sure that Ms. Sharpeton appreciates all the hard work you are doing. She's mentioned it to me a couple of times." Ryan figured a little praise might go a long way.

"She did? That's really nice to hear." Ashley quickly added, "Not that Emma doesn't tell me that herself. I don't want you to think that she isn't great to her employees."

Ryan leaned against Ashley's desk, which accentuated his muscular physique. "No, no. I didn't think that for a minute. She loves all of you guys here. It's quite a little family, she always says."

"Oh, good! She should only be a few more minutes. She's on with one of the suppliers for the gala."

"Not a problem. Will I get to see you at the gala?" Ryan started to work the charm.

Ashley blushed. "Yes. I'll be there."

"You'll need to save me a dance." Ryan winked at Ashley.

"My boyfriend will be with me. I'm not sure he'd be happy with me dancing with someone else. Plus, I'll kind of be working." Ashley looked down as she spoke.

"That's too bad, but I understand. I don't want to make your boyfriend jealous. I'll make sure to say hello to both of you. I'd like to see who my competition is." Ryan tried to sound sultry.

Ashley smiled. "I'm sure that you could have any woman you wanted there."

"Just because I could have any woman I wanted, doesn't mean that I want them. Remember that." Ryan stood up as Emma came out of her office, a questioning expression on her face. "Ah, here is the woman of the hour. Shall we chat about final details, Emma?"

Before leaving the waiting area, Ryan turned and winked at Ashley again, which deepened her blush. Ryan followed Emma into her office and shut the door. "Before you ask, I was using my immense charm to try to see what morsels of information might spill from the beautiful Ashley's sensuous lips."

Emma was in awe of the measures Ryan took to gather information.

"Just be careful, Ryan, she may actually take you up on your offer. Then what are you going to do?" Emma snickered.

"I can handle her—not sure she could handle me. She seems like a delicate flower," Ryan commented conceitedly as he sat in a chair across from Emma.

"That delicate flower is dating a possible stalker and vandal and God knows what else. I'm thinking she can handle more than you think."

"I did ask her for a dance, but she pulled the boyfriend card. I told her I'd at least say hello to them to size up my competition. *And* she blushed." Ryan leaned back in his chair with a self-satisfied grin.

"Interesting tactic. Let me see if I can get this. You want him to know who you are, and you're saying to him that you know who he is. Do I have that about right?"

"Very good, sweet Emma." Ryan quietly clapped.

Emma bowed as best she could in her chair. "And I didn't even need to go to spy school."

"But, you didn't get the whole logic."

Emma knew a lesson in how to be a spy was coming next.

"It may throw off his game—maybe only *slightly*—if he thinks I'm hitting on his girlfriend. Even criminals sometimes screw up over the basics. And what is a basic, primal instinct for men? Hands-off their women!"

Emma considered what Ryan had said. "I guess it does have some merit. But, wouldn't it piss him off even more and make him more dangerous?"

"I don't think so. This guy is calculating and very controlled. He's the type that thinks through every possible scenario before selecting the best option."

"How do you know all this?" Emma was genuinely interested in the psychology of her stalker.

Ryan humbly answered, "Because this guy is me."

Emma couldn't hide her shocked expression.

Ryan continued. "Not me in the literal sense, but me in that this is how I was trained. I can analyze a situation in a few seconds and determine all possible outcomes. When you go to 'spy school,' as you so eloquently put it, it really is a school. They teach you how to think: to be methodical, to be prepared for every outcome, and most importantly, not to make rash decisions." Ryan normally didn't like to divulge that part of his life, but it was important for Emma to understand.

"So they brainwashed you?" Emma was a bit frightened of what she just learned. For a split-second a voice in her head asked: Could Ryan be the stalker? She quickly dismissed it and let Ryan continue.

"Not brainwashed like the terrorist organizations or cults do. It literally was training. You need to be prepared for anything on any of the missions, and intelligence isn't always reliable. You must be able to think on your feet or risk getting killed," Ryan said matter-of-factly. "We're getting a bit off-track. I know you're super busy, so how about we focus on the safety measures?"

Emma knew that Ryan had just shut down the topic of his spy training. "Thanks for explaining this to me. I know you probably don't like to talk about it, but it did help me to understand." Emma grinned at Ryan. "I'm guessing the place will be more secure than the White House?"

"You could definitely say that. I'm not going to show you everything, because I don't want you searching for the security that's in place. That would kind of give it away." Ryan popped open the laptop that he brought with him and pulled up a floor plan of the lobby where the gala would take place. "Have you kept to your original plans? Nothing moved, like where the cocktails are or anything like that?"

Emma shook her head. "No. I kept everything to the original design that I reviewed with Hunter." She examined the image on Ryan's screen and reviewed every detail. "This looks right."

"If you decide to change any of the layout, tell me immediately. To you it may seem like a small detail, but it could have some fairly large ramifications." Ryan tried not to be melodramatic.

"Got it. No changes. Anyhow, it's too late to change any of the layout."

"One more thing—all guests and personnel will have to go through metal detectors before they can get in. We'll try to make it as non-intrusive as possible, but it has to be this way." Ryan watched Emma's expression to see if he was going to get a fight from her. To his surprise, she just nodded in agreement.

"It's not exactly stylish to go through the detectors, but I understand the need. People go through them all the time, and I think it gives people a sense of safety. There will be some heavy hitters there, and I'm *sure* they'll be sporting all kinds of crazy expensive jewelry."

"Thank you. Wasn't sure if you were going to fight me on that one."

"Contrary to what you may believe, I *can* be reasonable...sometimes." Emma sat proudly in her chair with her arms crossed.

"Here's the next compromise I'll need from you. We'll need to have bomb sniffing dogs onsite before, during, and after the event."

Emma almost jumped out of her seat and lunged at Ryan.

"Wait! Just hear me out. Let me give you a scenario. What if one of the workers got paid-off by

Greg, so when they were setting up the food stations, they put an explosive device under the table? No one would be the wiser, and we humans may miss it. What if it was set to go boom right when Hunter's employees were leaving for the day on Friday, or during the event, or clean-up?"

Emma sat back in her chair and rubbed her temples. "This is out of control." She managed to say.

"I know. I know. Please trust me on this. This is the only way to be safe."

"This gala is going to be the death of me!"

Ryan visibly cringed.

"*Sorry*—poor choice of words."

Ryan put his laptop in his bag and stood up. "Don't worry. It'll all be fine. Trust me. I've got to run back to the office to prepare for a meeting tomorrow." Before Ryan opened the door, he turned and asked, "Has your brother mentioned anything about Logan Industries by chance?"

Emma's curiosity perked up. "No. Do I even want to know?"

"Just curious. Forget I said anything."

Emma rolled her eyes at Ryan.

"Gotta run. I'll pick you up around five tonight." Ryan dashed out the door, blew Ashley a kiss as he hit the elevator button, and disappeared.

While Emma was finalizing the security precautions, Robert was in the middle of reviewing that quarter's financial projections and was happy with what he saw. The company was doing very well, partly because of the market conditions and partly because of their investment choices. He put down the reports, rubbed his eyes, and pulled up his emails on his laptop. After scanning through a myriad of non-essential emails, he came to the one that instantly made his blood boil. After reading it, he slammed his laptop shut.

CHAPTER 26

E mma was surprised that Robert was already in the suite when she arrived. "Hi. Didn't think you'd be here this early."

Robert's foul mood surfaced. "Whatever."

"Whoa. What's up with the attitude? Rough day at the office?" Emma was perplexed.

"You could say that."

"Are you going to elaborate?" Emma suddenly had a bad feeling about where this conversation was heading based on Ryan's comment earlier in the day. She hated when her brother got in these moods.

"Fine. You know how I thought I'd mix business with pleasure and extend my stay?"

Emma nodded and let him continue.

"Well, I got a meeting invite for tomorrow morning at none other than fucking Ares Logan Industries!"

Emma's mouth fell open, but she shut it so that Robert would resume with the story.

"There have been rumors floating around about

my company possibly being acquired, and then subsequent layoffs. But up until now it's just been rumors. Now, I'm guessing the rumors are correct, since I've been summoned to that motherfucker's office tomorrow morning!" Robert was pacing around the living room area of the suite to the point that Emma thought she saw a wear pattern in the rug.

"But you don't know for sure if that's why you got the meeting invite, right?"

"The title of the invite was 'Acquisition Proposition', so I'm going to go out on a limb and say that the rumor has been confirmed." Robert wished he could throw something.

"Oh. I guess that sums it up." Emma struggled with what to say. "Who else is invited to the meeting?"

Robert sighed because he knew he shouldn't take out his frustrations on his sister. "It's just myself, the legal team, and his majesty."

Emma tried to come up with something helpful. "That's interesting. My guess is it's some kind of job offer. You don't work for him, so he wouldn't be telling you that you were fired. *And*, since there isn't anyone else from Authentic Financial Investments at the meeting, it says that Hunter wants to keep this on the down-low. Of course, I'm just guessing."

Robert contemplated what Emma had said. Deep down he knew that what she said was logical, although he was still furious that he might have to work for his archrival. Robert engulfed Emma in a hug. "Thank you. You're probably right. But you and I both know that Hell will freeze over before I work for *that* asshole." Robert kissed Emma on the forehead and trotted down to his room.

All Emma could think about, standing alone in the living room, was that there must be a full moon out tonight because the werewolves were coming out in full force. She sat on the couch and sighed. The idea of Hunter and Robert working together would be an epic disaster.

Emma's mind drifted to summers gone by when Robert and Hunter had been inseparable. It was because of her brother that she even met Hunter, so technically it was Robert's fault that she had fellen completely head over heels for Hunter. Robert never wanted Emma to start any kind of relationship with Hunter, or any other guy for that matter, but he knew he couldn't stop puppy love.

The more Emma thought about it, the more she was convinced that Robert probably knew more about their father's past affiliation with the Logan family than he was sharing. She wasn't convinced Robert understood what the affiliation might mean. She wasn't going to broach the subject tonight but made a mental note to try to coax more information out of Robert.

After a quick dinner that consisted of buffalo chicken tacos, the rest of the evening was spent with

Robert silently brooding on the couch while Emma tried to find something to watch. She finally settled on the Bruins playoff game, thinking that it would cheer Robert up. The Bruins were winning, but the game seemed to drag on. After taking as much as she could of the game, Emma kissed her brother and headed to her room.

Robert knew he had taken out his career frustrations on his sister and suffered pangs of guilt. The job he currently had was almost a dream job. The only thing that would make it better is if it was in Boston instead of London. This wasn't how he wanted to end his career at the company—being pushed out by his opponent. This was going to be a night that he wouldn't get much sleep, Robert surmised. He would need to play the potential scenarios in his head before his career-ending meeting in the morning.

As Robert predicted, the night was filled with unsettling dreams, which caused him to toss and turn all night. His fears rose to the surface of his subconscious mind, like lava spouting from an erupting volcano. The dream sequence began with Robert sitting alone in a dark room without windows. He quickly realized he wasn't alone when he heard snickers and whispering behind him. Something held him in his chair facing forward so he couldn't turn around.

Suddenly, a spotlight illuminated a podium in

front of him. Hunter stood behind the podium, glaring at Robert. Hunter's deep British voice boomed throughout the room as he called the meeting to order. When Hunter spoke, it was in a foreign language that Robert couldn't comprehend. Unexpectedly, Emma appeared out of the shadows and stood next to Hunter. Both stared intently at Robert until two uniformed guards came into the room and stood on either side of where Robert sat. Hunter gave them a nod, and they released Robert from his chair. A box of personal belongings was shoved in Robert's direction and he was escorted out of the room. Before he left, he caught a glimpse of Emma beaming at Hunter.

The buzzer from the alarm jolted Robert awake. He felt clammy and unsettled from his dream. The most disturbing part was Emma's role in the nightmare. He knew that blood was thicker than water, and that Emma would always be on his side. What he wasn't sure of was how much Hunter may have influenced his sister into believing that this acquisition was in everyone's best interest. Procrastination wasn't an option, so Robert bolted out of bed to start what he thought of as the last day of his career.

CHAPTER 27

Several blocks away from the hotel, Robert walked into the lobby of the Ares Logan Industries headquarters. Even Robert was amazed by the building, both inside and out. He hated to admit it, but it was the perfect location for the Boston Children's Hospital Gala. Robert shook off his admiration and strode up to the security desk.

"Good morning. I have an appointment with Hunter Logan."

"Good morning, sir. Name please?" the uniformed security officer asked politely.

"Robert Sharpeton."

"Thank you." The security officer typed in Robert's name into the computer. "Oh, yes. I see you are on the list. Let me get you a visitor badge, and then you can have a seat while I call Mr. Logan's assistant to notify her you are here." In a few minutes, the security guard presented Robert with a generic, clip-on visitor badge.

Robert accepted the badge and sat on a comfortable dark brown leather couch to wait for the pissing match to start. While he waited, Robert admitted to himself that if it was anyone else who would be his boss, he could definitely see himself at a company like this. It would be a dream job to work for a Fortune 100 company of this stature.

A petite, plump, older woman with dark hair that was going grey planted herself in front of Robert. "Mr. Sharpeton?" she asked curtly.

"Yes, that's me." Robert realized when he stood up just how much taller than this woman he really was.

"Come this way. Mr. Logan will see you now."

Robert followed the woman to the elevator that whisked them to the top floor in a matter of minutes. Normally, Robert would try to be friendly and chatty, but he got the distinct impression this woman was all business. Robert was surprised Hunter chose a mature woman as his assistant—he assumed the assistant would've been a voluptuous twenty-something. The woman knocked on the closed solid mahogany door and turned the scroll-patterned, brushed nickel lever. Once Robert had been deposited into Hunter's office, the woman discreetly left without saying a word.

Robert tried as hard as he could to not seem impressed by both the décor and the view as he entered the office. Hunter was finishing up a conference call and motioned for Robert to take a seat on the same dark brown leather couch that, unbeknownst to him, his sister had occupied during her first business meeting here.

While Hunter wrapped up his call, Robert studied the office and noticed the same things that Emma had. There were floor-to-ceiling windows throughout, and it was decorated with a sophisticated, masculine style, which had plenty of dark wood, leather, and muted colors. The space was clearly divided even though it didn't have walls that separated the space. A large, mahogany executive desk with matching credenzas and bookshelves were in one corner. On the opposite side, where Robert now sat, was a dark brown leather couch, two matching leather wingback chairs, with coordinating cherry coffee table and end tables. And, on the floor was a cream-colored plush area rug.

Hunter ended the call and walked over to where Robert sat. "I'm sorry that my call ran over by a few minutes." He extended his hand, which Robert decided to ignore. Hunter sat in one of the leather wingback chairs opposite Robert. "Thank you for coming in today. We have a lot to talk about. I decided it should just be the two of us today, if that's okay with you."

"First off, I didn't really have a choice. I was summoned here. Second, I'm not sure how much we really have to talk about—I'm out of a job. And third, I don't care who you invite to this meeting or any other meeting."

"Whoa! Not true at all. I apologize if you felt summoned—that was *not* my intention."

Robert started to protest until he saw Hunter's pleading expression.

"Please give me a chance to explain. If, after that, you want to storm out of here and hand in your resignation, so be it."

Robert rolled his eyes in contempt.

"As I'm sure you've heard—since it was literally the worst kept secret—I'm in the process of finalizing the takeover of Authentic Financial Investments. The Logan conglomerate has always had their eye out for acquiring a strong financial institution and, until now, hadn't found one. The challenge has been that Authentic has been a family owned and operated company for over forty years and that means they weren't exactly overjoyed to sell the firm."

Robert nodded at Hunter to let him know to continue.

"I tried it the nice way and offered them a more than generous proposal, which they basically put in the shredder. So I then had to play hardball. It's now a bit of a hostile takeover, although still at a fair price. The leadership has been struggling for the last few years with expenses on the rise, and they know that there are other sharks circling the waters. Long story short—the deal will be finalized on Friday morning." Hunter paused to let this sink in. "I'm asking for your discretion as it won't be made public until Friday afternoon."

"I can be discreet. All of this is fascinating, but I'm still not sure what this exactly has to do with *me*."

Hunter grinned. "I'm getting to that part. I know you've spent the last several years basically running their London office. Word on the street is you've done an incredible job. You're a huge asset to the company—one that the company can't afford to lose."

"Flattery will get you nowhere with me, Hunter." Robert began to lose his patience with the conversation.

"Always a battle with you, isn't it? I must be starting to go senile for even offering this. I want *you* to run Authentic Financial Investments."

Robert's mouth hung open. This was not something he had expected or, for that matter, even thought about. He figured, given their turbulent past, this was his swan song. "I, um, ah…"

Hunter let out a hearty laugh. "Now that I have your attention, maybe we can stop jabbing at each other and get down to business?"

All Robert could do was nod.

"I want you to be president of Authentic. It would obviously be under the Logan umbrella, but would operate as its own company. My father used to try to absorb companies and ended up ruining them because he didn't let them flourish. That's not what I'm going to do. The one catch is that you would, of course, report up to me. If you can get past that, you'd have a seat at one of the largest conglomerates in the world." Hunter thought that Robert might pass out. "I know this is a lot to take in. I've had the legal team create, what *I* think, is a very generous package. I know I'm not giving you a lot of time to think about this, but I really would need an answer by Thursday morning. Does that work?"

Robert felt dizzy. "I really don't know what to say. I hadn't expected this. I have to ask you—are you offering me this because you think it will get you into the good graces of my sister?"

"I can honestly say 'no'. I'm offering you the job because I think you're the most qualified person for the position. This deal is all about *you*—it has nothing to do with Emma," Hunter replied earnestly.

Robert was satisfied with Hunter's answer and grabbed the thick folder of materials Hunter offered him. "I'll let you know my decision on Thursday."

Like magic, the mahogany door gently swung open and the same unfriendly woman was there to escort Robert to the lobby. This time, Robert shook Hunter's hand when it was offered and quietly left with his head whirling. When the elevator glided to a stop in the lobby, Robert barely noticed. The woman held the elevator door for him and was then whisked back up to the top floor.

Robert handed in his temporary badge to the same security officer from earlier and headed outside in a daze. The sun was shining brilliantly, turning the building into a giant prism. Robert soaked up the sun on the sidewalk for a minute as he tried to wrap his head around the events of the last hour.

This was an opportunity of a lifetime, but he also had major reservations about working for a man he loathed. Emma wasn't going to believe a word of this, Robert thought. He knew his sister was more than busy, and he also knew that he couldn't wait another minute before telling her. Robert hailed a cab and headed to Emma's office to get her logical and honest perspective on his potential new career path.

Fifteen minutes later, Robert entered Emma's office building and headed to the security desk. Robert faintly remembered Emma talking about a nice security guard named Stan. The nametag of the guy on duty said "Charlie," and he was all business. Once Robert provided every piece of information possible, Charlie called up to Emma's office to get clearance.

"Sir, you've been approved to go to Sharpeton Consulting. Do you need directions?"

Robert tried to hold down his sarcastic remarks, "No, thank you. I think I know where my sister works." With that, he took his second temporary badge of the day and headed to the elevator. Once in the office waiting area, Ashley greeted him with a smile.

"Hi, Mr. Sharpeton. It's nice to see you again."

Robert chuckled. "Please call me Robert. 'Mr.' makes me feel old." Robert winked at Ashley and gave her a million-dollar smile.

Ashley blushed as if on cue. "I'll let Emma know you're here. You're lucky. She canceled most of her appointments today so she could concentrate on some of the last-minute details."

Once Robert was given the go-ahead to enter Emma's office, he smiled again at Ashley. On the short walk to his sister's domain, he thought that Ashley was the type of woman he could settle down with. She was obviously smart and enthusiastic, plus she had that demure personality that drove Robert crazy in a good way. Maybe if he decided to take this job offer, he'd have to consider the Ashley situation, he thought, not knowing the hidden dangers that surrounded Ashley.

"You have quite a happy look on your face. Do tell, big brother." Emma was busy typing on her laptop when Robert came in.

Robert plopped himself in one of the chairs facing Emma's desk. "Yes, I've had a very interesting morning and needed to share it with you."

Emma cocked an eyebrow, not sure where Robert was heading. "I'm intrigued."

"I've had a very lucrative job offer which would

require me to move back to the States—specifically back to Boston."

"Don't screw with me, Robert! Are you serious?" Emma tried her best to hold down her enthusiasm.

"Why yes, dear sister, I am a hundred percent serious. I wanted to talk to you about it, though. Would you mind me moving back here?"

"Are you kidding? That would be incredible!" Emma jumped out of her seat and smothered Robert with a big hug and kiss on the cheek. "What's the job? Have you decided to take it? I didn't even know you were looking. Wait. Was this the meeting you had this morning?" Emma dialed back her excitement.

"Yes, it was the meeting I had this morning. I thought I was going to get canned and instead came out of it with an offer to become president of Authentic Financial Investments once the takeover is complete." Robert let this penetrate Emma's brain.

"President? Wow!" Emma was visibly stunned.

"What, don't you think I'm a financial rock star?" Robert teased. "Emma, this is honestly my dream job. The only catch is that I'd be reporting to Hunter. I need to make a decision by Thursday."

"I think you'd be the perfect president for the company. I'm just a little worried that you'd be fired within the first week given the, let's say, tumultuous relationship you have with Hunter."

"I know, and that's something big that needs to

be considered. He said I'd have autonomy to run things my way, but we all know that can change. I admit I like his management ideas better than his father's. His father used to swallow up companies and basically tear them down to their nuts and bolts. Hunter wants to keep the integrity of the company and just add more resources from within the Logan conglomerate."

Emma started to laugh, and Robert eyed her quizzically, "What?"

"Oh, nothing. You already seem to be drinking the Logan Kool-Aid, that's all."

"This is why I love you so much. I need to review the offer package they gave me—that should tell me a lot about what I'm potentially getting myself into. I also want to do some research on Logan Industries, especially when his father was running things."

"Company research is always a good thing. I'll save you the trouble—I have some research on the company." Emma could tell that Robert was confused. "When I knew that I'd be working with Hunter, and ultimately his company for the gala, I did my own research. Nothing clandestine—just good old Google. I'll bring it back to the suite with me tonight. Now, I'm very happy for you, but I'm kicking you out so that I can get out of here at a reasonable hour tonight." Emma walked Robert to the elevator, gave him a kiss on the cheek and sent him on his way.

"Your brother sure is a hottie." Ashley looked completely smitten.

"Oh, brother! No pun intended. I thought you only had eyes for Greg."

"A girl can window shop, can't she?" Ashley resumed what she was doing, and Emma did the same.

The rest of the day was a blur for both Emma and Robert. Emma dove into the remaining tasks for the gala with a vengeance, while Robert went back to the hotel to study Hunter's offer packet. It seemed as if both siblings were moving toward their career dreams, although neither of them truly understood how quickly those dreams could turn into nightmares.

CHAPTER 28

———

When the elevator doors slid open to the suite, Emma could hear symphony music playing. In an instant, any stress from the day was washed away with the soothing sounds emanating from the Bose SoundTouch system in the living room.

"Ah, my sweet Emma. I've taken the liberty of ordering us dinner. Should be here in a few minutes. Tonight, we will feast like the carnivores we are!" Robert bowed in Emma's direction.

Emma dropped her bags on the wet bar and stared at her brother. "Who are you? And, what have you done with my brother?"

Robert hummed to himself as he uncorked a bottle of Holloran 2012 Pinot Noir—Cuvee Gran Jean. He gently smelled the cork before pouring an ounce in his glass. Emma watched in amazement as Robert assumed the role of sommelier. All she could think of was that this was a far cry from his beer guzzling days in Hardwicke. Satisfied with the finesse of the wine, Robert poured himself a full glass and one for Emma. Emma did her best to put her limited wine tasting experience to the test. She absorbed the aroma of the fruit before taking a sip.

"Wow! This is fantastic! I've never heard of this wine before."

"It's from a winery in the Willamette Valley of Oregon. Some of the world's best pinot noirs are from there. A husband and wife own the winery and have been making great small production wines for several years. I came across this at a business dinner in Portland a few years ago and was hooked with the first sip."

Emma tried to sip the wine slowly and enjoy each robust mouthful. "Now I know what to get you for Christmas—a case of this wine."

Robert laughed. "I definitely wouldn't turn that down."

Both sat on the couch with their glasses of pinot noir. Emma was the first to dive into the subject of the job offer. "So, given any more thought to the job offer?"

"It's *all* I've been thinking about. I ended up working from here the rest of the day, because I was so distracted."

Emma nodded.

"I read through the offer package. Holy shit! And, it's not just the money—which is outrageous— it's the benefits and the contract."

"Contract? Like a non-compete?" Emma was mystified.

"No, no, nothing like that. Hunter drew up a contract that outlined what I would have control over and what would need his approval. He left no stone unturned," Robert replied.

"I take it that's a good thing?"

"Yes! A very good thing! A *great* thing!" Robert was bouncing around the room like a child who just ate a pound of chocolate. "He knew I would have reservations about reporting to him. This contract effectively removes that from the equation. Everything is very clearly outlined, so there aren't any mistakes on either of our parts."

Emma could see how excited Robert was at this opportunity. "I'm very happy for you!"

"I didn't make up my mind that I'm taking it yet, little sister."

"Oh, yes you have. *But*, you're going to make Hunter sweat a little bit and not tell him until whatever deadline he gave you. That's how well I know you," Emma responded smugly.

Robert laughed. "You do know me too well and I love you for it." He planted a kiss on Emma's forehead. "Before I make my final decision, I wanted to ask you something."

Emma looked at Robert, puzzled. "Go for it."

"Would it be a problem for you if I accepted the job? What I mean is, I don't want you to be uncomfortable. Hunter would be back in our lives."

"That's very sweet of you, Robert. I would be perfectly fine with it. I never want to stand in the way of your career. If Hunter is part of the package, then so be it. I'll deal with it." Now, it was Emma's turn to give her brother a kiss.

Dinner arrived, and the siblings continued with their early celebration, which included a second bottle of the same robust wine. Soon after dinner, Emma started to yawn and knew it was time that she tried to get some sleep. After kissing her brother on the cheek, she padded down the hall to her bedroom. Instead of risking a restless night, she elected to take a little blue pill so that she could get a solid eight hours of sleep since the gala was at the end of the week.

For the first time in weeks, Emma had a restful sleep. There weren't any strange dreams to occupy her sleeping mind, and she felt a sense of contentment. She thought about how wonderful it was going to be to have Robert home again and, for a few hours, she thought that everything was going to work out as it should.

On the other end of the city, Hunter grudgingly tried to sleep. Between the acquisition and the danger that reared its ugly head at every turn, Hunter's psyche was in overdrive. He slowly fell into a restless slumber and dreamt of Emma.

Hunter's mind went back to the day he and

Emma drove to Hardwicke several weeks ago. Once at Emma's family's house, she began to sultrily tease Hunter and gave him glimpses of her very expensive black lace lingerie. Emma dashed out of the car and giggled as Hunter chased after her. The pair ran into the basement through the bulkhead door on the side of the house.

With each step, Emma managed to discard another piece of clothing and threw it in Hunter's path. Hunter followed the trail until he saw the delicate curves of Emma's naked body standing in front of him. When he reached out to touch her supple skin, Emma's image vanished. Full of confusion, Hunter desperately searched for his beautiful vision. Instead of finding Emma in all her beauty, he glanced down to find her lifeless body on the floor in front of him with the word "Whore" written next to her.

Hunter woke up with in a cold sweat. Counting to ten, he tried to regain his composure and remind himself that it was only a dream. He just prayed that it wasn't an omen of things to come. Little did Emma and Hunter realize, the storm brewing on the horizon was now even closer. The next phase of the plan was being put in motion and was now like a runaway train with no hope of being stopped.

CHAPTER 29

After having a quick continental breakfast with Robert, Emma flew out of the suite and downstairs to meet Ryan at the hotel entrance. The elevator ride took longer than in past mornings and stopped at almost every floor. Emma felt like a pancake up against the back wall and was getting a bit claustrophobic. With the passing of each floor, she grew more anxious. Finally, they landed safely at the lobby and Emma could breathe again.

The warm rays radiated off Emma's golden hair. For a few seconds, she soaked up the sun and grabbed her Ray Bans from her bag. After putting her sunglasses on, Emma caught the tiniest movement in her peripheral vision. Gently floating around her was the most beautiful American Lady butterfly she had ever seen. Its wings were perfectly symmetrical with tawny brown and creamy white colors transitioning into brilliant canary yellow. The graceful creature circled Emma until it briefly rested on her right shoulder. Emma felt this was a sign that good things were on the horizon. The butterfly fluttered off, high into the sky as if trying to reach the sun and disappeared from view.

Emma noticed Ryan patiently waiting for her in the car. She cautiously opened the door and buckled herself in. Without a word, Ryan headed towards Emma's office building. Many mornings they rode in comfortable silence, and this was one of them. She wondered how foolish Ryan thought she was for being fascinated by the butterfly and feeling the slightest bit of hope.

Ryan pulled up in front of Emma's office building. "Have a good day, my lady. See you at quitting time."

"See you later," Emma responded.

When Ryan got back to his own building, instead of going to his office he went straight up to the king of the castle. Without knocking, Ryan entered Hunter's domain. "Hey, I think we might have a problem."

Hunter was reviewing the final contracts for the Authentic acquisition. "What kind of problem? Want some coffee?"

"No, thanks. I just dropped Emma off at work." Ryan could see the vein in Hunter's forehead pulsating. "Relax. It was all very mundane. She just seemed off this morning. I can't put my finger on it, but something didn't seem right. She was watching this butterfly like it was something she'd never seen before."

"I'm guessing she didn't enlighten you as to what might be on her mind?" Hunter continued to review the contracts.

"No, she didn't. It could be nothing. Did she mention anything to you?"

"I'm the last person she confides in these days. Look, she's had a lot to deal with over the last few months. Remember that she's not accustomed to all this cloak and dagger stuff like you are. I'm sure she and Robert celebrated his promotion last night, so maybe she's just being a little whimsical this morning."

"You're probably right. Just want to make sure she isn't about to go over the edge or anything."

Just before Ryan got up to head down to his basement sanctuary, his phone vibrated with a phone number he didn't immediately recognize. "Hello?"

"Hey, Ryan. Detective O'Reilly. I have some news on the cab driver for you. Looks like you were right, it was that Smallwood guy."

"Hmmm. How'd you get the results back so quick since there were no fingerprints?"

"I called in a favor—got the dental records rushed, and they matched. We're still waiting for DNA results, but I'm ninety-nine percent sure this is the guy."

Ryan had known it was Maxwell Smallwood but the confirmation from the detective made him shudder slightly. "Thanks for keeping me in the loop."

"Ryan, this seems to be escalating. Vandalism is one thing, murder is a whole different story, and I'm not sure we're going to like the ending."

Ryan grunted in agreement and both men hung up.

Hunter quizzically studied Ryan.

Ryan responded to Hunter's unspoken inquiry. "Detective O'Reilly. He's confirmed the cab driver, Maxwell Smallwood, is the dead guy they found in Roxbury."

Nothing else needed to be said about the confirmed dead end. Ryan left to go back to his office to try desperately to figure out what was going on. The security office was going full force again this morning, he noticed, when he went to the kitchen to make a cup of New England Full City Roast coffee. He tried desperately not to spill the scalding cup of coffee on the way into his office. Once in his haven, he noticed a stack of new reports that had been left on his desk late last night or early this morning. Ryan really wished he had stopped at the cafeteria to get a muffin and contemplated sending one of his minions upstairs with the task.

Before he could ponder this any further, his desk phone rang. "Yes, I see the stacks of files on my desk. Yup. Thanks. I'll let you know. Keep digging."

Ryan leaned back in his chair and sipped his slightly cooler black coffee. His 'secret weapon', as Hunter called her, may have cracked the code on Emma's father's files.

"This could be interesting reading," he said to himself and started with the top file. Ryan opened the plain manila folder to find copies of Craig Sharpeton's formulas and notes that Emma and Hunter had retrieved from Hardwicke. There were also additional pages of notes, not in Emma's father's handwriting. Ryan surmised it was his associate's handwriting, although wasn't sure since he had never seen it previously.

Two hours later, Ryan was still in the same spot flipping through files, wishing he paid better attention during science class. The folders were organized in chronological order similar to the way Emma and Hunter had found them. They were telling a story, and the reader needed to be patient and let it develop. Each folder provided a little more information, another piece of the puzzle. It was time to let Hunter know what was going on, and then they'd have to decide if, and when, to tell Emma, Ryan concluded. After he sent Hunter a text telling him to join him in the security office, Ryan decided he had earned that muffin.

Hunter made his way down to the depths of the basement soon after seeing the text. Ryan's door was open, so Hunter went inside the empty office and made himself comfortable in one of the chairs opposite the desk. A few minutes later, Ryan came through the door holding a very large blueberry muffin with melted sugar on top and one bite already gone. With mouth full, Ryan greeted Hunter. "Hey. Got some interesting info you should see."

Hunter waited patiently for Ryan to devour the muffin. "Now that your tummy is full, can we get on with this?"

"Sorry. I was starving. I came in this morning to find that my 'secret weapon' had basically cracked the code of Emma's father's files—at a high-level."

Hunter looked stunned, so Ryan continued. "These were definitely pharmaceutical formulas, except not what we were thinking."

"What exactly do you mean?" Hunter's curiosity was piqued.

"This is far beyond my realm of knowledge but let me try to start with the basics. Bear with me."

"Let's just get on with the science class." Hunter wasn't in the mood for Ryan's antics today after his unnerving dream from last night.

"No need to be snarky. Did you know that there are more than 3,000 species of plants reportedly used in cancer treatments?"

Hunter was astonished.

"Well, neither did I! Seventy percent of these are found in rainforests. Researchers think that there are many more plants just waiting to be discovered and turned into life-saving drugs."

Hunter didn't know how to respond. "Go on."

"All plants apparently produce chemical compounds as part of their normal life cycle. Companies have been synthesizing these plants to create drugs for years, so that isn't anything new. But what your father found, or should I say Emma's father found, was astounding."

Hunter gave Ryan a look to keep things moving.

"Dude, it was like her father unlocked the secret to preventing cancer!"

Hunter almost fell out of his chair. "Wait a minute. you mean *curing* cancer."

"No. I mean *preventing* it all together. This isn't science fiction any more. The guy was a rock star, as Emma put it, but I don't think anyone knew how much."

"Well, I know someone who knew how much— *my father*." Hunter let that hang in the air for a few seconds. "We all know that my father was interested in cancer research after losing his sister. *But*, we thought it was all about helping someone once they had the disease. If all of this is true, this would be something to kill for."

"My thoughts exactly. Here's what I think happened. Your father literally stumbled on this plant and figured they'd see what could be done with it, never guessing its true medicinal potential. That part was a hundred percent pure luck. Craig Sharpeton worked at Philip's lab, so he figured if anyone could find something to do with it, Sharpeton was the guy. Then Sharpeton starts dissecting, or whatever it is these guys do, and finds that the chemical composition would theoretically block cancer cells from ever forming. Emma's father also knew what an ass Phillip was, so to protect himself, he makes copies of his research and hides it just in case anything was to happen to him. How am I doing so far?"

Hunter nodded in agreement. "I think you're on the right path."

"Good. Then, fast forward to a cold and snowy night in Hardwicke—the perfect scenario for a staged accident. The road is dangerous on a good day—mix in a little snow and ice, and you have the perfect recipe for an unquestioned fatality."

"But, why would my father kill Sharpeton? He had all the leverage."

"This is where it gets a little murky. I'm thinking that your father was paranoid that the competition would find out this massive discovery. And, your father definitely didn't want to share any of the mega profit this was sure to generate. So he silenced the main witness."

"But he would need someone to make the magic potion, so there were going to be others that ultimately knew about it."

"But those others may not have known exactly what they were making. Once they had the formula figured out, maybe he could have some lower-level technicians do all the grunt work."

"Go on." Hunter's head was spinning with the information.

"Obviously your father doesn't do the dirty work himself. He farms it out to some low-lifes. We know that Sharpeton called your father's cell phone the night of the accident. The call lasted long enough to leave a message, and it doesn't seem like the call was returned. My guess is that your father already knew the discovery was imminent and the voicemail message was confirmation. Probably all of Sharpeton's emails and work saved on the company computer was monitored. Of course, we'll never know exactly what was said on that voicemail."

Hunter felt dizzy.

"Anything Sharpeton had with him in his Jeep burned up when the vehicle exploded. Doesn't get any cleaner than that from an evidence standpoint."

Ryan takes a deep breath before he continued. "Or, the other scenario could be that Sharpeton, being a very smart man, realized the potential and got greedy. Your father was a cheap bastard, so he wouldn't have taken kindly to extortion. The accident was a way to eliminate future monetary obligations. I'm not sold on this theory. Everything I know about Emma's father says he wasn't out for financial gain."

Hunter put his head almost between his knees

with both hands on his forehead. "Let me see if I understand all this. One—we both agree that it looks like my father and Emma's father miraculously found a way to prevent cancer."

Ryan nodded.

"Two—it's likely, given how diabolical my father was, that he hired some thugs to arrange a car accident that killed Sharpeton."

Ryan nodded again.

"And three—we probably have the formula, or part of it, and this could be why Emma's life is in danger."

"That about sums it up," Ryan said solemnly.

For the next several minutes, the pair tried to digest all that they had learned. Neither one of them had expected this turn of events and weren't exactly sure what their next move should be.

"This needs to stay between you, me, and your secret weapon. No one else can know about this. I want every file locked up tighter than Fort Knox!" Hunter exclaimed.

"On it. I'm not sure that the people after Emma, and you, for that matter, realize that Sharpeton had copies of the files at his house. I really think that they thought they were in his car and burned in the accident."

"I tend to agree, but let's not take any chances. This is a whole new ball game now."

Ryan swept the remaining muffin crumbs into

the wastebasket. "So, the six million dollar question—do we tell Emma?"

Hunter rubbed his temples. "I don't think that's prudent right now. She's been under enough pressure and this would just add to it. Plus, I'm not ready to tell her my father probably had her father killed."

The pair were silent for a minute while Hunter's last statement hung in the air.

"I can brush her off if she asks if we've made progress deciphering the notes. But I won't be able to hold her off forever," Ryan said.

"I know. She's always been tenacious to a fault, like a dog with a bone."

"And, remember, we only have half the answers for this breakthrough."

Hunter was puzzled. "What do you mean?"

"I mean, that's great that we have what looks like the formula, but the formula means nothing without that damn plant. And, unless you know otherwise, we haven't found any plants lying around or a map from your father with a big 'X' on it."

Hunter stood up and paced around Ryan's office. "You've got a point. This whole mess just keeps getting more complicated."

"Can you stop pacing? You're making me dizzy. One thing at a time—let's make it through the gala and the acquisition, then we can focus on saving the world." Ryan leaned back in his chair and clasped his hands behind his head as he examined his friend.

"Agreed. I'm heading back upstairs to work on the acquisition. Call me if anything else comes up." Hunter strode out of the office and disappeared out of Ryan's view.

Ryan grew more perplexed with each passing moment during this progressively confusing game. His sixth sense told him that the danger just increased exponentially. If these people knew what he and Hunter had just learned, no one would be safe. Suddenly, Ryan recalled his classified bioweapon briefiings. They only added to his paranoia.

As much as this drug could help people, might some sinister mad scientist somehow turn it into a weapon? Or, if it fell into the wrong government's hands, could it be held for ransom, only allowing the very wealthy to have access to it? Ryan didn't like where his mind was headed with these questions and decided to keep them to himself for now. Although, he did wonder what something like this would cost on the black market—the profit potential would be astronomical.

CHAPTER 30

———

Ryan picked Emma up at precisely 5:30 p.m. to take her to the hotel. Fortunately, Emma didn't notice that Ryan was more preoccupied than usual. Emma used the opportunity to quiz him a little on Robert's job offer. "So, I heard that the takeover of Authentic seems to be in full-swing."

"Ah, yes, it is. Just wish it didn't need to be a hostile takeover, but Hunter has all that covered. I'm going to go out on a limb and say you're inquiring due to your dear brother." Ryan merged into traffic, which was moving at a snail's pace.

"Is this offer really as good as it sounds? You need to tell me the truth, Ryan."

Ryan focused on the road since there were crazy commuters, honking their horns, in every direction. "Hunter gave Robert the job of a lifetime—if you're into that sort of thing. Look, Emma, you know as well as I do that Hunter will always do what's best for his company. He knows Robert's skills and thinks that he's the best person for the job. Now, it will be up to both of them to see if they can call a truce, find some common ground, and work together."

Emma sighed. "I know—that's going to be the tough part. I just don't want to see Robert throw away this chance because of the past. Robert holds a long grudge, in case you couldn't tell."

"Well, I can't blame him. If you were my sister, I probably would've found a way for the guy to disappear. *And*, given my background, not really that hard to do." Ryan flashed her his pearly whites.

A chill went up Emma's spine at this admission. "I don't doubt you could do that, which is a tad bit scary, truth be told."

More horns honked to the right of the Mercedes as traffic merged due to the never-ending construction. "Don't mean to scare you, sugar. Just saying that I get where Robert's coming from. My personal opinion, since you asked, is he should take it. The pluses outweigh the minuses. And before you ask, I've had this same conversation with Hunter."

"I'll talk to Robert tonight. Ultimately, it's his decision, but I really would love having him home again." Emma looked out the window as a black, mid-sized sedan with tinted windows pulled up next to them. The driver must be an idiot to weave in and out of traffic like that, she thought.

Suddenly, Ryan jerked the wheel. He grabbed Emma and pushed her down, so her head was practically in his lap.

Ryan managed to shout: "Gun!" seconds before the front passenger side window exploded into a spider web of cracks from two gunshots. The glass didn't shatter since it was ballistic glass, but there was still enough damage that could allow a bullet inside if the shooter tried again. Ballistic glass, or "bullet-proof" glass, was multiple layers of tempered glass, polyurethane, and polycarbonates. These various layers can stop up to five direct impacts, depending on the caliber of gun and the configuration of the glass. The entire fleet of Ares Logan vehicles was outfitted with this type of glass.

Ryan's evasive maneuvers took them onto a side street behind a high-rise luxury apartment building before the shooter could try again. Ryan headed to the adjacent parking garage and found an empty spot. "Are you okay?" Ryan asked hastily.

Emma didn't even realize she was shaking. "Y-y-y-es. I think so. What the *hell* was that?"

"Looks like we were followed, although from a distance. I didn't even notice until it was too late. FUCK! What did you see?" Ryan didn't mean to yell at Emma. He was mad at himself for being so preoccupied that he didn't even notice they had a bullseye on them.

"All I saw was that dark car weaving in and out of traffic behind us, then suddenly they were next to us. That's when you pulled me down and it sounded like an explosion," Emma replied shakily.

"Here's what we're going to do. I'm going to bring you to the Logan headquarters. I need to switch cars and then get the team working on this. Why don't you text Robert and tell him you're going to be a little late due to work, okay?"

Emma said unsteadily, "Yes."

When Emma got on her cell to text Robert, Ryan called the security team to provide a quick run-down of the events in hopes the team could start pulling street camera footage. Once safely inside the Logan headquarters garage, the duo rode the elevator down in silence to Ryan's lair. When the doors opened, Emma was shocked to see Hunter standing there.

Hunter inspected both, sizing them up for injuries. "What the fuck *happened*? Are you both all right?" Hunter gently brushed a strand of hair from Emma's face and caressed her cheek. It was his intimate way to confirm she was all right. He wondered if his dream was becoming a reality.

Ryan did the talking. "Yes, we're fine. Just a little shaken up. The car has some glass damage on the passenger side but is otherwise unscathed. Would you mind taking Emma to my office? I think she could use a stiff drink. I'll be in after I get some preliminary details from the team." With that, Ryan went over to where his team was actively combing through camera footage, trying to piece together the sequence of events.

As Ryan suggested, Hunter brought Emma into Ryan's office, and sat her down in one of the chairs. After pouring her two fingers of Glenlivet 18-year-old single malt scotch, he turned the empty chair so that he was facing her. Hunter watched as Emma tried to steady her hands. She held the Waterford tumbler with both hands and sipped the amber-colored liquid slowly. The warmness slid down her throat and through her body. Hunter put his hand gently on Emma's knee. "Are you sure you're all right?"

"Yes, I'm fine. Just a bit wobbly. Hunter, *why* is this happening?" Emma peered at Hunter pleadingly.

Hunter felt physical pain in his heart when he looked into her begging green eyes. "I wish I could tell you. My gut is telling me that this doesn't have anything to do with the here and now. It all started in the past."

"You mean with our fathers?"

"Yes, that's *exactly* what I mean. It feels like vengeance for something, but I don't know how it's all connected yet."

Emma finished her drink, which significantly calmed her nerves. "Has Ryan made any more progress in deciphering my father's notes? I do agree with you that this all started in the past, and I think those notes are the key. My father wasn't a secretive man, so for him to have hidden that information…it must mean something."

Hunter removed the glass from Emma's hands and placed it on Ryan's very cluttered desk before very diplomatically answering her question. "I know Ryan is still working on your father's notes. I just can't believe that someone would go to these measures for some pharmaceuticals. But then again, the pharmaceutical industry is cut-throat, so who knows."

Ryan entered the office and Emma rose.

"I know you want to go to the hotel. Give me five minutes to tell you both what I know so far," Ryan said.

Emma nodded and let Ryan continue. "I'll drive you back after our quick chat." Ryan took a deep breath. "So, the car was a rental. No shocker there. Based on the street camera footage, we have the car heading down Seaport Boulevard toward the Black Falcon Pier where the cruise ships are. Just before the end of Seaport Boulevard, he takes a right and that's where we lost him. There are a lot of empty warehouses plus a parking garage down there, so that's where we'll start our search. I've notified our friendly police detective as well. Emma, he'll call you tomorrow at your office so that your brother isn't in the vicinity to overhear the conversation."

Emma felt spent. "Okay."

Hunter solemnly watched Ryan take Emma to the elevator and then disappear. He sat back down in the same chair he occupied a few minutes prior, thinking about the past. His memory wasn't always that clear regarding his relationship with his father. It was clouded with anger and resentment, which blurred the truth. Something deep within the cobwebs of his memories kept nagging at him, but Hunter couldn't bring it to the surface.

Before he could go down memory lane any further, he got a text from an unknown number. "See how close I can get to your precious Emma?"

Hunter hurried out of Ryan's office and handed his cell phone to one of their top technicians. "Can you find out where this came from?"

The engineer plugged Hunter's phone into his computer system and began typing furiously. Hunter could see things he couldn't begin to fathom pop up on the monitor before the engineer replied, "Sorry, Mr. Logan. It was from a throwaway cell phone with no GPS. There's no way to track it—the guy could be next door or in Poland for all we know. I downloaded the information to my workstation, so let me keep digging. Just no promises." He unplugged Hunter's cell and returned it to him.

"Thanks." Hunter headed back up to his office in the clouds to think about the past and how it potentially influenced the present.

Emma and Ryan used one of the other Logan Mercedes to go to the hotel. Both rode in silence—there wasn't anything that needed to be said. Tonight, the tentacles of danger reached out and touched them. What started out as strange coin-cidences turned into stalking and now a tangible threat. Ryan was thankful that Emma didn't know about the murdered cab driver—she was shaken up enough about this shooting. Just before pulling up to the front entrance, Ryan received a text from his engineer notifying him of the text sent to Hunter.

"Something about what just happened?" Emma looked at Ryan with wide eyes.

Ryan lied effortlessly. "Nope. Sorry. Just the commander-in-chief making sure you get into the hotel safely. I'll wait here until I see you get in the elevator." He still wasn't sure if this was a warning or if the shooter intended to make Emma his next victim, and that troubled him.

"Thanks." Emma got out of the car and slowly walked into the hotel. She knew that Ryan was watching her, and it made her feel like she was exposed, on display. She knew it was just her nerves, but it was unsettling when she glanced over her shoulder to see Ryan still watching her when the elevator arrived. Before the doors closed, she got a quick glimpse of the Mercedes before it disap-peared amongst the other commuters.

The elevator ride gave her a chance to collect herself, so she could put on an Academy Award-winning performance for her brother. The drink in Ryan's office had calmed her nerves, but she found herself being hyper-aware of every person in the elevator. What she really needed was a long, hot shower to get lost in a world of steam with the water cascading over her body, washing the filth of the world she was now exposed to down the drain.

CHAPTER 31

E mma pulled off the performance of a lifetime with Robert. It helped that Robert was
preoccupied with his job offer. Because of
the job offer, he was trying to secretly clean up as
much of his work in the London office as possible.
After dinner, Robert retreated to the study while
Emma pretended to watch TV. Not even QVC's *In
the Kitchen with David* put her at ease. Usually, David's
jovial spirit put a smile on her face, especially when
he did his happy dance. But not that night. Emma
decided trying to cheer herself up with TV was
futile and went to her room.

The shower steam filled the marble bathroom.
She left her clothes in a pile on the floor, wondering if she'd even wear them again after tonight's
events. They would remind her of what could have
happened. The multiple jets streamed water over
every crevice of her naked body. Emma hoped the
searing hot water would wash away tonight's events.
Each time she closed her eyes, all she could see was

the passenger window exploding. Emma switched to the rain shower setting, hoping it would be more calming. The water softly cascaded through her hair, over her breasts, down her buttocks, and onto the shower floor. Thoughts of Hunter seeped into her mind, a pleasant distraction before she had to step back into the dangerous reality that was now her life.

As Emma relaxed into sleep, aided by her little blue friend, the dreams came fast and furious. It was the only thing that couldn't be prevented with her sleeping pills, which she knew wasn't advisable given the drink she had earlier. Most of the dreams replayed someone shooting at her in the car. Both the shooter and the person she was in the car with were faceless blurs. It was like an annoying song that she couldn't get out of her head until she heard a new song. Unfortunately, the new song started to play and the tune had drastically changed.

This time, she knew exactly who she was with, and that wasn't a comfort. Emma was in the Mercedes with Ryan travelling down Seaport Boulevard, which eventually turned into Northern Avenue toward the cruise ship terminal. On the left was the Massport Marine Terminal and next to it were several old, decrepit piers no longer in use. She knew this wasn't the direction they should be going and tried to ask Ryan why he was heading this way. Quickly, she realized she couldn't speak. Duct tape across her mouth prevented any of the words from coming out. Her wrists were also wrapped tightly in duct tape, and she was securely belted into the seat, unable to move.

Panic set in, and her eyes pleaded with Ryan not to do whatever was to come next. Ryan's demeanor was cold as ice, and he barely acknowledged her except to tell her to stop struggling. He was no longer the witty, charismatic guy she thought of as a friend. Everything about him radiated callousness and a disregard for her well-being.

They continued to the end of the street and turned left, heading toward some dilapidated, long-forgotten warehouses. Emma grew more agitated with each passing second. She knew that there weren't many options down this desolate street, and there wouldn't be anyone to save her.

In her peripheral vision she saw Ryan's hand move slowly toward a black metal object that was resting in his lap. Emma began to get hysterical as she realized what the object was. She desperately tried to break free of the bonds that held her. Tears streamed down her face as her fear escalated. The car slowly came to a stop next to one of the abandoned warehouses, facing the water. The front passenger window exploded into thousands of pieces of glass.

Emma jolted awake to find herself tightly wrapped in her sheets to the point where she wasn't sure she was going to be able to escape. Her pulse was beating at an exceptional pace and she was drenched in sweat. Emma tried to adjust to the early morning light peeking through the drapes as she tried to calm down. When she finally untangled herself, she rolled over to see that it was 6:30 and the alarm was seconds away from going off.

Emma knew that her subconscious was still shaken up from the terrifying attack, which caused the awful dreams. She found it strange that her mind transformed Ryan into an assassin. Once again, she thought about how dreams were sometimes the truths our minds were too afraid to acknowledge.

CHAPTER 32

———

E mma's palms were sweaty, and her pulse was fluttering as fast as a hummingbird's wings as she peered out of the lobby doors to the waiting Mercedes. She never felt awkward with Ryan until this morning and scolded herself for being foolish. Ryan was protecting her and would never harm her. Or would he if the need arose? Emma knew this whole situation was larger than herself, although she seemed to be the primary target. If push came to shove, would Ryan defend her or throw her to the wolves as the sacrificial lamb for the greater good? Emma contemplated these questions when she got into the car.

"Morning, my lady." Ryan was his normal self.

"Morning." Emma couldn't think of anything else to say.

"How are you holding up after last night's escapades?" Ryan asked, concerned.

"I'm fine. I just don't understand why any of this is happening," Emma replied.

"I know. I'm sorry about the shooting last night happened. I take full responsibility for not being able to prevent it."

"Ryan, you couldn't have known that some maniac was going to shoot at our car. This isn't your fault. It's the fault of this lunatic and whatever sick fantasies they are having."

"Okay." Ryan still felt guilty.

Unlike a typical weekday morning, the traffic wasn't heavy, and they reached their destination quicker than normal, which helped Emma stop contemplating the evilness of the world. Emma hopped out of the car, waved to Ryan, and headed in to her office building. Stan still wasn't back to work at the security desk. Emma started to worry about him. Over the last few years she had gotten to know Stan. She couldn't remember the last time he wasn't at work other than for planned vacations. Emma thought about mentioning Stan's absence to Ryan, just in case it had something to do with the current situation.

Ashley poked her head into Emma's office and startled Emma. "Everything good, boss?"

"Sorry. Yes. I'm fine."

"You just seemed preoccupied when you came off the elevator and didn't say hello."

"I'm sorry. Just mentally going through the list of things I need to do today."

Ashley seemed satisfied with the answer and

went back to her desk. Emma was putting her things away when her cell phone rang. The number's area code was from Boston but didn't provide any more information.

"Emma Sharpeton."

"Hi, Ms. Sharpeton. It's Detective O'Reilly."

"Good morning, Detective. Ryan said you'd be calling."

"Is now a good time? Shouldn't take more than fifteen minutes or so."

Emma wanted to get this over with. "Sure. Now's probably the best time."

"Great. Ryan gave me most of the details. I want to get your version of the events."

The last thing Emma wanted to do was to relive the shooting, especially after her dream last night, but knew that the detective was only doing his job. "I'll help any way that I can. Although, I'm not sure how much help I'll be. Ryan definitely saw more than I did."

"Just tell me what you do remember." The detective gently prodded Emma.

Emma recounted her version of the events—the dark sedan coming up fast next to them, Ryan pulling her head down and the sound of the gunshots smashing into the window.

"That coincides with what Ryan said. Good thing that car was as secure as it was. I'd hate to think about what could've happened."

"I'm right there with you, Detective. So, what are the chances that you'll catch this guy?"

The detective thought about his answer. "We'll pull any camera footage from the street. See what we can come up with for witnesses."

"Doesn't sound promising," Emma said realistically.

"You know, a lot of police work is luck, so you never know what will pop up. I'll do my best."

Emma started to get a migraine. "I know you will. And I appreciate it. I have to ask you—do you think this is related to the break-in?"

"If I was honest, I'd have to say yes. I can't see how these two incidents wouldn't be related. I'm not big on coincidences."

Emma chuckled. "Now, you sound like Ryan."

"Oh, no! That's not good." It was the detective's turn to laugh. "I don't want to take up any more of your time. Be extra vigilant, especially this weekend at your event. I know I don't need to tell you that, but it makes me feel better saying it out loud."

"Thank you. I will."

When both disconnected, Emma leaned back in her chair, rubbed her temples, and desperately wished she could go back to last weekend with Morgan, Hannah, and Robert. She couldn't remember the last time she had felt so relaxed. Emma hoped they would all have the opportunity to have more of those carefree weekends in the future.

People always said to live each day to its fullest, and Emma now understood what they meant.

Emma dove headfirst into the rest of the day and didn't give herself time to think about any of the events over the last several months.

For the rest of the week, she focused on the final preparations for the gala. Even at night in the suite with Robert, her mind was absorbed with the final touches for the big evening. Robert knew his sister well enough to stay out of her way when she got like this—she had tunnel vision regarding her latest mission.

Robert occupied himself with finishing up the projects he had left in the London office. After accepting the position offered by Hunter, he felt a wave of relief. He hadn't realized how tense he had been about the pending acquisition, mostly due to the fact that, until recently, he hadn't known what was going on. The acquisition of Authentic was announced on Friday as planned and it created a firestorm in the financial news. None of the analysts expected Logan Industries to be the potential buyer, which Hunter was pleased about.

The press release announcement included Robert taking on the role of president of the firm. Robert still had to pinch himself each time he read the small paragraph announcing his promotion. This was the boost he wanted in his career, and the thought of moving back to Boston was icing on the proverbial cake. As far as Robert was concerned, it seemed like he and his sister were getting what they deserved. Unfortunately, Robert didn't realize the price that they may need to pay for these rewards.

CHAPTER 33

———

Robert knew how hard his sister had been working, especially this last week, and decided to let her sleep in on Saturday morning. What he didn't realize was all the extra stress Emma had been under from the unknown assaults on her from multiple directions. He had managed to tear her away from work long enough to grab pizza and a beer the night before and thought it helped her relax a bit.

Sitting in the living room area watching the morning news, he braced himself for the tornado that was about to come out of the bedroom. "One. Two. Three," he silently counted.

"What the *hell*, Robert? Do you have any idea what today is? I can't afford sleep!" Emma flew into the room in her pajamas, hair disheveled.

"Good morning, sunshine." Robert continued watching the news.

"*Good morning*? You let me oversleep by an hour."

Robert patted the seat next to him on the couch

for her to sit down. "It was only an hour, and you needed it. You've been running yourself ragged, and I didn't want you falling over tonight from exhaustion. Now, come, sit. I'll bring you breakfast."

Emma reluctantly sat down with her arms crossed and pouted. "Fine."

Robert sauntered over to the dining room table and dished out eggs, bacon, and a croissant. Handing her the plate, he said, "I'll get your tea in a minute. Start eating before it gets cold." In less than two minutes, he put a steaming cup of tea in front of her on the coffee table.

Although she was fuming at Robert, Emma admitted to herself that he was probably right. "I probably needed a little extra sleep."

"Am I forgiven?" Robert tried to sound contrite.

"I guess. But, only because I need a date for tonight, and you look okay in a tux."

"*Okay in a tux*? Oh, my little vixen of a sister! I look astonishing in a tux and will be driving the ladies wild!" With that declaration, Robert went to his room to shower and change, so he could help Emma with any of the final pre-event preparations needed.

After both siblings were fed, showered, and dressed, they took a cab over to Hunter's office building just as the transformation started. Emma was amazed at how much had already been done that morning. What was normally a serene lobby was now filled with movers, tables, electronics, and flooring for the dance area. Emma felt a sudden panic attack, wondering how it was all going to come together in time for the festivities.

Robert could see his sister tense up and wrapped his arm around her with some brotherly support. "It'll all get done. There's a small army in here. Don't worry."

"I know it will. You know I live to be stressed." Emma tried to sound relaxed.

From across the lobby, Hunter watched Emma intently. Tonight was a big night for Emma and her company, but it could also be an explosive night in other, more sinister ways. Ryan joined Hunter in watching Emma interact with all the workers to make sure that everything was exactly as she had planned.

"She's amazing, huh?" Ryan commented.

"That's an understatement. All quiet on our side project?" Hunter asked.

"So far. I'm hoping it stays that way. We've done everything humanly possible to make sure tonight is as safe as it can be. My guess is that this would be too predictable of a target. This guy must know how tight security will be. I think he's going to be here to watch and observe. Kind of like an animal testing the electric fences to see if there are any weaknesses."

"I really do hope you're right. I'm going to head over to say hello. Are you coming?"

"I'm going back downstairs to make sure all the tech equipment is working properly. I'll be back up here in a bit." Ryan departed.

Hunter meandered over to where Robert stood, desperately trying not to get run over in the process. "Wow. It's getting a little dangerous in here."

Robert turned to see his new boss next to him. "That's for sure. You're taking your life in your own hands around here. And, definitely don't get in *that* tornado's way over there!" Both glanced in Emma's direction. She was overseeing each piece of the dance floor being assembled.

"Does your sister have you helping? If not, let's head up to my office to escape this."

"I told her I'd help if she needed it, but I like your idea better. Let's go!"

The two men made their way through the throngs of activity and into the sanctuary of the elevator. Emma was still busy ensuring every detail was done to her specifications and didn't notice as they left. In the elevator, both men sighed with relief.

"That was getting a bit dicey down there. Your sister is a little...um..."

"I think 'crazy' is the word you're looking for."

Once safely inside Hunter's office, Robert inquired, "Anything new on the acquisition?"

"You saw the scuttlebutt in the financial news. I've gotten some congratulatory calls last night, some from a few folks who will be here tonight. I know you're attending with Emma, so I'm hoping that I can show off my rock star to a few folks, if you're up for it."

Robert was very pleased at this suggestion. "Absolutely! It'll be good for me to start building relationships in Boston again."

"Excellent! I'll try to make sure that I don't take you away from the fun for too long."

As the two started cautiously rebuilding their relationship, Emma was focused on getting everything perfect. As the last piece of the stage was being put together, Emma felt a light tap on her left shoulder. She turned around to see Joe Bonamassa smiling at her.

"Sorry, I didn't mean to startle you."

"Hi, Joe. I'm wound a little tight today. So, what do you think?"

Joe examined the whole scene. "This is fantastic! You should be very proud of yourself."

Emma blushed at the praise. "Thanks, but it was the whole team. I'm just the traffic cop."

"You are too modest. I can't wait to play here tonight. What time should we do the sound check?"

"Let's see. Guests will start arriving at 7 p.m. How about 5:30? Does that give you enough time?"

"That's perfect. I don't anticipate any problems. I need to dash. I'll see you here later, Emma." Joe shook Emma's hand and then maneuvered through the obstacle course leading to the front doors.

"Who was that?" a British voice said from behind Emma.

She turned to see Hunter's ice blue eyes staring at her. "That was Joe Bonamassa. I'll introduce you to him when he comes back for the sound check."

Hunter was a little star-struck. "Wow! Can't believe I'm going to have a blues legend playing in my lobby in a few hours. Amazing."

"Someone's got a 'man crush' going on." Emma smirked.

"Shush. He's just the best and it's a little intimidating."

"Stop the presses! Hunter is intimidated by some-one. I have to write this down!" Emma mocked.

Hunter couldn't help but smile. For the first time in weeks, the two were bantering and it felt good. "Okay, okay. Forget I said anything. On another note—Robert is up in my office, and I'm having lunch delivered for us plus for every-one down here."

"That's very nice of you. You didn't need to do that."

"Why don't you go tell the troops that lunch will be here in about ten minutes, then come up to my office and the three of us will have lunch together?"

Emma was reminded of years past when it was the three of them taking on the world in the small country town of Hardwicke. "Sure. I'll be up there in a few minutes. Thanks again."

With his mission completed, Hunter made his way back up to his office unscathed.

CHAPTER 34

———

Emma entered Hunter's office cautiously. She still wasn't quite sure what to make of the sudden thawing of the relationship between Robert and Hunter. Although it was better that they were being civil, she wasn't completely sold on them working together—the years of animosity didn't just go away overnight. They had been like brothers each summer in Hardwicke and complimented each other's personality. But she knew her brother and the wounds of the past ran deep. Emma recognized that this merger was also putting both siblings in the spotlight. She wondered if that was going to make her brother a target by default. Then again, she considered the fact that he was probably already a target since he was her brother.

Both men rose as Emma entered the room. Robert pulled the chair out for Emma, and he placed the linen napkin on her lap once she was seated. Emma doubted that the workers downstairs were dining on fine china or drinking champagne for lunch.

"Hunter, this is a bit over the top. Pizza would have been fine."

Without responding, Hunter raised his glass indicating he wished to make a toast. Both Emma and Robert followed suit with their glasses. "We have two important milestones to celebrate. One— the Boston Children's Hospital Gala and all the work that Emma and her team has done to make it happen. And, two—Robert accepting his new position at Authentic Financial Investments. Here's to the Sharpetons! Cheers!"

The trio clinked glasses and then dug into their lunch, which consisted of Caesar salad with grilled shrimp and crab cakes on the side. For dessert, they enjoyed a spice carrot cake with light cream cheese frosting. The conversation focused around that evening's event and Robert's pending move back to Boston. Once they were done, Emma politely excused herself to head back downstairs.

Before Emma reached the door, Hunter inquired, "Robert, if Emma doesn't need you downstairs, I'd like to continue our strategic planning conversation."

"It's fine if Robert wants to stay up here. I've got it under control downstairs," Emma said.

"Then it's settled. Robert, make yourself comfortable. Emma, let me walk you to the elevator." Hunter escorted Emma out of the office and called for the elevator. Emma was a bit perplexed but decided she didn't have the mental capacity to argue. As the elevator arrived at the top floor, Hunter implored, "Please don't jump to conclusions tonight."

Emma wasn't in the mood for more of his cryptic messages. Before she could respond, the elevator doors opened, and Hunter gently nudged her inside. Emma's head started spinning again as she was zipped down to the lobby. When the doors opened, Ryan was standing there as if on cue.

"Hello, my lady! Did you just come from the castle in the clouds?"

Emma tried to focus. "Yes. Hunter invited Robert and I to have lunch with him."

"You seem a little mystified."

"Time spent with Hunter has that effect on me."

Ryan cringed. "I don't even want to know, do I?"

"Lunch was good. He's just doing his cryptic one-liner thing again. It's nothing. I've learned to ignore him these past few weeks and it's served me well." Emma didn't wait for Ryan to jump to Hunter's defense and went back to where her team was busy adjusting the lighting.

By late afternoon, the entire space was converted from a pristine business lobby to an elegant ballroom. Emma was in awe of the work that everyone had done to make the place magical. She noticed the elevator speeding down to the lobby with her brother inside.

Emma grabbed her belongings and met Robert as he exited the elevator. "Ready to go? We need to get ready and be back here by 5:30."

"Yes, ma'am!"

Before leaving, they turned to admire the space one more time before it was filled with guests. The wide smile across Emma's face made her green eyes radiant. Robert put his arm around his sister and walked outside to hail a cab back to the hotel. He knew that Emma wanted to be just as dazzling as the location for the event tonight, even though he thought she already was.

The pair was so preoccupied they were completely unaware they were being watched. Across the street, the shadowy stalker captured the duo's every move on camera while pretending to be just another Boston tourist. Satisfied with the surveillance, he hailed his own cab, so he could make the final preparations for the evening.

CHAPTER 35

A t precisely 5:20 p.m., Jared arrived in one of the Logan Mercedes. He waited for Emma and Robert to emerge from the hotel. Jared, who was like a butler only with very special and deadly skills, was a man of few words. He preferred to do his job to the best of his ability and not get involved with the passengers. The one exception was Hunter and Ryan. Although, he was curious as to the role Emma played. She was a fascinating woman who always took the time to acknowledge him, and never seemed pretentious. This would be the kind of woman who could be the missing link for his employer, Jared thought.

Before his thoughts could go any further down that path, Jared noticed several passersby stopping to gaze at the couple that was leaving the hotel. The stunning woman was dressed in a Georges Chakra single shoulder strap, high-front slit full-length gown in pale pink. Her striking companion was dressed in a classic Armani tux that accentuated his broad frame. This was Jared's cue to open the rear doors to the Mercedes for Boston's newest power family.

Once the pair was comfortably situated in the back seat, Jared eased into the light traffic. "Good evening, Ms. Sharpeton. Mr. Sharpeton."

"Hello, Jared. Thank you for picking us up. We really appreciate it," Emma replied sincerely.

"It's my pleasure. And, may I say, you both look spectacular this evening."

Emma blushed and admired her brother. "Thank you very much. You are too kind."

Robert chimed in. "Yes, thank you, Jared. Will you also be taking us back to the hotel later tonight?"

"Yes, sir. I'm at your disposal for the entire evening. Ms. Sharpeton has my cell phone number—just text me when you are ready to leave, and I'll bring the car around. Oh, and I hear that congratulations are in order for you, Mr. Sharpeton."

"News travels fast. Thank you. Yes, big new job, so hopefully I won't screw it up too badly." Robert winked at Emma.

"I'm sure you'll do just fine, sir."

Emma was still in awe of the Ares Logan Industries headquarters, especially at night. Tonight, Hunter had done something she hadn't known possible. The lights on the building changed colors from blue to purple to green to yellow, making the building one giant prism. It was absolutely beautiful and would be even more fantastic as it grew darker.

She smiled to herself in wondrous amazement.

Jared pulled up to the front entrance and opened the doors for the duo. "Have a pleasant evening. Just let me know when you're ready to go back to the hotel." Both Emma and Robert nodded and stepped on to the red carpet that lead them to the front doors.

Once inside, there were beautiful trellises with pale yellow roses directly in front of them. Emma guessed this was one of Hunter's added touches. The fragrance from the roses was subtle, but distinctive, and added a touch of elegance to the scene. Emma didn't realize until she was walking through the trellis that, in reality, they were the metal detectors.

"Do you like how we've dressed up these drab old metal detectors?" Ryan said from behind her.

"This is amazing! What a brilliant idea," Emma said, very pleased.

"We were trying to figure out a way to kill two birds—have the necessary protection and make it pretty. It was the big guy's idea, but I'm happy to take the credit on his behalf."

"Thank you. This is great!" Emma noticed again how ruggedly handsome Ryan was, especially in his tux. Her weariness from the other day had dissipated and things were back to normal.

"Robert, come here. I'd like you to meet someone."

Robert strolled over to Emma and Ryan.

"Robert, this is Ryan, Hunter's head of security."

Robert shook Ryan's hand. "Very nice to meet you. I guess we'll be seeing more of each other in the coming weeks."

Ryan chuckled. "Yes, we will. Welcome aboard. It sounded like a great opportunity for you. Especially moving back to Boston."

"That was the best part, being here to keep an eye on my baby sister." Robert maneuvered out of the way of Emma's left elbow.

"I'll leave you two to whatever it is you need to do. Emma, Joe is here and is getting ready to do the sound check. And, the dogs have done their initial sweep, so we're good."

"Thanks, Ryan. I'll see you in a little while." Ryan headed back to finish briefing the team while Emma and Robert soaked in the view.

The 30-story lobby atrium, with its koi pond and real park surrounded by the brilliant grey Italian marble floor, had been transformed into a Cinderella style ballroom. It was everything that Emma had imagined—elegant and enchanting. The warm, white twinkle lights in all the trees were magical—it was like the stars had fallen from the sky and landed in the indoor park. Next to the koi pond, a string quartet softly played in the background, which only enhanced the mood.

To the left, past the metal detectors disguised as trellises, was the stage where Joe Bonamassa was doing his sound check. The dance floor was immediately in front of the stage. To the right were the bar and food stations. Scattered around the open space in front of the food and beverages were cocktail tables for people to mingle at. All the tables were covered in black linens and had different colored, mini-twinkle string lights strategically positioned on the tables. Also on each of the tables were five-inch high clear crystal square vases that had more of the string lights in the bottom of the vase with pale-yellow roses covering the top.

The bar was sprinkled with pale yellow rose petals that coordinated with the trellis and vases. Emma guessed it was another one of Hunter's touches and smiled. Hunter knew that yellow roses were something that she and her father enjoyed. Emma's eyes began to get misty at the kind gesture.

The featured beverages for the evening consisted of a sophisticated selection of wines, champagne, and beer. Emma had made a last minute change to the wine selections to include some of Robert's favorites, including the Holloran 2012 Pinot Noir—Cuvee Gran Jean. She also found a small central Massachusetts winery, Agronomy Farm Vineyard, that made an excellent white wine, the 2015 Vidal Dry. A variety of local beer favorites were also on hand for the non-wine crowd.

The food stations consisted of hors d'oeuvres and desserts. There was everything from mini-crab cakes to shrimp cocktail to prosciutto wrapped pineapple and mini-flatbread pizzas. The desserts were elegantly displayed on pedestals and boasted everything from mouth-watering chocolate delights to more health-conscious fruit concoctions.

In between each of the food stations and in the corners of the space were floor candelabras, which glistened in the light. They were a modern all-crystal style that boasted four candleholder arms with crystal chains dropping below each arm. Emma thought these added the final piece of elegance to the space and was pleased at how they completed the scene.

Robert was fascinated watching his sister admire the hard work her team had done. "You did an amazing job, little sister of mine. I'm very proud of you!"

"It wasn't just me—I had a whole team but thank you." Emma glanced up as Hunter strolled past the park towards them. She had to catch her breath—he was devilishly handsome in his Joseph Abboud tux. Just like Robert, the tux did him justice and accentuated all of his features.

"Emma. Robert. This place looks amazing. You did a great job, Emma. Your team as well."

Emma blushed at Hunter's praise. "Thanks. Let's just hope we get lots of donations tonight." She couldn't think of anything else to say. She was mesmerized by the exquisite male in front of her until she saw who was trailing not far behind him.

"Emma, I believe you know Wendy Aucoin. Robert, I'm not sure if you've had the pleasure. Wendy is one of our top business reporters for the Boston Times and just completed a series of articles on your sister's company."

Robert extended his hand to shake Wendy's. "Wendy, very nice to meet you."

"So, you're the famous secret that Hunter's been hiding with his recent acquisition. I'd very much like to meet with you sometime for an interview. I promise it will be painless."

Robert raised an eyebrow at Hunter. "I'm always happy to do an interview as long as the boss gives his approval."

Emma wanted to throw up in her mouth. Not only was this witch obviously Hunter's date for the evening, she was now zeroing in on Robert. "Wendy, I didn't realize you'd be here this evening. You didn't mention it when you were in my office the other day. Obviously, the more the merrier as long as you brought your checkbook." Emma forced a wide smile for her small audience.

"This was sort of a last-minute decision, but I absolutely brought my checkbook. It's such a worthy cause." It was now Wendy's turn to smile for the men.

Robert could feel the tension and decided it would be best to steer his sister away from the impending explosion. "Emma, how about you introduce me to this famous blues guy you've been gushing over?"

"Sounds like a good idea. Hunter. Wendy. I'm sure we'll see you later."

As they walked toward the stage, Robert asked, "What the hell was that all about? You were like a tiger about to pounce."

"Oh, nothing. That woman just gets under my skin. It's fine."

"I have a feeling there's more to the story, but I'll curb my curiosity for now."

Joe waved when he saw them approaching. Emma made the introductions between Joe and Robert, and soon the conversation moved to the London music scene, specifically Royal Albert Hall. Emma tried her best to remain interested while she watched Hunter and Wendy across the room.

"You might want to be a little less conspicuous. You wouldn't make a good spy," Ryan whispered in Emma's ear.

"Ha, ha. Did you know she was going to be his date tonight?"

"Nope. Between us, I can't take that woman. Something about her makes my skin crawl."

"That makes two of us, but probably for different reasons. I have no claim on Hunter. He can do whoever he wants. I just need to get through tonight without any catastrophes and all will be well."

"That's my girl! To put your mind at ease, the security sweeps haven't found anything to be worried about. Try to relax and enjoy yourself tonight. You deserve it!" Ryan gave Emma a quick hug and then disappeared behind the trees in the park.

A waiter appeared out of nowhere with two flutes of champagne for Emma and Robert. "From Mr. Logan."

Emma smiled and raised her glass across the room to Hunter while secretly willing his date choked on hers. As she sipped the very expensive champagne, Hunter's parting words to her after lunch hit her like a slap in the face. She wondered if this was what he meant by not jumping to conclusions. Guests would be starting to arrive soon, which didn't give Emma time to dwell on Hunter's mysterious words. She downed the rest of the champagne, then fluttered off to make sure everything was ready for when the first guest walked through the doors.

CHAPTER 36

The onslaught of wealthy guests started arriving in their glittering gowns and black tuxes. Hunter greeted each guest after they made their way through the covert security measures. Emma watched the charisma pour out of Hunter, and although he seemed perfectly at ease, she knew it had to be a bit tedious. To Emma, it felt like a receiving line at a wedding. Given all the money that was hopefully being donated tonight, it was worth it.

Emma strolled over to where Hunter stood while there was a small break in the line. "It looks like we have about half of the invited guests here so far."

"The big money folks will want to make a grand entrance, so they'll be fashionably late. I'm not standing here all night to appease them," Hunter responded gruffly.

Emma decided not to comment on his choice for a date. Instead, she tried a different approach. "Thank you for all the yellow roses. It was a very nice touch."

"I know you wish your father could be here,

so I thought that might help." Hunter gazed at Emma warmly.

Emma's eyes again got misty, like when she had first seen the flowers. "Thank you. And thank you for remembering. I better go make sure everything is running smoothly." Emma didn't wait for Hunter's response.

Hunter watched her walk away and hoped that she wasn't walking away forever. He knew it was a big risk to invite Wendy Aucoin, but he also knew it was safer to keep his enemies close. By the end of the night, he hoped to find out what Wendy was up to and how it played into his current situation.

"Don't worry. She's not walking away from you forever." Ryan popped up beside Hunter.

"I hope not. She's not pleased about Wendy being here."

"Neither was I. By the way, I lied to her and told her that you did this on your own without my expert advice. I think one of us needs to stay in her good graces, and who better for the job than me?"

"That's wonderful," Hunter said flatly.

"Gotta do what you gotta do. I'm off to do another security sweep. Catch you later." Ryan melded into the crowd without another word.

Emma returned to let Hunter know that it was show time. He had insisted on kicking off the event and saying a few words. Emma figured that should at least help persuade the female portion of the audience to donate, given his dashing good looks and British accent.

Hunter climbed the three steps onto the stage and took over the microphone. "Welcome, ladies and gentlemen. I'm deeply honored that you accepted our invitation for a night of good food, drinks, and music. We have a very special and talented guest who will surely bring the house down starting in a few minutes. Before we find out who in the audience can dance, I'd like to thank you in advance for your generous donations to Boston Children's Hospital.

"As you all know, the hospital gives outstanding, life-saving care to children in need across the globe. We are so lucky to have this world-renowned institution in our back yard. I hope and pray that none of us ever needs their services, but if we do, they are here to help. There will be many opportunities for you to donate tonight, so I hope you brought your checkbooks. Now, without further delay, please give a Boston welcome to Joe Bonamassa!"

The crowd erupted in cheers and clapping both for Hunter's poignant speech and for the entertainment that was about to rock the stage. Emma felt a wave of relief—the crowd seemed to be enthralled with the musical talent. She had been worried given that this crowd was known to have conservative musical tastes. The dance floor quickly filled, and the remainder of the guests mingled around the cocktail tables, having a good time.

Hunter cautiously approached Emma. "The hospital would like some pictures of both of us. They want to do a **PR** thing with them."

Emma hadn't been expecting this. "Um, sure. Where do you want to do them?"

"How about by the park? With all the lights in the trees, it might be a nice backdrop."

Hunter ushered Emma over to the park where a photographer was already waiting. Emma felt like she was having prom pictures done. Head-on shots, then side shots—it was a bit much. Throughout the fifteen minute ordeal, Hunter had his arm tightly around her waist. A sudden flash to a specific photo of Philip Logan and Wendy Aucoin shocked Emma's brain like déjà vu.

"That should do it. Thanks, folks. Really appreciate it." The photographer left to go take pictures of the crowd.

Before Hunter could say anything, Emma noticed Wendy glaring at her. "I think your date is feeling neglected." Emma headed toward Wendy on the way to catch-up with Ashley, whom she saw on the opposite side of the room.

"He's all yours. I'm done with him," Emma stated as she walked past a very perturbed Wendy.

By the time Wendy realized the dig that was thrown her way, Emma had already disappeared into the crowd. Emma tried to control her blood pressure and her attitude before she introduced herself to Ashley's boyfriend. She noticed Ashley, and presumably her boyfriend, at one of the cocktail tables while doing the mini-photo shoot.

From across the room, Ryan kept an eye on the unfolding situation. He had immediately taken photos and video of Greg when he arrived with Ashley. There were so many unknown variables in the room it made Ryan edgy. He didn't like situations he couldn't control. Unpredictability is what got people killed in his past line of work.

Ashley was dressed in a long, black gown with a low-cut back and strappy rhinestone sandals to match. "Ashley, you look absolutely lovely tonight." Emma provided a wide smile to the couple. "And, I'm guessing this is Greg?"

"Yes! I didn't want to bother you before to introduce you." Ashley was busting with happiness.

It was time for Emma to put on another Academy Award-winning performance. "Greg, it's very nice to finally meet you. Ashley has told me so many wonderful things about you."

Greg extended his hand to shake Emma's. Emma tried not to recoil in disgust given what she thought she knew about him. "Likewise. Ash talks about you all the time. I feel like I know you already." Greg chuckled and took a swig of his beer. "This is a righteous thing you're doing tonight. I'd like to make a small donation. Won't be as much as these other folks, but I'd like to do my part."

"We take any donations—big or small. And that's very kind of you."

Greg handed Emma a personal check for two hundred dollars, which Emma folded and put into her clutch purse. "Thank you again. Now you two go enjoy the evening."

"Are you sure, boss? Do you need me for anything?"

"Nope. You've earned it. Go have some fun."

Emma tried to calmly walk back to where she had last seen Ryan a few minutes earlier. He knew by Emma's expression that she had information for him. Emma hadn't realized that he had been watching the entire scene or that she would be depositing the check with him shortly. On the other side of the indoor park, Emma handed the check to Ryan without a word and then looped back around by the bar so no one would be the wiser.

When Ryan was safely in the elevator heading downstairs to his office, he examined the check carefully. He doubted that there would be any fingerprints on it and was sure that the bank account would also be a bust. Even so, he had to follow-up on these strings dangling in front of him or it would drive him crazy. He quickly put the team to work to uncover even the tiniest bit of information from the clues they had been given. Little did the wealthy guests a few floors above realize that a malicious and dangerous game was in play, and one that could have catastrophic consequences.

CHAPTER 37

The party was in full swing and the guests appeared to be having a good time, Emma noted. She strategically mingled as best she could, accepting donation checks along the way, wondering what the final count would be for tonight. After she finished talking with the mayor, Emma noticed an elegant older woman talking to Hunter. Even from behind, Emma recognized Hunter's mother, Katherine Logan, immediately.

A knot quickly tied itself tight in Emma's stomach. With any luck, she'd be able to avoid talking with the woman. Emma had always felt uncomfortable with Katherine Logan. Back in Hardwicke, she always had the distinct impression that Katherine didn't think Emma was good enough for Hunter. Emma always went out of her way to be pleasant, which was usually met with veiled snobbery that she guessed the wealthy must learn at birth.

Hunter had assumed that his mother would be attending, although she had not responded to his personal invitation. Katherine was famous for making grand entrances and considered herself royalty amongst this crowd. The relationship between mother and son had always been strained due to his father, but Hunter knew that deep down his mother loved him in her own way.

"Mother, I wasn't sure you would be able to make it tonight, since I didn't hear back from you." Hunter couldn't resist a little jab.

"Well, dear, I wasn't sure what my schedule was like until the last minute. My other plans fell through, so here I am." Katherine wasn't going to give her only son an inch.

Hunter knew that was a lie, but it was all part of his mother's persona. "Lucky for us your other plans didn't work out."

"I haven't seen that little minx you seem all enthralled with here tonight. Did you finally come to your senses?" Katherine barely tolerated Emma on a good day.

"If you mean Emma, she's here tonight and presumably mingling with the guests." Hunter decided to let his mother's distaste slide for now.

"I thought I saw you with a tall blonde woman when I came in. She seems familiar, but I can't place her."

Hunter sighed when he finally realized it was going to be a long night. "Yes. That was Wendy Aucoin. She's a business reporter for the Boston

Times. You may have seen her at other charity events perhaps." Hunter didn't know how much his mother knew about the picture with his father and wanted to tread lightly.

"Oh, yes. Now, I remember. I think she interviewed your father a few times." Katherine tried to be coy.

Just like a well-choreographed dance routine, Wendy appeared from the crowd and headed straight toward Hunter and Katherine. "There you are, Hunter. I've been looking all over for you. You still owe me a dance." Wendy ignored Katherine, focused solely on the catch of the day.

"Wendy, may I introduce you to my mother, Katherine Logan." Hunter was very interested to see the interaction between the two formidable women.

Wendy extended her hand. "Nice to meet you, Katherine."

"Likewise. So, how do you know my son?"

"I'm a business reporter, and he runs the largest business in town. In addition, it doesn't hurt that he's the city's most eligible bachelor." Wendy stroked Hunter's arm.

"I believe you also knew my husband." Katherine's facial muscles were clenched.

"Yes. I was lucky enough that he chose me to do several interviews on him and his conglomerate. He was such a charming man and died too young." Wendy was getting into her stride.

"Philip was definitely charming when he saw something he wanted. Hunter, I'm going to go say hello to a few friends I haven't seen in a while. Excuse me." Katherine elegantly sauntered across the floor to mingle with the elite.

"That was quite interesting," Wendy remarked as she interlocked her arm in Hunter's. "Now, let's go dance. You've been neglecting me all evening. Don't worry, I know countless ways you can make it up to me later." A sly smile formed on Wendy's mouth.

Hunter reluctantly led Wendy to the dance floor just as a slow song started playing. "Just my luck," Hunter muttered to himself. Within seconds, Wendy was wrapped around Hunter like a boa constrictor. Other people on the dance floor moved slightly to the side to let the event's benefactor have more space. Hunter was hoping to blend in with the crowd, but it seemed like the crowd wanted to make him a spectacle. He did his best to keep smiling until he saw Emma scowling on the sidelines.

Emma and Robert join the dance crowd, which provided Hunter a slight reprieve. Something strange happened. Hunter followed Wendy's gaze to Robert. She tried not to show her interest, although Hunter caught her in the act and wondered what it all meant.

"What can you tell me about Robert Sharpeton, besides what's in your press release?"

"Are you interviewing me?" Hunter was

always overly cautious with the press, no matter how beautiful.

"Let's call it curiosity. I'll have to decide later if what you tell me is newsworthy."

"Not much to tell. Emma's older brother now works for me and will be relocating back to Boston."

"Interesting. He would be a fine specimen to interview." Wendy licked her lips.

"I doubt you'll get any dirt on him, Wendy. He's clean as a whistle." Hunter didn't like the direction this was heading.

"We'll see about that. I have a talent for getting what I want." Wendy's tone turned wicked.

A chill went up Hunter's spine. Wendy went from overly friendly to cold as ice in a matter of seconds. "My money is on Robert. Unfortunately, I need to cut the dance short. I just noticed some business acquaintances that I need to speak with. Thank you for the dance." Hunter quickly strode over to a few people at one of the cocktail tables like he was escaping the plague.

Emma couldn't help but notice the relief on Hunter's face as soon as he left Wendy on the dance floor by herself and a small smile formed. Robert watched her inquiringly. "Nothing, Robert. I just really don't like that Boston Times reporter. There's something about her, that's all. I know it's petty."

"Not in the least. I do think it might have some-thing to do with how she was trying to wriggle inside Hunter's tux while they were dancing. It was quite the display. But, to give my new boss credit, he looked like he wanted to crawl under a table."

"She doesn't have much class. Just be careful if she wants to interview you. Not sure her motives are pure. I saw how she was salivating when gazing at you."

"Will do. And I'm not going to do any interviews without Hunter. It's his company, plus I may need the protection if she's as much of a viper as you say." Robert laughed. "C'mon, let's go get some drinks."

Wendy watched from the opposite side of the room as Emma and Robert made their way to the bar. The plan was in full motion. She would get what she wanted, she just needed to be patient.

In the meantime, Wendy decided to sample the people who were here to see if any would be interesting enough for a story. At least when she had accompanied Philip Logan to a few of these events, she had the pre- and post-event activities to look forward to. It was the only thing that helped her not die of boredom. She thought back to those encounters—Philip was distinguished and powerful, but his son was becoming more powerful than his father. For Wendy, power was an intoxicating drug that she couldn't get enough of. This was her chance to end up on top.

Wendy noticed Evan Stewards talking to some other people from Emma's company. Evan had served her well in the recent past. Maybe she could widen his usefulness. Wendy would probably need to sweeten the deal with Evan, she realized. This wasn't something that she was opposed to, although she had walked away from that part of her life a long time ago with the help of Philip.

"Oh, Evan, I'm about to teach you things you only watched on your computer or dreamed about," Wendy whispered to herself.

CHAPTER 38

——

Emma's watch said midnight and the crowd had started to disperse. Unexpectedly, Hunter got back on stage to close out the evening. Emma, and the rest of the crowd, turned their attention toward the eye-catching Brit.

"Ladies and gentlemen, tonight has been absolutely brilliant! I'd like to take this time to thank a few folks who truly put their heart and soul into making this all happen. Emma, can you come up on stage?"

Emma wanted to crawl under a table. She prayed that she could make it up the three steps and onto the stage without falling flat on her face. The crowd was focused on her as she made her way onto the stage—happily without incident.

"Emma and her team of miracle workers were the ones who made tonight possible. Through her leadership and her team's dedication, this evening was spectacular. Please join me in showing her and her team our gratitude."

The crowd followed Hunter's lead with the applause. He gave Emma a quick kiss on the cheek before she departed the stage.

"I'd also like to sincerely thank Joe Bonamassa for an incredible night of the best blues music in the world! You were definitely the life of the party and helped us raise over a million dollars!" The crowd, including Joe, erupted in applause with hoots and hollers.

Emma almost fainted when Hunter announced the total for the night—it was more than she had imagined.

"Hey, boss. That's amazing!" Ashley and Greg approached Emma on the side of the stage.

"I have to say, I'm stunned. Ashley, you and the rest of the team should be very proud of yourselves."

"I think we're all proud of what we did. Greg, if you want to go back to the hotel, you can. I need to help cleanup and it will be a little while."

"Ashley, why don't you go with Greg to the hotel? I can manage the cleanup."

"Are you sure? I don't want to leave you in a lurch. I'm happy to stay. Although, I need to change out of these killer heels." Ashley bent down to rub her right ankle.

Emma chuckled. "I told you those things were dangerous! It's fine—really. Go and enjoy yourselves."

Greg stepped forward with his hand extended. "It was very nice to finally meet you in person, Emma."

"Likewise. I hope we'll be seeing each other again."

"You can count on it." Greg stared directly into Emma's eyes, and she swore there was an evil glimmer.

"C'mon, Greg. My feet are killing me, and we have to walk to the hotel. Bye, Emma!" Ashley grabbed Greg's arm and led him to the front door.

A shiver went up Emma's spine like she had just been in the presence of the Devil himself. Emma jumped when Ryan put his hand on her shoulder.

"Sorry, darling. Didn't mean to startle you."

"I felt like I just shook hands with the Devil. That guy is evil to the core. I could see it in his eyes."

Ryan guided Emma to one of the cocktail tables to sit down. Before he sat down, Ryan went to the bar and grabbed two glasses and a bottle of champagne. While he poured the two glasses, he said, "I tend to agree with you. I was watching him all night. He always had you in his sight. It was a bit creepy."

"Great. Love to hear that." Emma took a large swallow of her champagne.

"Not much on the check he gave us, which I expected. Bank account was opened two years ago. The name on the account, as you could see on the check, was Greg Smythe. There are hundreds of Greg Smythe's in Massachusetts alone. The address is a warehouse down by the cruise ship dock, so that is obviously bogus. I'll keep digging, but don't expect much. The good thing is there is money in the account, so the check will clear." Ryan wanted to give Emma a silver lining.

Emma rubbed her temples just as her brother and Hunter strode over. Robert grabbed two more glasses from the bar and sat down. "Great job tonight, little sis! Hopefully now you can relax a little bit. Your stress is over and mine is just beginning." Robert flashed a smile in Hunter's direction while Hunter rolled his eyes.

"I would agree with you, Robert. Maybe your sister can take a little time off and go back to London with you to help you pack up?" Hunter suggested.

Ryan piped up. "That sounds like a great idea!"

"I'm beginning to feel a tad unwanted." Emma had a feeling that Hunter wanted her out of the country while they tried to figure out why Greg was stalking her. "I'll think about it, but I also have a company to run. It may not be a conglomerate, but it still needs my attention."

Hunter held up both hands in defense. "Okay. Was just a thought."

Ryan decided to change topics. "So, a million dollars? That's incredible!"

"I know. I'd say it's all Emma." Hunter smiled affectionately in Emma's direction.

Emma realized that someone wasn't stuck to Hunter like white on rice. "Hunter, where's your lovely date?"

Hunter rolled his eyes again. "She decided to call it an evening." He sounded relieved.

Emma got up from their pow-wow. "I need to make sure that the cleanup is moving along. Thank you, guys, for all your help tonight. Glad it was a success. Robert, if you want to go to the hotel, I can take a cab back there. I know you're flying out tomorrow."

"I'll wait for you. I'm in first-class so I can lie down and sleep the whole flight if I want."

"Shouldn't be too long." Emma walked across the lobby where the dance floor and stage were already almost completely dismantled.

For the next hour, Hunter, Ryan, and Robert drank more champagne and talked about Robert's plans to move back to Boston. They had finished the bottle by the time Emma came over, exhausted.

"Everything is done. I'm bushed. Let's go so I can sleep for the next twenty-four hours."

The men laughed and agreed. Emma had texted Jared that they'd be ready to leave shortly, and Jared was already waiting out front. Both she and Robert headed back to their hotel while Hunter and Ryan went to their separate residences. No one dared breathe a sigh of relief just yet that there hadn't been any major incidents at the gala. What the threesome didn't realize was that the next phase of the master plan had been put in place that evening.

On a computer screen across the city from the Logan headquarters, the image of Hunter and Emma taken by the professional photographer at the gala, filled the screen. Surrounding the picture was the outline of a bullseye, as if it would be used for target practice. Next to the computer was an advanced copy of the Sunday Boston Times, turned to the society page, where there was a large article on the gala with the same picture as a centerpiece, minus the bullseye that was on the screen.

CHAPTER 39

The next morning, Emma dropped her brother off at Logan Airport for his long flight back across the pond. Robert expected it would take a month or two for him to appoint someone to his prior position at the company and then pack up to move back to Boston. Emma was tasked with finding condo options for Robert to check out—either in person or virtually.

With all the heightened security at airports, Emma couldn't go to the gate with Robert. Instead, they said their farewell at the check-in area amongst the throngs of other passengers. For the first time in the last few months, Emma felt safe enough to relax a bit. She even got the chance to make friends with one of the German Shepard security dogs while she waited for Robert to check his bag.

Emma thought how normal this all felt. She wondered if things would calm down now that the gala was over. The gala had gone off without a hitch and no new signs of any danger had arisen last night. Her biggest fear had been that a bomb would be detonated during the event, but besides a few extra boisterous partygoers, it had been a mundane evening from a security standpoint.

Robert approached his sister, interrupting her train of thought. "Okay, Em, I'm all checked in. Back to the fog and murkiness. I'll text you when I land. Don't forget to send me anything that looks suitable for a living space." Robert kissed Emma and headed towards the first-class security line. After showing his passport and boarding pass, he turned and waved to his sister, then disappeared into the screening area.

Emma met Jared outside at the waiting car, and they arrived at Emma's condo thirty minutes later. Instead of dropping her off, Jared went inside with her. She knew by now not to question whatever orders Jared had been given. Jared instructed Emma to wait in the foyer while he checked every room, closet, and under the bed to make sure there weren't any surprises. Once all was deemed safe, Emma dropped her bags in the kitchen, thanked Jared for his thoroughness, and then locked the door behind him.

Although the suite at the hotel was spectacular, Emma was happy to be home. She decided that Sunday would be a day of rest. No laundry, no work, no phone calls—just lounging on the couch watching movies and eating junk food. Jared had given Emma a copy of the Sunday Boston Times newspaper, thinking she would want to read the article on the gala. After getting comfy under the blanket on the couch, Emma skimmed the newspaper until she found the article on the society page.

She should have expected the photo of her and Hunter to be front and center, but she still cringed a little. A similar photo from a charity event years ago with Hunter's father and Wendy crept into her mind. Emma noticed there wasn't a single mention of Wendy being Hunter's date for the event, which caused Emma to laugh out loud. "Take that, Wendy!"

The doorbell interrupted Emma's mini-celebration and Wendy bashing. She wasn't expecting anyone and the doorman didn't call to ask her about visitors. As she untangled herself from the blanket and made her way to the door, she realized who would be on the other side.

"Hunter, didn't expect to see or hear from you today." Emma motioned for him to come in.

Hunter surveyed the space, paying attention to the luggage in the kitchen and the newspaper on the coffee table in the living room. "Did I disturb you?"

"No, I got home a little while ago and just didn't feel like doing anything. I'm reading the article about the gala."

"I read it earlier. They did a nice job. The photo isn't too bad either." Hunter sat on the couch.

"It was a nice write-up. I'm sure Wendy has a nice, big ole bullseye around my picture," Emma said snarky.

"That's what I wanted to talk to you about—to explain things," Hunter said sheepishly.

"You don't need to explain anything. It's your life." Emma really didn't want to have this conversation. Any relaxation she felt earlier was now gone.

"I need you to understand. I wasn't purposely trying to hurt you."

Emma started to interject but stopped herself.

"I saw a picture of Wendy and my father at a charity event years ago. I don't know, I guess I was trying to see if she'd give me any insights. And, yes, I know that sounds stupid. I did witness an interesting exchange between her and my mother."

Emma lifted an eyebrow. "Do tell." Maybe her and Wendy had something in common after all—Hunter's mother's distaste of them.

"Let's just say, my mother was her typical ice queen. Wendy was no shrinking violet, especially with a jab about spending time with my father. For a few seconds, I was wondering if I should take cover. Then, my mother decided she'd had enough and went to mingle. Wendy didn't really say much after that."

"That's interesting. Sounds like Wendy wanted to make sure that your mother knew that she had been in your father's life with the innuendo that she was close to him." It wasn't anything that they all hadn't thought before, but why would Wendy almost flaunt it except to get a rise out of Hunter's mother? To Emma, this seemed like something a high school girl would do.

"It was definitely strange."

"What does Ryan think of it?"

"I haven't told him yet. I wanted to talk to you first." Hunter looked down at his hands on his lap.

"I appreciate that, but Ryan needs to know all this sooner rather than later. I know he's doing more digging on Wendy."

"I know. I'll tell him in the morning." Hunter paused. "I don't want this to sound conceited. What if she was putting my mother on notice that she was coming after me like she did my father?"

"Could be. Anyone in that room could tell she wanted you out of that tux and into her bed," Emma blurted out.

Hunter cringed. "Trust me, I know that. I didn't really want to be a spectacle, either. She did take a fleeting interest in Robert, too."

"I noticed her eyeing him. I told him not to do any interviews with her, and he agreed."

"That's good. She's a viper. I'm just not exactly sure what game she's playing."

"My opinion: she loves power and knows you have plenty of it, just like your father did."

Hunter let Emma's words sink in. "It wouldn't

surprise me. My father attracted women like flies, mostly due to his power and money."

"This really isn't any of my business, but she's coming after you. You're clearly in her sights, and she seems like a woman who's used to getting what she wants. I'd suggest having Ryan do some *deep* digging on her. Your father, with his many faults, wouldn't have let just any old gold-digger into his life."

"I'll get Ryan on it. To address your first comment—this is your business because you're *my* business. I hate this whole situation and the fact that you aren't safe being around me."

Emma hated the situation as well but couldn't allow herself to just fall back into Hunter's arms. She needed to keep her distance to see how everything unraveled. She still wasn't sure that, if given the chance, he wouldn't let Wendy take this all the way. "We'll figure all this out, and then we can get back to our lives."

Hunter knew that was his dismissal. He hated to leave Emma, but if he was going to make his way back to her, he couldn't be his usual aggressive self.

"I'm going to take off. You deserve a day of rest." Before Hunter got into the elevator, he smiled at Emma with his crystal blue eyes. The elevator closed before Emma could respond.

Back on the couch, under the blanket, Emma reviewed her conversation with Hunter, which was part of her routine lately. Emma kept coming back to the question of how Wendy was connected to Hunter's father and if it was just coincidence. The coincidences kept piling up. Emma shuddered. Wendy was going after Hunter, for probably obvious reasons, and Greg was going after Emma, for reasons unknown. The one common denominator was the Logan family. What deep dark secrets were they trying to keep buried?

CHAPTER 40

———

With a chocolate covered donut in one hand and a cup of steaming black coffee in the other, Ryan strolled into his office whistling a tune he couldn't quite place. Hunter sat patiently at his desk.

"Good morning, bro! I was going to head up to the clouds to see you after I dropped this stuff off."

"I figured I'd wait for you here to get an update on our favorite side project." Hunter moved to one of the other chairs so Ryan could sit at his own desk.

"Good news is nothing happened at the gala. I think we can all breathe a sigh of relief for that miracle."

"Agreed. Anything new on our friend Greg?"

"I looked into the check he gave us. Got zip, which isn't surprising. Bank account was opened a couple years ago. At least the check cleared." Ryan paused to blow on his hot coffee before cautiously taking a sip.

"Anything on his name? Now that we know his

last name." Hunter got more comfortable.

"Nothing yet. It's a very common name, so not expecting much. I did locate the social security number he provided when he opened the bank account. Don't ask me how, though." Ryan paused again to take a bite of his donut. While chewing, he continued, "So, the social belonged to a guy who died sixty-seven years ago in some tiny town in south Texas."

"This will be a stupid question, but could this Greg be from Texas?"

"Doubtful. You can get social security numbers on the dark web for a price. My guess is he bought these credentials so he could establish himself for this job. Professionals will discard the identity once the job is over and assume a new one." Ryan took another sip of coffee. "We figured this was how it was going to pan out. That's why he wasn't afraid to give Emma a check for the donation. He's taunting us."

"I hated how close he was able to get to Emma at the gala. It made my skin crawl."

Ryan knew how Hunter felt. "Right there with ya. Which is why I was no more than twenty feet away at all times. If that punk pulled anything, he wouldn't know what hit him. So, have you heard from your date?" Ryan snickered.

"No, thank God! She was like an octopus all night."

"Gee, I feel so bad for you." Ryan smirked.

Hunter recited the conversation between Wendy and his mother. "Your thoughts?" he asked Ryan.

Ryan leaned back in his chair for a minute before answering. "I think she definitely had something going on with your father and now she's after you. My gut tells me she likes power and money, and that you have a target on your back."

"That's exactly what Emma said."

Ryan leaned forward. "When did you talk to Emma?"

"Yesterday. I stopped by her condo. I wanted to try to explain the whole Wendy thing. She was gracious but I'm not sure she believed me. She did agree that Wendy is a viper who needs to be watched. And she suggested you do some deep digging."

"I've done the cursory probing on Wendy. I think Emma's right—now it's time to do the deep-dive and see what skeletons she's hiding. It could pull up some stuff you may not want to hear about your father, though."

Hunter got up and headed for the door. "Look, we both know my father wasn't a saint. There were always rumors of him having affairs. So, just do what you need to do."

"I'll see what I can find," Ryan replied before Hunter shut the door.

Ryan did as Hunter asked and started to conduct a more intense search of the reporter's life, specifically around the time that Philip Logan was in the picture. Something nagged at Ryan while he was pulling up the typical government databases, but he couldn't put a finger on it. What if Wendy was the person behind these incidents, the one pulling Greg's strings? What would her motive be? It had to be more than landing Boston's most eligible bachelor.

Ryan noted that there was no love lost between Wendy and Katherine, which could just be because of an affair long ago. Something about Wendy seemed vaguely familiar now that Ryan had had the chance to watch her in action. Ryan spent the rest of the day submersing himself in databases, trying to figure out the mystery that was the leggy reporter.

CHAPTER 41

————

While Ryan was across town trying to decipher the latest mystery, Emma was in her office trying to sort through the statuses of the projects for her other clients. It felt good to be able to put the gala behind her and focus on something different. Just as she was about to get another cup of tea, her cell phone rang.

It was a local number.

"Good morning. This is Emma Sharpeton."

"Good morning, Ms. Sharpeton. This is Detective O'Reilly. I saw your picture in the Sunday paper. Nice write-up, too."

"Hello, Detective. Thank you for the kind words."

"I was glad to see that all was quiet for your event. I can admit now that I was on pins and needles all night hoping my phone *didn't* ring."

"You and me both!"

"I wanted to call and give you an update. Still nothing concrete on the break-in at your office or the car shooting, sorry to say. This guy is a ghost.

Although, Ryan did give me an interesting scenario on who he thinks the suspect is. Has he shared this with you?"

Emma peered out of her office to make sure that Ashley wasn't in earshot. "Yes, he did. He thinks it might be my assistant's boyfriend, Greg. I met Greg at the gala. He was my assistant's date for the evening. But I can't tell you much. He was well-mannered, clean-cut with that military look, and rather quiet. Oh! He did give me a donation check, which I know Ryan was researching."

"Interesting. I'll give Ryan a jingle and see if he's come up with anything. I'm glad that your event went well. If I get any more news, I'll give you a call. And, please, even though the event is over, still be diligent."

"I absolutely will, Detective. Thanks again for calling." Emma hung up not knowing any more than before the call. She had a feeling that Ryan and the detective knew more than they were willing to share with her and that was probably for the best.

Ashley interrupted Emma's train of thought. "Morning, boss! Do you need anything?"

"I think I'm good for now. Just digging through our other projects to see if there's anything urgent, which it doesn't look like there is."

"Okay." Ashley hesitated at the door.

"Is there something on your mind?"

"Well, I just wanted to say that I thought it

was awfully rude for Hunter to bring that reporter to the gala."

"Oh, that. Don't worry about it. I've already forgotten it. Hunter is free to bring whoever he likes to these functions."

"But, still." Ashley looked like she wanted to pummel Hunter.

Emma laughed. "I appreciate you defending me, but it's not necessary. I knew he was bringing her so it wasn't a surprise." Emma decided the white lie might end the conversation quickly.

"Oh. I didn't realize. Still, it was wrong." Ashley walked out in a huff and went back to her desk.

Emma shook her head and tried to refocus on the tasks at hand, mainly getting another cup of tea. She didn't make it to the door of her office before her cell phone rang again. With a sigh, she leaned over her desk to grab the phone.

"Emma Sharpeton." Emma tried not to sound irritated.

"Emma, this is Chief Dyson from the Hardwicke Police Department. Hope I didn't catch you at a bad time."

She wondered why on earth the chief would be calling her. "Morning, Chief Dyson. How can I help you?"

"Well, I hate to tell you this but there was a break-in at your mother's house over the weekend."

"Oh, my God!" Emma was shocked.

"It looks like it was Saturday night. The alarm system tripped, and I had an officer go check it out. Nothing seemed out of place, so we just figured it was a crossed wire or something. I decided to go back over this morning on my way to the police station and noticed some of the bushes in the front were disturbed. I also tried the back door and it opened."

"Was anything taken?" Emma was heartbroken that someone had intruded on her sanctuary.

"I can't really tell. The only room that looks disturbed was your father's office but also the door to the basement was open slightly. It didn't appear that anything was gone, but you'd probably know better than I would. I'm hoping that you can come to Hardwicke today or tomorrow to let me know if anything is missing."

"Um. Sure. Let me clear my schedule, and I can drive out there shortly. What was done to my father's office?"

"Looks like they were going through the file cabinets. There were papers on the floor and the drawers were opened."

"That's a bit strange." Emma wondered if this had something to do with her father's secretive research.

"Please stop in at the station before you go to the house. I want to make sure someone is with you."

"I will. I'll see you in a couple of hours." Emma

disconnected. She felt stunned, but knew her next call needed to be to Ryan.

Emma quickly dialed Ryan's cell phone number and it went straight to voicemail. She left a brief message with what little she knew and that she'd be driving out to Hardwicke shortly. Although Emma knew that she should probably wait for Ryan or Jared to accompany her, she didn't know when they would be available. Ryan knew where she would be and, if needed, he could drive out there later.

With all her things gathered, Emma walked out to Ashley's desk to let her know that she would be leaving for the rest of the day and wasn't sure if she'd be in tomorrow. Emma could tell that Ashley was perplexed but was saved by the phone ringing at Ashley's desk. She didn't want to have to replay all the details of the disturbing situation to her inquiring assistant who might literally be in bed with the culprit.

Once back at her condo, Emma quickly packed a small bag in case she needed to stay overnight. She shuttered at the thought of staying in the house where an intruder had been not too long ago. Even though it was just a house, it was sacred to Emma. It was the house she had grown up in, had had holiday family gatherings, and held special memories of her father. Now all of that seemed tainted.

Emma went to her building's garage to get her Land Rover and start the trek out to the pristine country setting of Hardwicke. At this time of day, it should only take her about an hour and a half, depending on if she got stuck behind a farm tractor on one of the back roads. Usually the drive was relaxing, especially once she got off the highway. The landscape in that part of Massachusetts was breathtaking. Everything was so alive in the spring and summer—the wildlife, green grass, wildflowers in the fields. The air was crisp and clean no matter what season it was and made her lungs feel alive.

One of the many things Emma loved about Hardwicke was the town's historic roots and the way the townspeople worked to keep their heritage alive. It was believed that Hardwicke had first been settled by Nipmuck Native Americans after the King Philip War. In 1687 the land was purchased by a group of English settlers from Roxbury for twenty pounds. The center of town echoed its appearance from the early 1700s, with a large town common, surrounded by a school, tavern, and meetinghouse with residential houses sprinkled around the town center.

In 1739, the town had been incorporated and named Hardwicke, in honor of an English nobleman, Lord Hardwicke. The town's economy prospered with both manufacturing and agriculture well into the late 1800s. With more people coming to Hardwicke, the need arose for a library system. Hardwicke's first library association was founded in 1802 as a private library with subscribers. A hundred years later, the Paige Memorial Library was built. As jobs slowly moved elsewhere in the twentieth century, the town went from being a manufacturing and agricultural hot spot to a sleepy commuter and weekender town.

Emma always loved how picturesque and charming Hardwicke was. She loved living in the city, but there was something calming about driving west on the Massachusetts Turnpike and landing in the serenity of this community. Everyone knew everyone, and people were famous for "popping-in" at each other's houses. All of this made it hard for Emma to wrap her head around someone breaking into her family's home.

CHAPTER 42

———

Emma pulled into the almost empty parking lot of the Hardwicke police station, which was adjacent to the town hall. She sat in the car for a minute to calm herself before she entered the building. When Emma walked into the building, she realized that she didn't know the cops like she used to when she lived here. Luckily, Chief Dyson was coming out of his office and noticed her standing uncertainly in the lobby.

"Hi, Ms. Sharpeton. Thanks for coming out here today. Why don't we go talk in my office for a few minutes?" Chief Dyson escorted Emma to his small office in the back of the police station and motioned for her to sit down on one of the plastic stackable chairs in front of his double pedestal metal desk that was piled high with file folders.

"So, have you learned anything new?" Emma inquired.

"Unfortunately, no. We dusted for fingerprints and got zilch. Probably the intruder wore gloves.

Tracey L. Ryan

For once, the neighbors said they *didn't* see anything suspicious."

Emma found it strange that none of the neighbors noticed anything. That had never happened when she had a few friends over while her parents had been out of town. "Can we go to the house, so I can check if anything's missing?"

"Sure. I'll have Officer Wilson follow you there. Are you going to be staying the night or going back to Boston?"

"I'm not sure yet. I'll see how much cleanup there is to do and then decide."

"Just let Officer Wilson know. I'll make sure to have a car patrol by a few times tonight if you decide to stay over. I doubt the intruder will come back, but better to be safe."

A chill went up Emma's spine at Chief Dyson's last comment. When Officer Wilson appeared in the chief's office, Emma noticed how youthful the officer appeared. He was a little under six feet tall with a slim build and boyish face. Emma said good-bye to Chief Dyson and then followed the young officer outside to their vehicles. Luckily, the police station was less than a mile from the house. Emma took the lead. It was a little unnerving having the police following her.

The Sharpeton home was a two-story post-colonial style off the center of town during the building boom in the area. Much of the house remained in its original form with some minor changes. Additional rooms had been added for a pantry, a shed, and the room that served as her father's office. Her parents had tried to keep as much of the original features of the house, including the doors for each of the rooms with their old fashioned latch handles.

At the house, Emma walked around the perimeter in the hopes of finding something the police had missed. Nothing seemed disturbed except a few bushes, which could have been done by an animal. Emma put her key into the side door lock and slowly opened the door. At first glance, everything looked like it should. Nothing seemed out of place—the dust in the living room wasn't even disrupted. For a split second, she had a flashback of the last time she was in this house and her companion.

Emma moved cautiously through the kitchen to her father's office and couldn't believe what she saw. It was as if a tornado had torn through the small space. There wasn't an inch of floor that wasn't covered with paper. Her father's desk had been thoroughly searched, the contents dumped on the floor, as had all the file cabinet drawers. Her mind raced as she thought back to when she had been here with Hunter, specifically the files and flash drive they had found. Emma suspected this was what the intruder had been searching for. The question was—would the intruder be satisfied that they couldn't find anything or would they try a different approach?

Without a word, Officer Wilson followed Emma to the basement. All three of the five-tier heavy-duty wire shelving units were toppled over, their contents haphazardly dumped on the ground. Her father's old workbench at the opposite end of the basement was ransacked, the tools thrown in every direction. It seemed strange that the intruder would look in the basement. What could they have been searching for there?

Officer Wilson startled Emma. "Not sure what the burgler wanted down here. I can help you put this stuff back if you'd like. Looks like some of it could be heavy."

"That's very kind of you. I don't want to take any more of your time. I'm sure you have more important things to be doing," Emma replied sincerely.

"No problem. The chief told me to help you with whatever you needed. I can get started putting these shelves back up."

Without another word, Officer Wilson rolled up his sleeves and started putting things back in order. Emma tackled her father's workbench, putting all the tools back in their rightful spots. An hour later, the basement was back to normal and the two, now a bit dusty, trudged back upstairs to find Chief Dyson in the kitchen leaning against the counter.

"Chief, I hope you don't mind Officer Wilson helping me out a little bit with the big stuff." Emma really hoped that the kindhearted officer wouldn't get in trouble with his boss.

"Not at all. I told him to make sure he helped you anyway he could. Get everything back in order down there?"

"Yes, we did. I think I'm going to stay over tonight and go back to the city tomorrow. My dad's office is going to take a few hours to straighten out."

"I'll make sure a squad car does a few passes tonight. Officer Wilson, I'll see you back at the station."

"Yes, sir. Anything else you need, Ms. Sharpeton?"

"I think that after getting all dusty in the basement, you've earned the right to call me Emma. And, no, I think we've done enough for one day."

Officer Wilson chuckled. "Thanks, Emma. I'm heading back to the station. Call us if you need anything." The officer turned and left by the side door. Emma suddenly felt very alone and vulnerable.

Emma realized she hadn't checked her phone for messages. She grabbed her phone out of her rose-colored Coach Market Tote. She had forgotten how spotty the cell service in town was. Hardwicke seemed to be one of the last towns in the state to have updated cellular towers, which aggravated Emma.

Emma stepped outside on to the back patio and two bars magically appeared on her phone. She dialed Ryan's cell number and paced around the patio, only to find out that she needed to stay in one spot for the phone to work.

"Dammit." Emma muttered to herself as she hit redial.

"Emma! Is everything okay? The phone went dead before I could answer it." Ryan sounded exasperated.

"Everything is fine. I forgot that Hardwicke has barely gotten out of the last century when it comes to cell phone technology. I have to stand in this one spot outside on the patio for my phone to get reception."

"Phew. I got your text from earlier, and I'm *not* happy you went there alone."

Emma knew this was coming. "I know. I was hoping this would be a quick trip in and out, but I'm going to stay the night."

Ryan grunted.

"Don't worry. The police know I'm here, and they're going to do patrols by the house tonight. It'll be fine."

"I can be there in about two hours with traffic."

"I appreciate that, Ryan, but I'll be fine." Emma was getting tired of standing in one spot.

"Do the police have any suspects? Was any-thing taken?"

"They don't have any suspects yet. There were only two rooms disturbed—the basement and my father's office. It was clear that the intruder was searching for something specific. Both places were torn apart. Every drawer and crevice was searched."

Ryan contemplated what Emma had said. "I'm now even more concerned about you staying there alone."

"They obviously didn't find whatever it was they were looking for, so I doubt they'll come back." Emma knew the direction Ryan was heading and it freaked her out.

"I want you to make sure the alarm system is armed the entire time you are there. I don't like this one bit! I know I don't have to say aloud what they likely wanted."

"Trust me, my mind went directly there when the police told me what happened."

"How's the chief there? What's his name? Dennison?"

"No, it's Dyson. D-Y-S-O-N. I've known him forever. No love lost between him and Hunter, though." Emma let out a giggle. "The townspeople seem to like Dyson. He knew my dad fairly well."

Emma's last comment peaked Ryan's interest. "How well did he know your dad?"

"Ryan, everyone knows each other in Hardwicke."

"I realize that. Just trying to cover my bases given everything that's been going on. To put my mind at ease, I might do some digging on your fearless police chief."

"I doubt you'll find anything but go for it if it

makes you feel better."

Ryan could tell Emma had just rolled her eyes on the other end of the phone. "Okay, my lady, I must dash. Stay vigilant out there tonight. Text me so I know all is well tonight and tomorrow morning."

"Oh, one other thing, Ryan. I'm a little worried about the security guard at my office building, Stan. He hasn't been to work in days and that's highly unusual. With everything going on lately, I was wondering if you could maybe check into it," Emma said, concerned.

"Are you sure he just didn't go on vacation?"

"He has always told me when he was going on vacation in the past. It would just put my mind at ease if you could look into it."

Ryan could hear the worry in Emma's voice. "I'll let you know if I find anything. I'm sure he's probably just basking in the sun with an umbrella drink in hand somewhere." Ryan disconnected.

He now had two additional people to add to his growing list of, as the police would say, persons of interest, plus a missing person. Ryan figured that the police chief would come back untarnished, but he couldn't take the chance of ignoring a possible suspect. The fact that Dyson knew both Emma's family and Hunter's was cause enough for mild concern.

Anyone who knew the Logans also knew that Philip always got what he wanted. If Philip was indeed the cause of Craig Sharpeton's car accident, it wouldn't take much for him to pay the police to not look too deeply into it. The missing security guard was an interesting turn, Ryan pondered. Although it was more than likely nothing suspicious, Ryan understood why Emma didn't want to take a chance. The spider's web just got even more tangled in Ryan's mind.

CHAPTER 43

———

Emma's stomach growled, and she realized she hadn't eaten at all today. One of the other challenges, besides spotty cell service, was that fact there weren't any restaurants that delivered nearby. The local market was four miles away, so she decided to head down the hill to see if she could get the basics for her overnight stay.

The Land Rover was made to handle these country roads, Emma thought as she started down the hill from the center of town to the market. When she got to the hairpin turn on Old Ravine Road, she couldn't help but flashback to the night her father died in the car accident in this same spot, to the memory of her father's Jeep Grand Cherokee, a molten pile of metal and glass smoldering, at the bottom of the ravine.

Chief Dyson had told her mother that the tragic accident was a result of the unforgiving road conditions due to the snowstorm. There wasn't any foul play suspected, even though there were what looked like the remnants of another vehicle's tire marks on the side of the road and a half-smoked cigar found next to the Jeep. Craig Sharpeton didn't smoke cigars, but the police had said it was probably trash someone had thrown out their car as they passed by. There wasn't any way to tell how long it had been there, Chief Dyson had stated.

Emma always thought the cigar was out of place. It nagged at her even now. It was true that it could have easily been someone littering. What seemed strange to Emma was that there wasn't much snow covering the cigar. There had been quite a storm that evening, dumping eight inches of snow on the town, but the cigar rested only under an inch or so of snow. The chief had said that it could have been moved when the fire department was trying to extinguish the car fire. He had dismissed Emma's questions on the matter.

Being back in Hardwicke brought that terrible night back to the surface for Emma, especially with the break-in at her family's house. She slowed the Land Rover to almost a crawl around the turn and held her breathe a little. Once past the turn, it was smooth driving to the market where she picked up tea, milk, chips, and a chicken salad sandwich for dinner. She figured a nice bottle of dry rosé wine would complement the freshly made sandwich.

After resetting the alarm at the house and putting her groceries away, Emma opened the bottle of

wine. She preferred it ice cold, but room tempera-
ture would do for now. Wine was the only thing that
was going to help her through the task of putting her
father's office back together. It dawned on Emma
that she never called her mother or brother to let
them know what happened. She grabbed her wine
glass and went out to the patio to make the calls.

She decided to call her mother first in Arizona.
The phone rang several times and she almost gave
up when finally, on the last ring, Victoria answered.
"Hello, darling. I was outside tending to my little
garden and didn't hear the phone ring."

"Hi, Mom. How's the garden coming along?"
Emma was stalling.

"It's wonderful! I finally figured out which flowers work well with this desert heat and now it's thriv-
ing. Are you outside? The reception is a little fuzzy."

"I'm at the house in Hardwicke. That's why I'm
calling actually."

"Is everything okay?" Emma could hear the
concern in her mother's voice.

"Well, Chief Dyson called me this morning
to let me know there was a break-in at the house.
The alarm went off over the weekend, but the
police didn't see anything out of the ordinary. Chief
Dyson decided to check for himself this morning
and found that there had been an intruder."

"Oh, my God! Was anything taken? There's
nothing really of value left in there. Please tell me

they didn't vandalized the house!"

"No, no vandalism. They went through Dad's office and all the file cabinets. Made a real mess with all the files. And they went through the basement. Doesn't seem like anything was taken. One of the police officers who came to the house with me helped me put the basement back in order. I'm going to stay the night to clean up Dad's office."

"Oh, honey. Thank you for doing that. Are you going to be all right by yourself?"

"I'll be fine. The police are going to do some patrols by the house tonight just to be sure. I just wanted to let you know."

"I appreciate that. I got a text from your brother last week. He seems very happy with his new job and moving back to Boston. I'm really glad you both will be in close proximity again. I think it will do both of you some good."

"I'm very happy for him! It's a great opportunity and having him back on this continent is a bonus. I don't want to keep you from your gardening. I just wanted to let you know what was going on and that I'd be staying here tonight." Emma didn't want to alarm her mother, but she wanted to make sure that a few people knew where she was in case something happened. She chastised herself for letting Ryan get into her head.

"Okay, dear. Let me know if you need anything with the house. We'll talk soon. Love you!"

"Love you, too!" Emma was relieved the call was over. She didn't want her mother to worry, especially since she was halfway across the country in Arizona.

Emma sent a quick text to Robert about the break-in with basically the same information she just told her mother. Back inside the house, Emma swallowed a mouthful of wine and headed to her father's office. She couldn't decide where to begin, so she started with the papers closest to the door and worked her way into the office.

After almost two hours of sitting on the floor, Emma's body was stiff and her neck sore. Emma was able to separate the vast amount of papers into three main piles—bills and household receipts, work-related, and miscellaneous. She threw anything that she didn't know what it was into the miscellaneous pile, which quickly became the largest of the three.

Emma decided to take a break and stretch her legs by going out to the patio to check her phone for any messages. Two texts popped up—one from Robert and one from Ryan. She replied to Robert to let him know all was well. Ryan was checking on her welfare, and she replied that she was fine and not to worry.

Just after she hit "send" with the reply to Ryan's text and walked back into the kitchen, a loud crash from the basement shook the entire house. Emma's heart stopped. She waited for any other sounds coming from the bowels of the basement. The whole house was silent except for her breathing. She really wished her cell phone worked inside the house. Emma frantically scanned the kitchen for a weapon but didn't find anything. She remembered the large heavy-duty flashlight her parents always kept in the junk drawer in the kitchen.

She grabbed the flashlight and headed toward the locked basement door. Before opening the door, she put her ear against it to check if she could hear anything. All she heard was silence. Slowly, she opened the door and turned on the light. She scanned the area that she could see from the top of the stairs, looking for any movement or shadows. Again, nothing. Emma crept down the stairs as quietly as she could, all the time scanning for anything that would cause her harm. Her pulse was off the charts, and she was taking short, shallow breathes.

Once at the bottom of the stairs, Emma looked around. She was the only one down there. She breathed a sigh of relief when she identified the culprit that had almost sent her into cardiac arrest. One of the shelving units that Officer Wilson had reassembled earlier that day had toppled over.

Foundations in historic houses were generally made from rocks and then the gaps were filled with mud and dirt. The original dirt floor had been covered over by cement years ago, but the basement wasn't as symmetrical as a newly built house. As a result, the floor and walls were uneven, which caused things like shelving to topple over for no reason.

CHAPTER 44

———

Emma stared at the minor mess. Old paint
cans and cleaning products were strewn over
the floor amongst the shelves that had come
apart when they hit the cement. "I really need to
get rid of this crap," Emma muttered. No one had
used any of these in over ten years and most of the
things had more than likely been forgotten in the
bowels of the basement.

While bending over to pick up one of the paint
cans, Emma noticed something she had never seen
before. Behind where the shelves had stood, was an
outline of what seemed like a small door. Emma
was completely perplexed. The furnace was on
the other side of the basement, so it was doubtful
it was anything to do with that. The dryer had its
own vent, which was also not in the same area as the
mysterious door. Emma moved the old paint cans
and loose shelves out of the way for a closer look.

The door was about two feet tall and two feet
wide. It was too small for a person to fit in unless

it was some type of crawlspace. Many of these vintage houses had crawlspaces so that plumbers and electricians could get to the pipes and wires, if needed. It looked like it had been carved into the cement that now covered the uneven rock foundation, but there wasn't a handle to open it. Emma gently pushed on the door and to her surprise it sprung open.

A cloud of dust exhaled from the small, dark space as the door opened. Emma tried to see inside but it was too dark. She remembered the flashlight she had brought downstairs for protection. She had left it on her father's workbench after she realized there wasn't any threat.

Emma focused the beam of light into the space. She was puzzled by what she saw. The cubbyhole was probably about three feet deep and had been dug into not only the foundation, but into the earth beyond.

Even though Hardwicke hadn't received the typical amount of rain this spring, Emma could smell the dampness from the dirt. Emma decided to get closer to the hole in the wall. She studied every inch with her flashlight while her eyes adjusted to the semi-lit area. Emma really hoped there weren't any creatures living in the hole.

Instead of unknown creatures, there were remnants of potted plants, long ago dead, on the right wall of the hole. On the opposite side were metal

9x12 trays, filled with dried seeds, stacked on top of each other. It reminded Emma of when her mother would dry out the seeds from different flowers in the fall to plant the following spring.

If these were spring flowers, why had they been hidden in the basement? Emma was confused about what this meant, if anything. It seemed odd, but could this be what the intruder was searching for? The only reason Emma even noticed the door was because she was squatting down to pick up the paint cans and happened to look in that direction. The door was virtually invisible if someone was standing up with the shelves camouflaging it.

Dusk had overspread the country town and the natural light was fading from the basement's single window. Emma decided to tackle the rest of the cleanup tomorrow morning. Her stomach growled when she reached the top of the stairs, signaling it was time to quit. Before she dove into her hearty sandwich, Emma thought it best to text Ryan to let him know these latest events. She waited outside after sending the text in case he responded immediately.

For the next few minutes, Emma absorbed the sprawling fields that were the backyard while she listened to the birds chirping goodnight to each other. Her mind drifted to simpler times of frolicking in the hay fields and climbing trees. A gentle breeze fluttered through her golden strands bringing a hint of lilac with it.

Just as she was about to go back into the house, her cell phone rang. "Hi, Ryan. I had a feeling you'd call."

"Hello, my lady. Sounds like you had a bit of a scare tonight."

"Just my wild imagination getting the best of me."

"You said there were dead plants and dried seeds in your text?" Ryan asked.

"Yes. The door was well-hidden. I'm thinking this has to do with my father." Emma finally said out loud what she had been thinking the minute she found the hidden space.

"Sounds reasonable. Emma, my guess is the seeds are what that guy was searching for but couldn't find along with any of your father's research. I really don't like the idea of you staying there tonight."

"I'll be fine." Emma didn't want to admit that she was more than a little nervous.

"Emma, I don't want to alarm you, but I really think it would be best if you came back to the city tonight with those seeds. I need to tell Hunter what's going on, and then I'm coming to Hardwicke to meet you."

"Ryan, you're overreacting." Emma wasn't sure why she was fighting Ryan on this.

"I don't think I am. There have been too many strange incidents, and this guy is escalating."

"This can't be Greg. He was at the gala with all of us on Saturday night."

Ryan thought the same thing. "I know. That doesn't mean that he didn't send someone else to do this. It was guaranteed that you wouldn't be there this weekend."

"I hadn't thought of that." Emma started to get panicky.

"And that whoever he sent may be local. He could be counting on you going to the house because of the break-in and hoping you'll lead him to what he was hired to find. I just don't think we should risk it." Ryan was tired of trying to convince Emma to come back to Boston. "You always said you'd let me do my security thing, and you'd follow what I say. I need you to do that now. I don't have a good feeling about this. I'm coming to Hardwicke."

"Okay. No need for drama." Emma tried to sound lighthearted. "I'll pack up my stuff and wait for you to get here and then come back to the city tonight. I need to find something to put the seeds in."

Ryan was relieved he'd gotten through to her. "Call me if there's anything suspicious. I know service is spotty out there, so I want regular check-ins from you."

"Got it. I'm hanging up now, so I can get everything packed up and eat my sandwich before you get here." Emma ended the call.

Once inside the kitchen, Emma scoured the cabinets for a bag to put the seeds in. She finally found a few old plastic grocery bags tucked away under the sink. With bags in hand, Emma headed back to the basement to collect the unexplained seeds, trying her best not to touch them in case they were dangerous. With all the seeds dumped into the bags, she locked the basement door. Emma grabbed all her belongings and started to pack up the Land Rover. Since she wasn't sure if the seeds were unsafe, she decided to put them in the compartment under the rear passenger seat for safekeeping.

Emma realized she should let Chief Dyson know she decided to go home, so he wouldn't call out the cavalry if they drove by and didn't see any lights on. While she made the short drive to the police station, she called Ryan to let him know she had left the house and was stopping to notify the police about the change in plans. She thought she heard Ryan curse but it was tough to tell given the reception. Emma had a feeling that Ryan was closer than he let on earlier and probably had Hunter with him.

The parking lot at the police station was once again almost empty. Emma barely got out of her car when she saw Chief Dyson leaving the building. Once he saw her, he came over looking concerned. "Is everything all right, Emma? I was just heading home."

"Everything is fine. I wanted to let you know that I'm going to head back to Boston tonight. I have a few more things to do back at the house but no sense me staying the night."

"I'm glad you let me know. Did you find anything missing from the house?"

"Doesn't look like it. Just old papers thrown around and, unless they wanted ten-year old paint, there wasn't anything of value in the basement." Emma smiled.

"All righty then. I'll let you know if I find out any more. Drive safe back to the big city." Chief Dyson, instead of going to his Ford F-150 pick-up truck parked out front, went back inside the police station. Emma assumed it was to tell whoever was on duty not to worry about doing extra patrols tonight by the house.

Emma headed back to the house to finally have her chicken salad sandwich, which was a little on the stale side now. While she waited for Ryan, and presumably Hunter, she thought about the last few months. Both Greg and Wendy popped into her head almost simultaneously. Although improbable, Emma wondered if it was possible they were working together to get to her and Hunter. She dismissed it almost as quickly as she thought of it.

Her mind drifted to times gone by. The house felt lonely without her father. The memories of all the good times the family had together seemed to permeate from the walls. The house was always filled with laughter and smiles and friends popping in. Her aunt and uncle, who now resided in Florida, would come over for coffee and dessert after dinner.

Each year, the neighbors would take turns hosting a holiday party that was full of good cheer. Emma's walk down memory lane warmed her heart, despite how the house had been tainted by an unknown intruder's evilness.

CHAPTER 45

R yan and Hunter had been enjoying a
nice Italian dinner at Mario's Ristorante,
located on the next block from the Logan
headquarters, when Emma's first text chimed on
Ryan's phone. Even though Hunter owned his own
restaurant, he always enjoyed dining at Mario's.
It was a traditional, family-owned Italian eatery
where everything on the menu was homemade
and boasted recipes passed down generations. The
original location was in Southbridge, but they had
grown enough to open a second location in Boston.
The marinara was the best Hunter had tasted since
his trip to Italy several years ago, especially with
deep-fried bread for dipping. Both men were always
treated like family by the owner, Mario, and his staff.
Crystal, Kelly, Wendy Lee, and Anna always made
the meal enjoyable and relaxing. It was Hunter's
little escape and he had hoped to be able to share
it with Emma someday.

Now, Hunter was back to the evil reality of the

consequences of being associated with him. The feeling of contentment had quickly faded as soon as they left the restaurant in the middle of their main course. Tension and anxiety played a dominant role on the drive to Hardwicke after Ryan had given him the run-down on what Emma had found at the house. He was secretly glad that Ryan decided to make a preemptive strike and go to Hardwicke before Emma could disagree. The ride was a blur while Hunter watched the hint of scenery flash by. Hunter contemplated how things could have gotten to this point.

"Earth to Hunter. Anyone home?" Ryan shouted from the driver's seat.

Hunter turned his attention back to the here and now. "Sorry. Was just thinking about everything that's happened."

"I know. We're almost there." Ryan got off the exit on the highway and was immediately deposited onto the winding and shadowy country roads. "Shit! These roads are crazy in the daytime. At dusk, they are a bit spooky."

Hunter cocked an eyebrow. "The big secret agent is scared of some back roads? That's classic."

"I didn't say I was scared. It's just a little unnerving without any street lights for miles, that's all."

"Just go slow, and you'll be fine." Hunter stared out the window of the Mercedes to the rolling landscape. He never appreciated its beauty or tranquility during the summers he'd spent there. Hardwicke reminded Hunter of the English countryside with its endless hills and quaint village atmosphere. With the sun going down behind the hills, auburn faded to rose to gold like brush strokes on a canvas. The darkening sky illuminated the outline of the trees in the distance, and Hunter understood why Ryan called it spooky. The grass in the fields started to blend into the darkness, like a black hole was swallowing them up.

"Slow down a bit. You're coming up on Old Ravine Road and it's rather curvy."

"Isn't that where Emma's father had his accident?"

Hunter nodded. "Yes. Have you made any headway researching that?"

"Not much. I've been too focused on our new friends, Wendy and Greg. After talking to Emma tonight, I added Chief Dyson to the list of people to check into a bit deeper."

"That's interesting. He always struck me as a straight shooter. No pun intended." Hunter considered what Ryan had said.

"I'm sure he is, but something's bothering me. Emma said that he knew both the Sharpetons and your family very well. Could just be the small-town thing, but I'd rather be safe than sorry."

"It is a very small town where everyone was always in each other's business. Probably just coincidence on this one, pal."

Ryan kept his eyes glued to the road. All he needed was some wild beast to jump out of the woods and land on the hood of the car. "I agree. Just don't want to leave any stones unturned. From what I read in the accident report, and Emma confirmed, he didn't seem overly thorough in the investigation."

"I absolutely think you should do some more digging. But it was winter and the roads were icy. My guess is there really wasn't anything that would cause him to think it was anything *but* an accident. We know a hell of a lot more today than we did back then, so I think *we* need to do due diligence on it."

Ryan pulled the Mercedes into the Sharpeton's driveway behind Emma's Land Rover. His knuckles were white from grabbing the steering wheel on the last few miles of the drive.

Hunter took a deep breath and got out of the car.

Emma waited on the patio to greet them. "How was the drive? I don't even want to know how fast you were going to get here in record time."

Ryan was the first to respond. "We were speeding along nicely until about two miles ago. I was half expecting a deer or something to jump out of the woods and attack us!"

Hunter rolled his eyes in Emma's direction. "Our friend here is a bit of a scaredy-cat on the dark country roads."

Emma laughed and waved the men into the house. Ryan quickly glanced around without being rude to familiarize himself with the surroundings, something he always did when going to new places. Emma noticed and smiled as she motioned for the men to sit down at the kitchen table.

Emma noticed that Ryan didn't sit down.

"Ryan, I'm guessing you want to see where the break-in was?"

"Um, if you don't mind."

Emma showed Ryan the office first, with Hunter in tow. Ryan stood in the doorway and studied the entire scene in front of him—the remaining papers strewn all over the floor, drawers emptied—but no sign of anything destructive. He checked the lock on the window. It hadn't been forced open. There were the remains of what looked like fingerprint powder from the police investigation. He noted that they did the bare minimum and only did the surfaces like the desk, drawers, and window.

"Emma, have you started putting any of this back together?"

"Not really. I picked up a few things like pens and the tape dispenser and put it in the desk. As you can see, I started sorting the papers into piles. Why?"

"I'd like to take some of these papers back with me to see if we might get any fingerprints off them, if that's all right with you."

"Be my guest. From what I could tell, most of the papers are household things like old bills, at least by the desk. The ones in the back by the filing cabinet are my father's work papers."

"That helps. I'm going to take some of each and see what we can come up with. Want to show me the basement?"

Emma led the way to the basement and unlocked the door. Ryan always hated basements—it was where the dead bodies were both in his previous line of work and in the horror movies. Hunter grimaced at Ryan's hesitation and gave him a little push forward. Ryan shot Hunter a steely look before heading down the stairs.

Once again, Ryan scanned the area to try to find any clue left behind. This time he didn't notice any fingerprint powder and shook his head. Over the years, he'd learned that not everyone had a passion for the details of police work. They all liked to catch the bad guy, but most never realized the tediousness of the job. The amount of paperwork was incredible and most crimes weren't solved within an hour like on TV.

Emma could see the wheels of Ryan's mind moving fast. "The plants and seeds were over there, hidden in that cubby hole. If those shelves hadn't fallen over, I never would've noticed it. Scared the daylights out of me!"

Hunter stepped closer to Emma so their arms were almost touching. She could feel the heat from his body and breathed in his cologne. Both watched Ryan squat down to get a better look at the door.

He turned while squatting to examine the top-pled shelves. The shelves were heavy-duty, so they shouldn't have fallen over without any help. He supposed that when Office Wilson was putting them back up, he didn't position them on a completely flat area of the floor. Even so, without some help, they should have stayed put.

Ryan stood back up and dusted himself off. "Let's go back upstairs. This place gives me the creeps. No disrespect intended." Ryan looked thoughtfully at Emma.

"I'm right there with ya! I always hated coming down here."

Ryan led the way back upstairs with Emma second, followed by Hunter, his hand gently on Emma's back. Once again, Emma could feel the heat between her and Hunter, which made her pulse quicken. She needed to focus on the task at hand—packing and driving back to Boston. Once all three were safely out of the musty basement, Emma closed the door and latched the deadbolt lock.

"Let me make sure everything is locked up, then we can leave."

"Where are the seeds?" Hunter asked.

"I put them in my car, under the rear seat. I wasn't sure if they were dangerous so didn't want them just lying around."

Ryan jumped in. "I'll go get them and put them in our car. That way I can take them straight to my office and lock them up tight when we get back to the city. Hunter, why don't you help Emma lock up the house." Without another word, Ryan dashed out the door to Emma's car.

"Sorry. Ryan isn't the most subtle person around." Hunter stared directly into Emma's eyes trying to read her mind. "How are you doing with all this?"

"I'm fine. It's like something in a movie. I'm pissed off about someone breaking into my office and here. At least they didn't vandalize the house like they did with my office. That would've broken my heart."

"I'm sure Ryan told you the same thing he said to me. It was probably someone who knew you'd be otherwise engaged this past weekend."

"Yes, he did. I hadn't thought of it until he mentioned his suspicions and how Greg could've had help. Kind of freaked me out. Truth be told—I'm glad we're going back tonight. This house doesn't feel the same as it used to."

Hunter engulfed Emma in his arms and, for a few minutes, the rest of the world didn't matter. Emma instinctively wrapped her arms around his waist. She wanted to feel safe, even if it was short-lived. Although the moon would not be full until early the next morning, it seemed like the heavens had turned a light on that shined into the small kitchen, illuminating the two former lovers. Hunter bent down and kissed Emma like it was their last day on this earth. Emma gave in to the passionate kiss and let Hunter's lips lock onto hers with a fiery determination. At the sound of the Mercedes' engine revving slightly, the two pulled away from each others' grasp.

"I'm sorry. I just can't go on like we have been. I need you in my life—even if it isn't safe. But I know I'm being an ass and putting my needs before your safety." Hunter was conflicted about the emotions running amuck inside him.

"You don't need to apologize. We obviously both wanted this, needed this. I've done a lot of thinking, and I can't live in fear. I need to live my life. Let's talk when we get back to the city and see where we can go from here. I'm not promising anything—you hurt me with some of your stunts lately. But I think we both deserve to hear each other out. That's all I can do for right now." Emma tried to keep her tone even.

"I understand. I can drive back with you and we can talk." Hunter knew he was probably pushing his luck.

"Let's just agree to talk in the next few days. I'm exhausted and frazzled and confused right now. I need to clear my head first. The ride back to the city will help with that."

"Ryan and I will follow you back."

Emma was thankful Hunter didn't push things further and nodded in agreement. She wasn't sure she'd have the strength to hold her ground.

Both vehicles backed out of the small driveway and headed toward the center of town, with Emma in the lead. When Emma stopped at the end of the street, she glanced at the town common in front of her. In a few months, the Hardwicke Fair would be in full swing with all the arts and crafts, music, and food vendors. Her father had loved the annual fair as much as she did. Maybe she'd convince Hunter and Ryan to come out for this year's fair—it would be funny to see Ryan sashaying around the oldest fair in the country, she thought.

Emma started to head toward Old Ravine Road on her way back to the highway. As she started the decent down the treacherous dark road, all she could think of was being on an airplane when the flight attendants tell you to put your tray tables back in their upright position before landing. She looked in her rear-view mirror, but she had lost sight of Ryan and Hunter, which wasn't unusual given the curves on this road. Emma kept her speed down and her high beams on while she traversed the hill leading back to civilization.

CHAPTER 46

———

When Ryan pulled out of Emma's street, he hadn't realized that the police were waiting on the side of the road, hidden under the cover of darkness. As soon as Ryan forgot to put on his turn signal, the flashing blue lights came on. He silently cursed to himself and pulled over. Hunter couldn't help but roll his eyes.

Ryan lowered the window and got out his license and the registration while keeping his hands in plain sight. The officer cautiously approached the driver's side after he had plugged the license plate into the computer in the front seat of the police cruiser.

"Sir, do you know why I pulled you over?"

"I believe that I forgot to signal my left turn at the stop sign, officer."

"License and registration, please."

Ryan handed the young officer the documents and watched him head back to the police cruiser.

Hunter sat perfectly still with a small smile on his face, which drove Ryan crazy.

"You seem to be enjoying this a little too much," Ryan said flatly.

Hunter didn't respond, just smiled.

The officer walked back to the Mercedes. "Sir, can you explain why you are driving a car registered to Ares Logan Industries?" The officer had his hand on the butt of his gun in the holster.

Hunter decided it was time to end the fun. "Officer, I'm Hunter Logan, owner of Ares Logan Industries and this gentleman works for me. He's my driver." Hunter threw in the last bit just to aggravate Ryan.

"Can I see your identification, Mr. Logan?" Hunter leaned across the driver's seat and handed it to the officer. "I'll be right back, sir." Once again, the officer went to his cruiser. Both Hunter and Ryan could see him furiously typing on the computer.

When the officer returned, he had a written warning for Ryan and handed both men their paperwork. "In the future, signal when making a turn. I'm letting you off with a warning—next time I won't be so generous."

"Thank you, officer." Ryan was polite, but didn't like the condensation in the officer's tone.

Ryan made sure to signal before maneuvering back onto the road and to slow down at the intersection that had a yield for both ways. Without any warning, a large black SUV sped across the intersection. It would've broadsided the Mercedes if Ryan hadn't seen a glint of something in the corner of his eye.

"What the hell? Where was Officer What's-His-Face when something like this happens? Unbelievable. I get pulled over for a turn signal violation like it was a felony and this reckless jackass doesn't even get stopped!"

"Ryan, calm down. Let's just get going so we can catch-up to Emma and get home."

The Mercedes started down the hill with Ryan still muttering profanities at the other driver who had almost hit them. Ryan was amazed at how dark it was on this road. It was pitch black, except for the headlights of the Mercedes. For the first time, Ryan understood why the chief classified Craig Sharpeton's death as a motor vehicle accident. The road was immersed in total darkness, making it was nearly impossible to see where the road was compared to anything else. On the right side of the road was what seemed like a bottomless ravine and the left side a hilly forest. Craig Sharpeton hadn't had too many options the night of his accident, especially if there was another vehicle involved.

A light bulb went on in Ryan's head. "Oh, shit!"

"What's wrong now? Afraid of the dark?"

"No! That SUV that almost ran us over. Doesn't it seem odd that someone's in that much of a hurry on this road?"

Hunter didn't like where Ryan was heading. "I guess so."

"Emma is probably about a mile ahead of us."

"Oh, shit!" Hunter definitely didn't like this.

As Ryan decided to speed up as much as he could without going off the road, they heard a loud crash and metal grinding—the unmistakable sound of a car accident. Something everyone has heard at least once in their lifetime, metal against metal and the sound of an impact.

Ryan pushed the Mercedes to the limit—both men silently praying history hadn't just repeated itself.

CHAPTER 47

Emma saw the headlights behind her approaching fast. She shook her head at how irresponsibly Ryan was driving on roads he didn't know. As the headlights drew nearer, Emma realized they were too high to belong to the Mercedes. Just what she needed—some idiot going way faster than they should and being behind her with blinding lights.

All Emma could see were the two beams, which seemed to light up the sky, getting closer to her rear bumper with each second. She wished for a place to pull over and let this maniac pass her. Emma wondered how far behind her Ryan and Hunter were. She had thought they were right behind her but had lost sight of them when she started down the hill.

Suddenly, the Land Rover jerked forward with a thud. Emma glanced back. A black SUV had struck her rear bumper. Panic overtook Emma as her mind flashed back to her father's car accident. She sped up, but the SUV kept pace with her, all the while tapping her rear bumper. Both SUVs were about to come up on what the townspeople called "dead man's curve", the place where her father had died.

Emma threw the Land Rover into all-wheel drive and tried to put on her brakes, hoping that it would slow both vehicles down. The Land Rover started to fishtail at the sudden change in speed, which gave the other SUV the opportunity to catch the left side of Emma's bumper. At their combined speed, it was enough to send Emma into a 360-degree spin and down into the ravine.

Emma's world spun out of control. She was able to catch a glimpse of the black SUV idling in the middle of the road, as if waiting to see what happened to her and if they needed to finish the job. Tears rolled down Emma's face as the Land Rover went over the edge and was momentarily airborne. Her thoughts focused on how her father must have felt at this very instant. Disbelief consumed her that she would suffer her father's fate, in the exact same spot, just as the driver of the black SUV threw a cigar out the window towards Emma and sped off.

When the Land Rover landed, the front wheels hit a boulder, which caused it to roll over twice before coming to rest on the roof. Fortunately, the roof wasn't completely flattened, which helped protect Emma along with the airbags that blanketed her. The front-end was a mangled mess with both front wheels facing outwards, the tires deflated. Metal and glass fragments were scattered amongst the rocks and dirt where the vehicle finally rested. The protective undercarriage casing had been peeled backwards. Steam and smoke bellowed out of the engine block, while gasoline trickled out towards the rear of the vehicle.

Luckily, Emma was wearing her seat belt, which kept her suspended upside down. She knew that Hunter wasn't too far behind her and prayed that he'd come to her rescue. The ravine was deep, and in the darkness, it would be nearly impossible to see anything down here unless he had witnessed the accident—which she knew he hadn't. She prayed that the almost full moon would help guide Hunter to where she was. When the vehicle stopped moving, Emma slipped into unconsciousness. Her final thoughts on this deadly journey were of her family and Hunter.

As Emma floated away from reality, Ryan came upon the skid marks that led to the edge of the ravine. Both he and Hunter scanned the area but didn't see anyone else but themselves. Ryan desperately wanted to hunt the SUV's driver down, but knew the odds weren't in his favor. Before Ryan had come to a complete stop, Hunter jumped out of the car and ran toward the ravine.

"Get the flashlights from the glove compartment," Hunter yelled over his shoulder.

Ryan retrieved the roadside emergency car kit from the trunk. He handed a flashlight to Hunter and then set up three roadside flares to warn anyone coming down the road. Ryan grabbed his cell phone —only one bar of service, but it was enough. He dialed 9-1-1 and told the dispatcher where they were and what had happened. Within a few minutes, in the distance, sirens wailed.

By the time Ryan got to the ravine, Hunter was already making his way down to Emma's mangled Land Rover. Ryan aimed his flashlight to help Hunter see where he was going. The multitude of rocks plus the steep decline made it virtually impossible for Hunter to traverse into the ravine without slipping several times. Hunter wasn't dressed for the occasion with his charcoal grey V-neck cashmere sweater, black lightweight dress trousers and Joseph Abboud shoes. Hunter finally made it to what was left of the Land Rover after what felt like an eternity.

"Hunter, can you see her yet?" Ryan shouted down in the abyss.

Hunter, still trying to keep his balance, shouted back up to the road, "I've made it to the Rover. I'm going to try to get to the front of it. It's all rocks down here."

"I can hear the sirens. Keep talking to me so I know you're okay." Ryan wanted to be in the bottom of the ravine, but he knew someone needed to stay at the road to direct the EMTs to where Emma, and now Hunter, were. Ryan hated being on the sidelines but he knew that nothing would to stop Hunter from reaching Emma—dead or alive. Ryan saw the flashing blue lights heading their way.

Hunter steadied himself against the rear of the car while he tried to find more solid ground to make it to the front driver's side. The moonlight sliced through the darkness, and he could see the metal, glass, and plastic strewn around the area. He also noticed a half-smoked Macanudo cigar. Something about the cigar nagged at him. It seemed out of place, but he didn't have time to think about it.

"Ryan! I've made it to the front of the Rover. Going to check on Emma."

"Okay. Cops and ambulance just pulling up now. Be careful!" Ryan tried to remain calm and hopeful.

"EMMA! Can you hear me?" Hunter shouted at the front of the Land Rover.

He listened.

Nothing.

Slowly, Hunter came up to the remains of the front of the Land Rover. Emma's bloody hand rested on what remained of the driver's side window. Hunter's heart stopped, his mind went to the bleakest of all places. He dropped to his knees to peer inside the vehicle. Emma hung upside down, still in her seatbelt, her blonde hair, streaked with red, hiding her face.

"Emma, honey, it's Hunter. Can you hear me? Say something," Hunter pleaded.

Emma gave no response. Hunter didn't want

to unlatch the seatbelt in case she had neck and spinal injuries. Instead, he tried to move her hair to the side, so he could assess the damage. Blood stained Emma's face, likely from a head wound. Hunter couldn't tell if she had any broken bones, but everything looked normal.

Then he saw something that brought him to tears: her chest was ever so slightly moving up and down.

She was breathing.

Hunter said a silent prayer as the rescue crews carefully made their way down the ravine. Flood-lights were being set up on the edge of the road, so the crews could see what they were doing. The fire chief was the first to get to Hunter.

"Your friend up top gave us the run-down. My team is going to have to cut her out of the vehicle. I know you want to stay here with your girlfriend, but I'll need you to go back up to the road and let us do our jobs."

"I checked, and she's breathing, but I didn't try to do anything else in case of other injuries."

The fire chief nodded and waved over two of his crew who had tools to cut open the car.

On the way back up the ravine, Hunter noticed the damage to the rear bumper. That clinched it for him—this wasn't an accident, and neither was Emma's father's death.

Again, Hunter slipped on the rocks. He had to

crawl up to the edge of the road, where a few of the police officers helped pull him back onto the road.

Ryan walked over to Hunter. "I'm afraid to ask."

"She's breathing, but that's all I can tell you. They're trying to cut her out of the Rover now."

Both men flinched when they heard the power tools grinding through metal and glass.

"She was still held in by her seatbelt, but the Rover landed on its roof, so she's upside down. There is some sort of head wound that was bleeding." Hunter suddenly felt wobbly.

One of the EMTs noticed Hunter's unsteadiness and had him sit on the edge of the ambulance for a few minutes. As a precaution, the EMT took Hunter's blood pressure, which was extremely elevated. Given the circumstances, the EMT said it was perfectly normal. Hunter felt a little better sitting down, and a tidal wave of emotion came over him.

Hunter couldn't help but think of all the time lost—what his father had done to break up him and Emma, the numerous times he had picked up the phone to call her over the years but hadn't, even the last several weeks not being able to see each other because of the imminent threat. Despite all their precautions, that threat gotten to Emma—all their sacrifices had been for nothing, he silently fumed. The anger rose inside him like bile along with an enormous sadness that he might never get to hold Emma or kiss her again.

The world had gone silent—no more cutting metal or voices or even crickets. The light breeze had stopped, and it was dead calm. As if on cue, clouds obscured the brilliant moonlight, and they were shrouded in darkness. Hunter and Ryan glanced at each other. They heard a rustling sound and looked in the direction of the ravine.

Two somber-looking firefighters climbed out of the abyss. Both hung their heads, a look of despair on their faces.

At the sight of this, Hunter Logan broke down into a flood of tears.

ALSO FROM TRACEY L. RYAN:

Wicked Game of the Hunter

———————

Visit Tracey L. Ryan online:

WWW.TRACEYLRYAN.COM

Facebook.com/wickedgameofthehunter